Praise for MJ James

James's effective worldbuilding employs strong emotional and sensory descriptions ... often paralleling our society's own issues with neurodivergence, gender equality, economic disparity, and more.

— The BookLife Prize on The Immortal Part of Myself

Good world-building and a storyline I was quickly hooked into.

— Goodreads Reviewer on In-Between

I0562532

The
Immortal Part
of Myself

MJ James

Developmental editor services provided by Fiona McLaren
Proofreading editor services provided by Chey Mongeon and Erin Paige
Cover design by PurpawArt

E-book ISBN: 978-1-958175-04-0
Paperback ISBN: 978-1-958175-03-3
Hardcover ISBN: 978-1-958175-05-7
Audiobook ISBN: 978-1-958175-07-1

www.mj-james.com

To everyone who didn't see
themselves represented
but still found a way
to figure out who they are.

Trigger Warning

When I started seeing the world divide, I thought about where we could go. The Immortal Part of Myself is the result. Parts of the book are very dark, and I would not want anyone to pick it up without knowing what was coming. I tried to handle the topics as sensitively as possible while showing the harm they can cause. While there is a dark side to this story, there is also one of hope. I have faith in who we can be.

Physical Child Abuse
Spousal Abuse
Sexism/Genderism
Rape
Homophobia
Ableism toward Autism
Confinement

ALSO BY MJ JAMES

In-Between

NeurodiVeRse

The Ember Town Series

Lucas

Phoenix

Birk

Mika

CHAPTER 1

RILEY

PRESENT

RILEY WAS IMPRISONED in the shower. The doors had slid closed, locking until the decontamination process had thoroughly sanitized her. She held up her arms, allowing the disinfectant spray to reach every inch of her body. The skin along her ribs stretched, causing the bruises to throb with new pain. Riley ignored it and started a slow twirl, allowing the shower to decontaminate evenly. The spray misted her body, highlighting the scars across her torso. Her husband had made each scar deliberately so they could be hidden under her clothing. It was only when she was fully naked that they were visible.

Each scar was a reminder of her fight to live. But Riley was done fighting. She had finally won.

When the disinfectant stopped, Riley put down her arms and waited. The door unlocked with a soft click, and she finally opened her eyes. Riley walked out to a room that contained only a plastic stool and a drain. She grabbed a light gray jumpsuit off the seat and briefly held it to her chest. Her body relaxed, finally believing that she was safe. She slipped her legs in and then each arm, zipping it up, so the fabric pressed into her skin. It brought to life every nerve ending it touched, causing her pain that far outweighed the bruising.

Her reaction to clothing was unusual. It didn't make it hurt any less. But before her was the door to true freedom. She clutched her hands at her side and took a deep breath.

Riley reached out and pressed a small white button, causing the door to unlock. She opened the door and walked through. As she did, the door behind her sealed. Riley heard the decontamination streams turning on, preparing the room for the next passenger.

Before her was yet another room. This one had a biohazard suit hung on the wall, which Riley slipped on, securing it tightly around her wrists and ankles. Then she put on the feet covering and the mask. She checked the filter to ensure it was reset and then placed it on her head. The seal clicked into place. She took a few deep breaths to ensure the air flowed adequately. Lastly, she put on her hand coverings. Just like every child was taught in school.

She waited. This room would contain cameras hidden in the wall. Behind the cameras were technicians watching her put on her suit to confirm that she had done so correctly. Now they were reviewing her profile. They would be analyzing any pathogens washed down the decontamination shower. They would be checking the readouts from the biohazard suit. The filters were programmed to pick up all known viruses and bacteria. They ensured it was safe for her to breach their center.

So, she waited, keeping her breath even. She stood still to not increase her heart rate or body temperature. Then, when the last door opened, she let out a breath of relief.

Standing in the doorway was a man with dark skin dressed in blue. It was the color of the Reaper corporation, the conglomerate that controlled space travel. The corporate symbol was on his light blue button-down shirt, dark blue tie, and even his face mask. Fear spiked through her suddenly before she pulled herself back from panic. She never understood why the Reaper corporation used the radioactive mutant spider, nicknamed the reaper because it dealt instant death, as their corporate symbol.

"Riley Matherson?" the man asked. His voice amplified through the speaker built into his mask.

"Yes, that is me. I'm Riley Matherson." The name was new, and the unfamiliarity of it felt wrong. She could only hope he overlooked her awkwardness.

"Follow me," he said. Then he took off walking down the hallway, turning out of Riley's sight before she thought to follow him.

The hallways were a maze. Each one had a unique number displayed in elegant gold lettering. It reminded Riley of the hotels she had seen in old films. They walked towards the elevator. The man placed his hands under the decontamination box and stepped back. Riley instinctively went to do the same before remembering she had on the biohazard suit.

"Elevator, going up," the man said.

They waited. Each faced the elevator at a slant, so they were angled away from each other. When the elevator came, the man let her go on first. She walked in facing towards the back and stopped.

"Elevator, floor five," the man said.

It did not take long before Riley heard the ding of the elevator doors opening. She turned around and walked out. When the man exited, they walked a short way down the hallway until they stopped at room 546, her new home for the next few weeks.

"Have you quarantined before?" the man asked.

"I have," Riley said.

"This door will seal after you enter. It will unseal when the quarantine period is up. The quarantine period will last 14 days from when the last passenger enters their room. You elected to board early, so expect your stay to be closer to three and a half weeks.

"There is enough food for three months in the room so that you will have plenty available. We have also stocked your choice of extra food items. Unfortunately, they will not be available on the ship, so enjoy them now.

"Your clothing and personal effects are being decontaminated. You can expect your luggage quickly due to your early arrival. Housekeeping should have your items thoroughly decontaminated in 24 hours. However, do not worry if it takes up to four days. The wall screen has a built-in emergency contact channel. Please remember, if you leave quarantine for any reason, you will not be allowed to board the ship."

The man spoke the script like he had said it a thousand times before. He most likely had.

"Thank you. What should I do with the biohazard suit?"

"There is a hamper in the unit. You can leave it there. We will decontaminate it when we clean the room."

Riley gave a curt nod and waited as the door unsealed. When it opened, she walked into the gap between doors and remained as the door began to close. The air started filtering through rapidly, causing the suit to flutter against the jumper, reminding her of how uncomfortable it was against her skin. She closed her eyes and focused on breathing until the air stopped and the second door opened.

Riley stripped off her suit, dropping it piece by piece in the hamper by the front of the unit. Then she tore off the jumpsuit until every bruise and scar was visible. She just had to hope her clothing arrived quickly.

The room had the look of a hospital unit. Each item had been designed so they could clean it quickly and cheaply. The floor was a solid linoleum that seemed to make the room glow. On Riley's left was a small kitchen area with a counter and a microwave. Next to it was a food container full of packets of nutritional bars and rehydrated food meals. There was even a section devoted entirely to desserts.

Riley walked towards the space and picked up a compostable cup. She used the sink built into the counter and poured a glass of water. The water came out clean of contaminants due to the unit's purification system. The same system would be connected to her bathroom as well. It was a standard system in homes. The main difference was that a quarantine room's sink and bathroom could be deconstructed to clean it between uses. They could even replace the pipes.

She drank the water and pressed a button on the disposal unit. It was a smaller stainless-steel unit about waist-high. The lid opened, and Riley dropped in the cup. Once the lid closed, there was a light hum as the packaging was dropped, compressed, and sealed for disposal.

Riley took two steps and moved out of the kitchen to the living area. There was a small plastic table with a single plastic chair against the closest wall. It would serve as Riley's work and dining area. The wall above the table had a built-in screen. She would have to use touch or voice control until her pad arrived from decontamination. She missed her pad more than her clothing. A gap between the table and an open doorway led to a small bathroom. Riley ignored it and moved towards the bed.

It took up the wall opposite the kitchen and table. Riley was grateful to see that the bed had a mattress on it. Many quarantine rooms expected you to also sleep on a hard plastic slab. Riley imagined that most of the clientele able to afford a ticket off-planet would not be willing to sleep on such a hard surface. This bed had one of the new foam mattresses, the ones they could run through a decontaminated machine explicitly made for them.

Riley could walk across the room in less than five steps. But it was all hers for the next three weeks. She laid down on the mattress, relieved that she had made it. The plan had been months in the making, ever since the day she first realized that her husband planned to kill her

CHAPTER 2

MATTY

PRESENT

THE OUTSIDE of the quarantine center was as gray and lifeless as the rest of Earth. It was nothing compared to the wonders that Matty had grown up with on Mars. A wave of homesickness coursed through her at the thought. It had been three years of arguing with arrogant men, the air so polluted you had to wear a mask to walk outside, and disease everywhere. She was glad that the High Priestex had allowed them to leave for the quarantine center early.

The rest of her team had already left the transport, checked in, and started the decontamination process. Matty was stuck unloading the group's luggage. All because she happened to tell one of the new ambassadors about the senator that enjoyed squeezing the asses of new female arrivals. Once Matty had broken his wrist, he had never touched her again. Maybe telling this story in the middle of the senate chamber, in full session, was not the best idea, but perhaps the new ambassador would not have to break his wrist. She had done everyone a favor. Either way, Matty did not regret it, even if twenty-three people amassed a lot of luggage after three years.

After placing the last bag on the luggage transport, she stopped to take one last look at Earth. The sky was gray, and clouds of pollution nearly blocked out the sun. The picture books had promised her lush green forests, but the corporations had already destroyed it all. It was a mystery that humans could still live on this planet.

During their stay, they had traveled some. The trips were primarily diplomatic visits where the corporations tried to impress or intimidate them. They visited Earth's great wonders, the rainforest, the great wall, the pyramids, and the oxygen refinement plants. All Matty had seen were the scars that humans had left on the planet.

The corporations, the five major ones left running the entire planet, turned around and charged for Earthens to live with the damage they had caused. The Segadon Corporation, in an agreement with the rest of the corporations, was required to create oxygenation stations in the rainforest. Instead of taking the cost out of their profits, they passed it on to their members. At birth, individuals started getting taxed on the oxygen they needed to breathe. Most remained in debt their entire lives.

Matty was ready to return to a world where the basics -

food, healthcare, housing, and breathing - were all considered rights, not privileges. Matty used to be pretty mild-tempered, but she had lost most of her control since arriving on this planet. How could people just let this planet die?

She turned away, ready to leave it behind, when she noticed the other shuttle. She couldn't help wondering who else was so willing to get away from this planet that they volunteered for an extra week and a half of quarantine. The shuttle doors opened, and a woman walked out. She appeared to be older than Matty by a few years. Her clothes looked like those of a high-ranking government wife, but they were out of date and dirty. Her hair was blonde, with reddish-brown hair growing out at the roots. It fell in a straight cut along the woman's shoulders. The only corporations that allowed women to wear their hair short were the Reapers and the TKR. She was not a Reaper, but she didn't seem to carry herself like she was from the TKR.

Matty found she couldn't take her eyes off the woman. She was tall and thin, like she had skipped too many meals. It was at odds with the clothing that she wore. Matty knew she should turn around and mind her own business, leaving the Earth woman alone. But there was something about her that called to Matty. For a brief second, the woman made eye contact. Her eyes had a ring of exhaustion, her face was gaunt, and it looked like she may have never smiled. But there was something in that sharp gaze, a quiet strength, a defiance, that charged through Matty like a shock, rooting her in place.

"Theia mania," Matty said, quoting a common Martian phrase when two souls connected. "The Goddess has sent me to you, and my life will never be the same."

Then a man stepped out of the shuttle and wrapped his arms around the woman's waist in a possessive gesture. The woman turned away from Matty and tried to escape the man's grasp, but he held on tighter. When the woman continued to struggle, Matty started walking towards them, her fists clenched. She was ready to vent all the frustration building over the last three years.

Then the woman stopped struggling and reached up and touched his cheek. She whispered something in his ear, causing his hands to loosen from around her waist. When he let out a laugh, Matty stopped walking.

The man left the woman, entering the registration building, where the Earthins checked in. Matty started to go to the woman but paused. If she had turned and looked at her or acknowledged her existence even briefly, she knew she wouldn't be able to stop herself. Instead, the woman took the bags and walked into the registration building.

"Theia mania," Matty said again. Then she focused on her work and started steering the luggage rack inside.

CHAPTER 3

RILEY

PAST

RILEY WASN'T ALLOWED out often. So, when her husband, Nesili, suggested that she go out to the theater with one of his lieutenant's wives, she was suspicious. Nesili had given up on using her to navigate the women's games. She gave away too many of his secrets and gained nothing in return.

The wives were pathetic. Instead of pulling together to fight for respect, they quarreled and outmaneuvered each other to push their husband forward in the company. She didn't blame them, not really. They had as little control as she did. Setting herself apart just came naturally to her. She wasn't one of them.

The lieutenant's wife was young, skinny, and blonde. Her skin was a porcelain color that was rarely seen. Riley vaguely wondered if her parents had illegally tampered with her genes before birth. They wouldn't be the first to use a child to rise in the ranks.

The couple was newly married since the lieutenant's first wife had accidentally slipped in the shower after failing to father him a child. The woman, barely out of girlhood, was full of nervous energy trying to impress the wife of one of the company heads. The poor woman must not have been appropriately initiated. It would be a while before her smooth skin and bright eyes stopped reminding the wives how easy it was to trade them in for younger models. If they had included her in their social lunches and teas, the new wife would know tonight was a waste of time. Riley had no social standing, and what little her husband had would be gone as soon as their son turned sixteen.

Still, being out for a night on the town was good.

The woman pulled on her arm and then looped through, connecting them. Riley tried to remember her name. It was Puppy, Kitten, or some other extinct animal with a lot of fur.

"Kitten," Riley said. The woman ignored her.

"Puppy," Riley tried again.

"Oh, where?" The woman looked around the square even though Riley had not seen a dog in the city in years.

"I'm sorry. I have forgotten your name."

"It's Bunny."

"Right, Bunny. Let's head inside the theater now. It is not a good idea to be outside for too long."

"We should be fine. This is the third tier. No one will hurt us here. Isn't tonight beautiful?"

The statement confirmed Riley's suspicions. The girl must have been raised on one of the lower tiers. She hadn't yet learned that danger and beauty could coexist.

"I'm thirsty. I want to go get a drink."

"Oh, of course," Bunny said. "You are probably tired and want to sit down. How inconsiderate of me. A drink before the performance sounds delightful."

They walked towards the door, where an usher scanned their ID. Then they had to remove one of their gloves and place their finger on a pad to confirm that their bio signature matched. Riley knew they coated the bio-reader with an antiviral and bacterial substance, yet, she could not help but feel tiny creatures crawling over her skin until she thrust her hand into the decontamination machine and put back on her glove.

Satisfied with their identities, the usher opened the door and let them in.

Bunny walked straight through the lobby and directly towards the lounge. They sat at a small table, and before they had typed in their drink order, Bunny had unhooked the straps to her face mask and put it away in her purse.

"Do you plan on keeping it off for the entire play?" Riley asked.

"Isn't the building up to date?"

"It is." The building had current filters that cycled the air every minute, cleaning out pollutants. The air filtration system scanned the air for all known viruses and bacteria. And if it found any, the theater would be closed down and cleaned thoroughly. But it still did not seem worth the risk to Riley.

The menu was displayed on a touch screen built into the center of the table. Bunny flipped through pages of drinks until she selected a bright green cocktail called Toxic Snot. When Riley saw the name, she couldn't help but grimace, her expression safety hidden behind her mask. But she ordered the same. A few minutes later, a bot rolled up to their table. It used its one-clawed arm to remove their drinks from its tray and placed them in front of the women.

Riley's glass sat untouched as Bunny went off on the virtues of her husband. When Bunny finished her drink, Riley pushed her cup toward the young woman. It was unladylike for a woman to drink more than one drink, but Bunny did not hesitate before bringing the cup up to her lips.

"Do you know what alcohol is?" Riley asked abruptly. Bunny stopped talking, thrown by the sudden change in conversation. "It is a poison. It travels up to your brain and kills the neurons that live there. I have always wondered why we seem to enjoy poison so much. We have made our air so toxic we cannot breathe in it without a filter. We send viruses to hurt each other until they have taken over our world. Then, for enjoyment, we gather together and ingest poison. I suppose it doesn't matter much to us. We are women and probably won't be allowed to live that long, anyway. Shall we find our seat?"

Riley stood up and walked away from the woman.

The play was a classic Shakespeare. His works had come back into fashion in the last few years. Unsurprisingly, the men would enjoy a play full of assassination attempts, jealousy, and political plotting. But this play seemed too familiar. The wife of Othello's ensign betrayed Desdemona, a young daughter of an important man. Then she was killed by her husband.

"Did you pick this play?" They were sitting in boxed seats, just the two of them.

"I'm sorry; what did you say?" Bunny did not pull her face away from the stage. Tears glinted on the side of her eyes.

"Did you pick this play?"

"It was my husband's suggestion. Isn't it marvelous?"

"Have you ever seen a play before?"

"Not like this. Look at the actor's costumes. They are all so talented. It is nothing like what I saw where I was raised."

Riley resumed her silence, letting the girl get swept back up in the play as she watched with a more critical eye. Why had her husband let her come out tonight with his lieutenant's new wife? *He must need her occupied. It must be something important if he could not chance to leave her at home. What would the lieutenant gain by sending a message through the play? Or maybe it was all a joke that he thought her too stupid to understand.*

When the play ended and the lights turned on, Bunny sat motionless, transfixed by the empty stage.

"Wasn't that beautiful?" she asked.

"It was very well performed."

Bunny turned and looked at Riley, then jumped to her feet. "Oh, I'm so sorry. Where are my manners? Here, let me help you up."

"I am fine to get up on my own."

Bunny put back on her face mask and then walked up to Riley. Since Riley had already risen from the seat, she again linked their arms, attempting to assist Riley.

"Is there some reason you think I am incapable of walking on my own?" Riley asked.

"No...I mean...my husband told me you were not feeling well and that I should do my best to help you. I didn't mean to offend you."

"Who told him that I was not feeling well?"

"Everyone knows you do not have the best of health." Bunny said casually as they joined the procession of people leaving the theatre. "It is why you hardly attend public functions and spend so much time at your house. However, your husband said you had a bit of strength and wanted to have a night out in case things took a turn." They had made it outside and were standing on the walkway. A few guards stood near the theater, but most attendees had already moved on to their following destinations. "Should we go to one of the social lounges? I hear that the Pink Teacup is currently popular."

"I'm afraid you will have to attend on your own."

"I can't. I haven't gotten an invitation yet."

"At this rate, you never will." Riley was frustrated and distracted by her own thoughts. The words came out of her unfiltered. "You have to learn how to play the game and with whom to play it. If you were hoping to use me to increase your standing, you have been mistaken. I am out, an old model. My son turns sixteen next month, and all the assets I hold will go to him. I have no more value. My husband is using you as a convenient excuse to cover up my eventual murder."

As Riley spoke, Bunny's face had become more and more crestfallen. At the mention of murder, she let out a gasp and clutched at her heart like a southern belle in an old movie. "No, no one would be that cruel."

"How do you think you got your current position? Stay beautiful and young or find a way to be of use, or one day you will never wake up, and someone else will be in your bed."

The girl's already white skin was so pale that you could nearly see through it. She stood frozen except for a lip that seemed to tremble. Riley almost felt sorry for her.

"Where did you say my husband was this evening?"

"I don't know. I wouldn't be told that kind of information."

"No, you wouldn't. But you are young and opportunistic, so you would have tried to figure out as much information as possible. There is more that you are not telling me." Riley moved forward until she was towering over the child.

"All I know is that he had a meeting you were not supposed to find out about. I was to keep you busy as late as possible."

"Where was this meeting to take place?"

"It was at one of the second-tier restaurants, a new one just past the gates." At this, the trembling lessened, and a look of desire passed on the girl's face. "It serves seafood, actual seafood. I asked to get the lieutenant to take me, but he told me no. I'm hoping that he will change his mind if I do a good job tonight."

Riley had just told her that her husband had murdered his first wife, and the child was still dreaming of seafood. "I hope you figure out the game before you become too much of a liability," she said. Then she turned and walked away.

CHAPTER 4

RILEY

PRESENT

ON THE FIRST day of quarantine, Riley had sorted through all the food. There was enough to last for months, making it easier for Riley to indulge in multiple meals a day. She even took advantage of the desserts. She also took some packets and lined her suitcase, just in case. It was always good to have food saved away.

When her pad arrived, she started covering her digital tracks better. There had been too many last-minute changes in the plan, and Riley worried her husband would find her hidden bank accounts and track the recent transactions. He wasn't a very bright man, but then again, she hadn't anticipated him catching her before. Underestimating him had nearly cost Riley her life.

After a few hours, when the silence became unbearable, she turned to the entertainment feeds. She stared transfixed at the hundreds of options, each as unfamiliar as the last. Finally, she selected a show about a deep space crew. When Riley finally took a break, five hours had passed, and she understood why her husband had banned her from the entertainment feeds. She stood up, made some food, and continued watching the show.

When the screen froze the next day, reminding her to do her mandatory exercise, Riley pulled out her pad and wrote a quick program. The message disappeared, and Riley went back to watching.

As the weeks passed, Riley's body changed. The bruising disappeared, and she started to put on some weight. When they came to release her, she felt like a new person.

"Come with me." It was the same crew worker who'd shown her in. He was dressed in a biohazard suit this time, and she was allowed to walk around in just her clothes. She didn't even need her mask, although she put it on out of comfort. "Your bags are packed and ready for transport?"

"Yes," Riley managed.

"Good, good," he said as he led her past the identical doors and into an elevator. "Medbay," he instructed the elevator. At his command, it began to move. A few seconds later, the doors opened again, and they walked down a short hallway into a large room partitioned by curtains. Around the room, various nurses and doctors were walking around. They only had on face masks and gloves, leaving Riley wondering how they could allow such contamination, until she realized the doctors and nurses must be joining them on the ship.

The crew member led her into one of the curtained-off rooms. The room was empty, with just a plastic holder on the wall. The crew worker put a datapad into the holder and turned to face Riley.

"Wait here until they can get to you." Then he walked away, leaving Riley alone. Anxiety bubbled up instantly. She hated being in such unfamiliar situations, but she just had to make it through this. Then she would be on the ship, finally headed away from this planet.

So, she waited. The wait seemed to drag on, and the doubt crept in. *Did they forget about her? Maybe the crew worker forgot to tell them she was here? Maybe they knew who she really was, and were waiting for her husband to come and bring her home?*

When the nurse opened the curtain, Riley jumped. She then scanned the hallway to make sure that he was alone. Once Riley was satisfied, she turned her attention back to the nurse. He was slightly shorter than her, with cropped black hair and light brown skin. The nurse walked over and picked up her pad. He studied the information, not once looking at her. He motioned her to stand in front of the machine that read her vitals and watched them appear on the pad.

"Did you experience any symptoms?" he finally said.

"No," Riley said.

"No diarrhea, constipation, night sweats, sneezing, congestion, loss of appetite, or increased appetite."

"No, nothing."

The nurse finally looked up at her, giving her a skeptical look. "Did you exercise?"

"Yes," she lied. "I did the standard workouts."

He looked at the pad and nodded, the data falsified before his eyes. Riley knew she would have to go back to working out on the ship, but the break was nice.

"You are done." He threw the pad into a sanitation bin and waited by the door. It took a moment, but Riley realized he was waiting for her to exit. The nurse headed off as soon as she started walking, and Riley found herself hurrying to catch up. He led her to another elevator and called for the lift to arrive.

"This will take you to the departure room. You will be able to meet up with your party there. Your items will be moved onto the ship and waiting for you when you can enter your cabin." Then the nurse turned and left.

Riley stood waiting for the lift to arrive. More nurses came, dropping off additional passengers. They found themselves doing the complicated dance of giving each other space in the small hallway. When the lift arrived, they walked on one by one facing the wall. No one called out a floor, and Riley wondered if there was something she should say when the doors to the lift closed and they began to rise.

It was a short ride before the doors opened into a spacious

room. About a hundred people, all from Earth, were already standing around. Riley stepped inside, at a loss for what she was supposed to do next. She gazed around at the vast circular space. There were numbered gates evenly spaced around the area. Each gate had a waiting area in front full of blue plastic seats. A few gates were filling with people. Then she noticed people from the elevator had already wandered off. Riley found them lined up at a check-in counter off to the side of the elevator. Riley quickly joined them.

"Name?" a bored voice said. Her mind had wandered; Riley hadn't noticed she'd reached the front of the line. There was a person in a biohazard suit sitting behind a counter, a woman. She had heard that women could work in other corporations, but she had never seen it before.

"Riley Mi-. Riley Matherson," she was glad to have caught herself just before giving away her real last name.

"You are in gate 14." The woman gave some vague wave over towards the left of Riley and then turned her attention to her pad.

There looked to be 38 sections, so Riley headed directly across the room and veered right until she found the gate.

Riley walked up to the viewport overlooking the gate. A ramp led off to a large bus that would take them to their shuttle, where they would board through a hermetically sealed walkway, ensuring that they would not contact Earth's air again before leaving. The shuttle would then take them out of the atmosphere and dock with the ship.

The Reaper company had become hypervigilant after nearly losing everything in a disaster ten years ago. They had lost more than half of their passengers to a virus that had managed to get on board. Even Mars made the passengers stay aboard the ship until the medical staff had developed a vaccine. The ship was out of commission for over two years, and the Reapers revamped their space travel procedures to stop another catastrophe. The only reason the Reaper corporation had survived was that they had a space travel monopoly. Even Martians had to use them to travel back and forth between the planets.

Suddenly, arms wrapped around Riley's waist. A face pressed against her ear. "Hello, wife. Did you miss me?"

Riley acted instinctively. She went limp and pulled into herself, trying to distance herself from the situation.

"Oh, that is no way to act," the voice said. "We must make them think that we are happily married and on our way to Mars."

Riley allowed herself to relax. She focused on her breathing, although it didn't help until he finally removed his arms.

"You passed quarantine?" Riley asked, not yet turning to face him.

"You sound surprised. Were you hoping that I wouldn't? They would never let you board without your husband to escort you. It isn't allowed."

"I know I need you. I was only worried since I had no idea what viruses you picked up from the streets."

"Now, don't give me attitude. You need me. All it would take is for me to say one little word, and you would be locked up and shipped back to that man you're running away from."

"You need me too," Riley said. "They still talk about you in the upper tier. They call you the 'fallen one' and use you to give their children nightmares. The golden child of the third most powerful man in the Molbin corporation who managed to lose everything and become nothing more than a street vermin in the lowest tier."

Riley felt him pull back, felt the instinctual tightness between her shoulders. She braced for a hit, but instead heard him speak. "If I turn you in, they'll reward me. Maybe they'll give me my place back."

"If you think that, then maybe you should turn me in. See what happens. My fate will be easy. My husband will have me killed nice and quietly. Do you think you'd be so lucky?"

Riley was exhausted. She preferred looking at the code on a screen more than trying to hold her own in a conversation. Finally, she turned and sat down in one of the hard plastic chairs. Then she looked up at her old childhood playmate.

They were only a year apart, and their fathers had often thrown them together while they were working. His dark brown hair had grown back out slightly, and it looked like he hadn't shaved in quarantine. His frame had filled out, and he had put on some muscle in his upper body that pulled against his t-shirt. Riley noticed a slightly crazed look in his eye. Had she seen it before their trip, she would have found someone else to escort her. But there was no one else, at least not on such short notice.

It wasn't long before more people gathered at their gate. As the people arrived, Ron calmed down. He sat next to her and gently held her hand. He talked passionately with everyone around them, telling them about the job he had lined up on Mars, such a great job that he'd decided to uproot his new wife and take the voyage.

This will work, Riley thought to herself. *It has too. I hope that he can pull this con off.*

CHAPTER 5

MATTY

PRESENT

QUARANTINE HAD STARTED FINE. Matty's items arrived early the next day, and she had set up her alter first thing. Now that they were headed home, she wanted to disconnect herself away from the pain and close-mindedness of Earth. It was time to reorient herself towards the Goddess, the female representation of the energy in the universe. She planned to meditate the entire quarantine. Three weeks would have been enough time to cleanse herself thoroughly.

The first day was hard, but Matty was determined. She managed a total of six hours of meditation. On the second day, she started getting distracted. It was hard to sit still when her body was made to move. So she switched over to movement meditation. On the third day, she decided that fitness would reconnect her to the Goddess. She spent the day pushing her body to the limit. The fourth day she spent in bed, mostly asleep.

Then she got distracted by the entertainment feeds. Matty found Earthen shows comical. They had minimal plot, and were mostly just one long advertisement for the newest corporate product. The farther they got from the Earth, the harder it would be to stream, so Matty decided to take advantage of the situation.

When they came to let her out of quarantine, she was so desperate for human interaction that she hugged the Earthen in the bio-suit. He looked affronted, but his body leaned back into hers.

He escorted her straight up to the Martian viewing platform. As soon as Matty stepped off onto the elevator, she let out a sigh of relief. They were officially back on Martian territory. From here on out, they were no longer subjected to Earthen rule.

The viewing platform was crowded. The bodies pressed into each other to form a sea of bright clothing.

Off to the side, there was a scattering of people not yet conditioned to Martian culture. They had already been granted asylum, but they hadn't yet been picked up by families. There would not be many. Families adopted most new Martian citizens as soon as they submitted their applications. They were assigned families years in advance, so there was time for them to make the trip to pick them up. Sometimes the paperwork had to move faster, and a few citizens were unattached when the voyage started.

Matty walked around the crowd of people searching for the High Priestex. Instead, she found a group of her fellow ambassadors. They were huddled together with one of the Martian families.

"Hey, Triston," Matty said as she walked up and put an arm around his shoulders. He was one of the few Earth-born ambassadors, and at slightly over six feet, he could almost pass for a short Martian-born if it wasn't for his stocky build. "Do you think that maybe we should help those poor souls without families?"

He looked at her and then at the group he was talking with. Most of them were tech heads. "I think we should wait for the High Priestex to tell us what to do." His voice was deep and smooth. If Matty didn't prefer girls, she could imagine hooking up with him just for his voice. "Did they send you over here?"

"They didn't have to. Helping these people is in our job description. Now take out your pad and go find out who they are." Matty slapped him on the shoulder and walked over to the wall of people.

She stopped in front of the first person she saw. They were a masculine youth that looked to barely be of age according to human standards. *Sixteen was just too young,* Matty thought. Martians were not considered full adults until they were closer to 25.

"Hi, I'm Matty." Matty had stopped a few feet away from the youth, giving them enough space to feel safe. "I am one of the Martian ambassadors. Were you told about us in your briefing?"

The teenager gave a slight nod.

"What's your name?"

"Zeek." They slumped against the wall with their arms crossed. They were dressed in roughly used clothing and still wore a basic face mask. Their hair was short, but at an awkward length. Most likely, it had been shorn off in one of the Earthen camps, and they had let it grow back out during quarantine.

"Nice to meet you, Zeek. What are your pronouns?"

The teenager looked at her in confusion.

"What gender are you?"

"I'm a boy. I mean, I'm a man."

"Of course you are. I didn't want to assume. On Mars, people like to ask instead of making assumptions based on their looks. You've heard that Martians are different. So I assume you're coming to Mars because you are different."

The boy stared at her, unwilling to answer.

"I know there is a lot to learn. That is why all new citizens are adopted when they move to Mars."

"I'm not a kid. I'm too old to be adopted." His voice cracked as he spoke.

"It doesn't matter how old you are. The oldest person I

know to get Martian citizenship was 76, and she was also adopted. Do you know why she decided to move to Mars?"

"No, how would I know?"

"She decided to move to Mars because all her life, she was supposed to act like a man, even though she knew she wasn't. But you know how they treat women on Earth. Finally, she realized that she would end up dying as a man, and she couldn't handle that thought. So, she applied for Martian citizenship, and when she stepped out of quarantine, she dressed in the prettiest ball gown you ever had seen. She lived next to me when I was growing up and showed me all sorts of pictures."

The boy had started moving away as Matty talked, pushing into the wall like it could swallow him. "That's stupid. Men can't be women," he said.

"People come to Mars for all sorts of reasons. The one rule of Mars is to respect others. As long as people are not causing harm, they can be who they are. I'm not going to ask you why you are coming to Mars, but whatever the reason, everyone here will respect it. They expect you to do the same for them."

The boy stood slumped against the side of the wall. His eyes glanced down, trying to ignore her.

"Come on, let's find you a family."

"I don't want a new family," he said.

"I'm afraid you don't have much of a choice. If you want to go to Mars, you travel with a family." Matty glanced over the families until she found a couple with a group of native Martian teens. It looked like they had come to pick up half a dozen young orphans to bring back home. "Follow me."

She didn't look back to make sure that he was following her. On Earth, he had to keep his armor up, and she wasn't going to try to force him. He would open up when he felt like it. A family would make it easier.

"Do you have room for one more?" Matty said. "This is Zeek, and he doesn't have a family."

A middle-aged man stepped forward, his face scrunched in concern, then sprung back into a smile as if it couldn't handle staying serious. He was dressed in a pullover shirt and matching pants that were bright red on one side and faded into bright orange on the other, a traditional Martian outfit.

"That won't do at all," the man said. When he spoke, his whole body shook as if it could not contain his excitement. He reached out and put his arm around Zeek's shoulder. "Come on in; welcome to the family. I have a son and daughter around your age. There are quite a few cousins the same age back home, but they weren't up for the visit. These are all your siblings." He raised his free arm to gesture at the flock of children that were gathered around. The youngest were all wearing bright Martian clothing. "There are a few of them, so we appreciate your help. I bet they will be glad to have you around to help them. It's hard when none of the older family members have come from Earth."

The man guided the teen into their group. Zeek stood

awkwardly, but as the hollow-eyed children surrounded him, he seemed to recognize one of them. The teenager squatted down next to the child. They looked about ten years old, but they were so thin and pale that it was hard to tell. They fell into each other's arms, their eyes full of tears.

"Does this mean you will get to be my brother?" the younger child asked.

Matty's heart caught at the sight, but the young man was fine now, and there was still so much to do. She turned away, starting back towards the un-familied travelers when she saw the High Priestex exiting the elevator.

They were immediately recognizable from the long brown robes of their office. The High Priestex was tall and slim, although the robe hid their form under the fabric. They kept their head hairless, and their skin was a pale white typical of the people who lived for generations in the deep Martian cave towns. Matty headed over to them to figure out the plan.

"I see you are already assigning families," they said.

"They look so out of place. I couldn't stand by and do nothing."

"You did well, but we must ensure that we properly record the families. So go gather up the rest of the ambassadors and let's get to work."

Getting all of the passengers properly shuttled from quarantine to the ship took several days. Matty stayed in the observation room the entire time. She felt satisfied watching the new citizens get paired up with families. When the High Priestex left and took half the ambassadors to the ship, they left Matty in charge of the remaining group. She was proud that her skills were finally finding some value after a rocky three years on Earth.

When the last Martian shuttle took off, Matty was aboard it. She took one last look at the Earth, the pollution still visible despite the previous century of environmental reforms. It was night on the side of the planet that their shuttle was orbiting, and the lights flickered below, making the continent glow. It seemed unnatural, and Matty was happy to see it go. She turned to the opposite side of the shuttle as the ship came into view. She was struck with an intense longing to return home.

The ship was just like the one that had brought her to Earth. For all she knew, it was the same one. There were only five ships currently in commission, and at least one was getting repairs at all times. The ship reminded her of the Earthen cuisine known as pizza. Most of the ship was a round ring with walkways connecting it to the middle, leaving trian-gular gaps. The ship rotated around the center, giving them gravity for the nine-month journey.

Matty turned towards her seatmates, each showing the same joy as herself.

"We're going home," Tamiqa whispered. Her tanned skin glistened under the shuttle lights.

Matty reached over and grasped her hand. At one point,

that would have been awkward. They had had a brief but passionate fling on Earth when they had both been under the grip of homesickness. It had ended badly.

When the shuttle connected to the ship, they waited until the hatch decompressed. As the doors started to open, there was a collective cheer.

The ambassadors stayed back, letting the other passengers get off before them. When they finally left, they saw Jacques, a tall copper-skinned Martian-born ambassador, giving the Martians directions to their new quarters. He paused long enough to tell his colleagues to head to the conference room where the High Priestex was waiting for them to begin a briefing.

The ship layout came back to Matty quickly. It was like the last three years had never happened, and they had just had a brief stay on their trip to Earth. The ambassadors walked to the conference room like they had been there a hundred times before.

The conference room was rectangular, with a long table housing workstations on each side. On the walls, screens were mounted to allow projects to be projected for collaboration. For now, the screens were all tuned in to external cameras on the ship. Earth was visible in many of them, its placement adjusted based upon the camera angle, making a harsh harmony of its features.

Their group was almost the last to arrive. The only ambassador missing was the one that had met their shuttle.

However, his absence did not stop the High Priestex from their briefing. They stood up at the head of the table, making the room feel even smaller than it already did.

"Our work is not done," the High Priestex started. "This ship is its own world, one that is adrift between two very different planets. Here we are, Mars' representatives. We will continue to work for our people. This is not an abstract purpose, like our work on Earth, lobbying for resources and stopping wars. Here we represent the actual Martian citizens on this ship. You sit there believing that you know what to expect. After all, didn't you do the same on the way here?

"You are wrong. This situation is very different. From Mars, we traveled with humans that had spent time on our planet. Even if they had not liked our ways, they were exposed to them. They knew what it was like to interact with Martians. Now we travel with Earthens that have yet to learn our ways.

"You have spent the last three years trying to understand the earthen culture. Now is the true test of that knowledge. On Earth, we had to concede to their ignorance and intolerance. We ignored practices that were unjust and unacceptable. They are not our people, and all we can do is lead by example in such situations. Even then, some of us had problems with this." A few ambassadors turned and faced Matty. She continued to face the High Priestex, doing her best to ignore their gazes. "Now, we must protect our people. We are on Martian soil, and we cannot allow them to disrespect that.

Yet, we must handle it with the utmost caution. We are not separated by the vastness of space but by a few metal sheets.

"Many of these humans have never interacted with a Martian before. We must show them how to respect our ways before allowing them to step foot on our world. For those returning, we must remind them what it means to be Martian. I know I sound harsh, which goes against the teachings of the Goddess. Yet, all I am talking about is discipline.

"We would not permit a child to run unchecked, allowing them to grow into an ungrateful adult. Nor will we allow the Earthens to run unchecked, allowing them to bring down destruction on our planet. But, most importantly, we must protect our people. Our new citizens are fragile. They have suffered trauma at the hands of the Earthens. It is our time to show them that they are safe."

Matty heard the whispers of her peers trying to discount the High Priestex's words. What could be more demanding than the three years they just pulled on earth? Yet, the High Priestex was not prone to dramatics. Matty knew that if they said the ambassadors would be working hard, that is what she would do. After the nine months it took to return home, she would be given a six-month sabbatical. She could visit her family, do some hiking, and enjoy the sun on her face in one of the habitats.

As the High Priestex continued, Matty looked at the briefing on her pad. The first item was a summary of the Earthen passengers that security had flagged. There were a few corporate lieutenants and an Earthen judge sentenced to serve on the transport ship for undisclosed crimes. There were also the usual criminals, accused of minor offenses or just being different, that Earth had sentenced to work in the few mines that Mars allowed them to run.

Then Matty saw her. There were two pictures, one with the same striking green eyes and short blond hair that had caught Matty's attention at the quarantine hub. The photo looked more like a picture of someone about to head off on an exciting interstellar voyage. The second photo was the same person, only a few years younger. Her face was thin but not quite as gaunt, and her hair was auburn and so long that it hung well past her shoulders. The expression on this picture looked haunted. Matty read the name "Riley Matherson. Identity in question."

"Excuse me," Matty said. She realized she had cut off the High Priestex, but the words were already out of her mouth.

"Yes, Matty."

"What does 'identity in question' mean?"

"Ah, excellent question. The Earthen corporations are good at confirming identities. However, we are better. I assume that you are referencing the Matherson couple?" Matty shook her head in assent. "We are nearly certain that they are traveling under false paperwork. It is likely they are fleeing Earth and will apply for asylum once they reach Mars. However, someone needs to research the couple and determine the situation discretely. It is imperative that they not be alerted. It is possible that we are wrong, and they are something else."

"I'll do it," Matty said.

The High Priestex raised one eyebrow and stared at Matty. Then they broke off eye contact and said, "Very well."

Matty had difficulty focusing on the rest of the briefing. She kept going back to the pictures. Riley, now she had a name.

CHAPTER 6

RILEY

PAST

THE ROOM WAS DARK. The only light that entered came from the small cracks around the doorframe. It was not enough to allow Riley to see more than the brief outline of her hand. She knew that there was a light somewhere. Her father must have forgotten to turn it on when he put her in the closet. He was angry, so it was understandable.

She wasn't supposed to leave the house, but when she found the message, she couldn't resist. There were other people, like her, who saw the information in the data stream. The message was an invitation. Anyone who could read it was welcome, and Riley wanted to find a place where she was welcome.

Her father had pulled her out of school five years ago. Since then, she had been stuck alone with the tutors. Occasionally, she was allowed to attend a birthday party to practice her skills. Her tutors made her wear a lacy dress that hurt her skin. At the party, the girls had to sit quietly at tables, sip tea, and eat pieces of food with tiny silverware. The other girls made fun of her; she was sure of it. Only, she could never quite figure out how.

When she saw the message, she thought she might find a friend.

It wasn't hard to sneak out of the house. She just had to write a few lines of code into their home system, and the front door opened, letting her out. She had written a program to turn off all the cameras that came in contact with her pad. It was easy, as everything was connected to the same network. Her father would not be able to follow her.

It was harder to find the building. Riley was only ten and had never been allowed outside alone, and the streets were confusing. Some roads were just for walking, and others allowed transports down them. She had to find the right ones to walk on. She had to find the right way. Eventually, she walked off the path and hid in a doorway. She hacked into the public system, pulled up a city map, and wrote a program showing her location. It wasn't a complicated program, but it did take some time. Riley hoped the place would still be open. It was long past her bedtime.

The map took her to a set of fences. There were guards outside watching all the people as they went past. Riley almost turned away and went back home. She had never been allowed to go to this side of town, and the unfamiliarity of the situation made her heart race. But, somewhere on the other side of that wall were people like her. She was determined to get there somehow.

She gathered all her courage and walked up. In front of her were a man and a woman who removed their gloves and placed their fingertips on a scanner. It was a way of identifying them, Riley knew. The guard looked at his pad and let the woman walk into the body scanner. The scanner was something Riley understood. They were at the entrance of every guest door. You walked in, and the air rushed over you, decontaminating you. At the same time, it gathered up all the germs that came off you and ensured there was nothing new or flagged. If you were clean, you were allowed to continue past.

When the light flashed green, the door opened, and the woman was allowed to walk through. The chamber cleaned itself, and then the man stepped through. When he cleared, the man and woman started walking away. Riley was left standing at the gate alone.

"What are you doing here?" one of the guards asked her.

Riley's throat tightened, and she was unable to use her words. She stood there staring at the guards.

"It is a bit late for you to be out alone. Are those your parents?" He gestured towards the man and woman, now walking away.

Riley couldn't lie, but she also knew that if he thought she was alone, he would probably end up calling her parents, and she would be in trouble. So, she stood there staring at the man.

"Hey, is this your kid?" the man yelled toward the departing couple. He turned back towards Riley. "Can you talk?"

Riley shook her head. It wasn't a lie. She couldn't talk right now.

"No wonder they don't want to claim you," the guard sighed, scratching at his trimmed beard. "Having a defective kid around is no good to anyone. That doesn't give them the right to leave you with me. They think I'm going to take care of you, do they? I have too much to do already. Go on, get through the scanner and catch up to them. Next time you make sure they let you go first."

Riley nodded again. Then she stepped into the scanners and waited until the green light turned on and the doors opened. She walked fast towards the area where the couple had disappeared. When she turned past the building, she stopped and checked her pad. The message was from a place very near here.

She walked past the restaurants showing a glow of light behind closed blinds. Then the restaurants disappeared, shifting to shops that had bright windows showcasing their items even though they were closed. Then the shops disappeared, leaving metal-framed workhouses. The area became less lit, and the people disappeared until she found she was alone on the street. When she saw the building, it had no windows or a front door. There was a rolling door, like the one that moved to allow their transport to park.

Riley looked at the message and then double-checked the map. This had to be the right place. Tentatively she reached out and knocked on the rolling door. Nothing happened. Riley looked back at the message and realized that there was one more thing she had to do. She pulled some code from the message and ran it on her pad. The door lifted, stopping a few feet off the ground.

From the other side, Riley heard music and talking. She saw lights of all different colors bouncing off the ground. She froze. It was too loud and bright, and she hadn't even gone in.

"Either come in or go away," a voice shouted from behind the door. "Now, before you let more air in."

Riley nearly turned and ran. Then she thought about the message. Only those that could read it were inside. These were people like her. She leaned over and crawled under the door.

The room was even brighter on this side. There were lights of every color strung from the ceiling. They were moving around, so the colors never seemed to stay in the same place. Riley watched the colors dance across the floor and noticed the tables. There was a handful of them scattered around the room. On the tables were drinks, and some held food. Most had people sitting on them, all of them were on their pads. There were screens hung up on the wall so everyone could see. Lines of code were running across them.

It took Riley a few seconds to realize that many people were working on this code together. She stood transfixed until the door behind her closed, and she jumped.

"Who the fuck is this?" one of the people said. One by one, people turned away from their pads and stared at her. In the corner of the room, Riley saw someone stand up. The man was as old as her father but dressed in dirty overalls like a workman, his hair short and spiked with grease.

"How did you wander in here?" he asked her.

Riley held up her pad with the message showing on the screen.

"You found the message? Who helped you?"

"No one," she managed to say. "It was easy to see."

The man laughed. Others in the room laughed, and Riley turned to follow the sound. Men filled the room. Some were young, and some were old enough to be grandfathers. None were young like her. She looked around closely and found a few women sitting around the room. They were hard to see as most wore clothing just like the men. Riley stared at them and then down at her dress. It was a simple cotton one that hung down to her knees. She hated it, but it didn't hurt as much as the fancy dresses her tutors forced her to wear.

"What is a pretty young thing like you doing with the invitation?" The voice was deep, and Riley looked to see a big man with brown skin and a deep frown.

"I found it."

"A little girl found the code? We must be losing our

touch. Someone better start building a better one." The man was talking to the room, ignoring her. Riley moved towards one of the women sitting on a chair against the wall.

"Hi, I'm Riley." The woman didn't speak. Riley could understand that. "They let you wear pants?" At this, the whole room burst out laughing.

"Did you really find the code?" the woman asked.

Riley nodded.

"Prove it." The woman looked up towards the screens. Riley followed her gaze and became lost in the code. She had to read through what they had done before she began to understand. They were moving currency from one place to another. The money was all digital, only existing virtually, and Riley had never understood why it had such importance when it was so easy to manipulate. However, this money was behind some tight protection.

"Why do you want to move it?" Riley asked.

"We are taking it from people who have too much and sending it to an orphanage in the third tier."

Riley stared at her, her face blank.

"Do you know what an orphanage is?"

She shook her head.

"It is a place to go when you no longer have a mom or dad. They don't have anyone to pay for them, so they don't always have a lot of food to eat. We want to help them out."

"It's a good thing to help them?" Riley asked.

"Yes, it is a very good thing."

Riley turned back to the screen and connected her pad to their secure line. She went back over their code, repairing what wasn't quite right, and then took off where they left off. No one joined in to help her. They just watched as she moved the money over.

Riley was never quite sure how much time passed when she was working on a project. Once she was caught in the grip of something, time ceased to be important. She was at work, and the work made her happy. When she finished, Riley felt like she was emerging from another realm, remembering she had a physical body. The people in the room must have felt the same way. They all started pulling themselves away from the screen and looking at her.

"The little girl did it," someone screamed.

"I'm not a little girl," Riley said.

"Then what are you?" the woman asked.

"I want to wear pants."

The room laughed again, and Riley looked around to see if she had done something wrong. But everyone seemed to be happy. They went back to drinking and talking. They turned the screen to the newsfeed, where newscasters started talking about boring stuff. Someone left and returned with a pair of pants that were a little too big for her. She put them on and tucked in her dress. People would come up to her and talk to her about code. Sometimes they would tell her stuff she didn't know, and she would sit while they explained it to her. Then she showed them how to make it better.

They stayed talking until Riley could no longer keep her eyes open. Someone shook her awake. It was the same woman.

"I'm Splicer," she said. "Do your parents know that you're out?"

Riley shook her head.

"You had better get home before they find out. You know not to tell them about us, right?"

Riley shook her head again. "I have to get past the gates."

"You're from first-tier? I wouldn't think they would let any of their girls-" the woman paused, "I mean, their kids, hack."

"They don't let me. They don't know."

"I bet there's a lot that they don't know. Do you know how to make a fake ID profile?"

Riley stared at her, unsure of what she meant. The woman pulled up Riley's profile and read through what it said. She looked at Riley again but did not say anything about it.

"We need to hide this profile. Then we create a new one. It won't hold up too much, but it'll be enough to get past the gates. It's easier for boys to travel through, especially if they think you are tier two. Of course, we will have to find you a hat to hide all that hair, but you will be able to pass well enough."

"I'm not a boy."

"If you're not a girl and you're not a boy, then what are you?"

Riley wasn't sure what to say, so she said nothing.

"Well, for now, you will have to pretend to be a boy, like you pretend to be a girl in those pretty dresses."

That much, at least, Riley understood, so she nodded. They worked together to create a fake profile. Someone gave her a hat, and they hid all her straight auburn hair under the cap. Splicer even put some dirt on her face and clothes. It worked easy enough. Riley was able to get back through the gate and to the house. She made it back in the door without setting off the alarms. She had taken off and hidden the pants and hat before her father stormed into her room and dragged her off to the closet, locking her in.

CHAPTER 7

RILEY

PRESENT

RON AND RILEY'S quarters were small. Riley knew this; she had booked the tickets. Only, that was before her real husband had locked her in. Before Eliot had disappeared.

Eliot, her friend who should have been her fake husband, would have understood. He would have stayed hunkered down in their cabin the entire trip, helping her through her panic attacks and insisting they keep a low profile. He would have helped her finish her project to keep her mind occupied, so it was ready to release when they were safe.

Except her husband had locked her away, and when she was finally let out, Eliot was gone. She had to scramble to find someone to take his place and ended up with Ronald Bishop IV, her former betrothed.

When they boarded the ship, he held her hand as they walked to the cabin. He smiled and talked to her about his dreams for when they got to Mars. Riley knew it was all an act. It didn't surprise her that the minute they walked into their cabin, his smile disappeared, and his hand dropped from hers. They both looked around at the single bed, the tiny built-in desk, and an even smaller bathroom. It made the quarantine room look like a luxurious suite.

"I know it's small. But it's just for a few months, and then you will have enough money to buy an entire house once we arrive," Riley said.

Ron grabbed his suitcase, left conveniently inside their door, and put it on the bed. He reached under the bed and opened one of the storage drawers; it slid out soundlessly. From the suitcase he took his underclothing and a few other possessions they had managed to purchase before they left and stored them all neatly in the drawer. Then he took his few nicer clothing items and placed them on the hooks on the wall opposite the bed. They fit between the screen and the bathroom doorway. He looked at his few items, selected one of his shirts, and proceeded into the bathroom. Before he fully entered, he turned and looked at her. "You should get ready soon. Dinner is in less than an hour."

"Do you plan to eat in a dining room?" Riley asked.

"Yes, how else will we make connections before we get to Mars?"

"That's barbaric, eating in a room with other people. We have all finished quarantining, but there are not even separate pods. There are just tables together in a room. No one would eat there. I'm sure we can pick it up and bring it back here."

"If we stay in our room, how will we meet people? We need to build relationships before we get to Mars. I don't even have a job lined up yet."

"You don't need a job. I told you that I would take care of you. I have already transferred a sum into your account. That is to hold you over. Once we land on Mars, I will transfer over ten times that."

"I know you told me that because you were desperate to get me on this ship. Your father should have never married you off, not to him. I just needed one more chance." Ron took a step towards Riley, closing the distance. He reached his hand up and cupped one of her cheeks. "With his name, I could have earned back my reputation. He didn't listen, and now here we are. You found me on your own, and now I will take care of you. To hell with your father."

"I didn't find you to take care of me." Riley moved back against the wall, pulling away from his touch. "I just needed someone to get me on the ship. As soon as we land on Mars, we will go our separate ways. Your way will have a lot of money with it. What you do after that, I don't care, but for this voyage, leave me alone."

He moved towards her again, reaching his hand back to her cheek and stroking it. "Fine, don't go to dinner. I will tell them you are feeling unwell. Or maybe I will tell them how I married above my station to a tier-one woman who finds eating together barbaric."

"Tell them whatever you want." Riley moved sideways, climbing onto the bed to get away from him. "Remember that I am not your wife. If you want your money at the end of this trip, you need to keep your mouth shut about who I am."

She sat on the bed, her arms wrapped around her legs. Pulling her body together helped her to feel grounded. She stayed unmoving while Ron got ready. Then she watched him leave the room and tried to will herself to move. The walls were painted a blank white, and they were so close they felt like they were squeezing her together. She grabbed her pad and ran out of the room. The hallways trapped her in their grasp, so she ran aimlessly, unsure of where she was going but needing to keep moving. Then she saw a viewport. The Earth covered the entire frame. She went as close to the window as possible and sat with her arms wrapped around her legs.

They eventually fell into a routine. Ron would head out for a late lunch or an early dinner. He would stay out all night and come back in the early morning smelling like alcohol. The ship did not have an official bar, and bringing alcoholic beverages onboard was prohibited. However, a gentleman's club was open to all Earthen males regardless of social standing. No doubt they used it to overcharge on drinks, leaving men just that much more desperate for money when they finally arrived planetside.

Riley had programmed an alarm to notify her when Ron's pad started moving back towards their room. She would be awake and dressed before he arrived. She would listen to his drunken slurs, fend off his pathetic attempts at seduction, and leave him passed out on the bed.

On the first day, she explored. The hallways were mostly empty. Each deck seemed to have a few small mess halls, two gyms, and a handful of themed social centers. She found her way back to the observation deck and was pleased to see it mostly empty. There were just one couple in the corner, and a group of men huddled near the window.

Seeing so many people walking around without their face masks was uncomfortable. She knew that everyone had passed quarantine and that the ship's ventilation was the best. However, after habitually wearing the contraption every time she left her house for the last 32 years, she found that she could not just leave it off now. She might as well be walking around naked.

She turned her attention to the Earth. It still filled up most of the window. They were facing the night side, and the lights below sparkled under the blanket of haze. After watching for a few minutes, she settled down to work. She had left before her program was finished, and Riley wanted to take advantage of the time they had while still being in better communication range of Earth.

Her silence lasted less than an hour before a portly gentleman sat beside her. She scooted away from him, put away her pad, and then looked at him. He wore the Segadon corporation symbol, a firebird. His jacket had a small patch and a full-color rendering on his back. Their corporation specialized in trade and resources, and the ship would most likely be full of their men going to work off some debts at the mine. Riley did not know much about them, just what she had overheard from her father and a few history books she had managed to download. They did not believe in marriage. Instead, they treated women as commodities that the men shared until they became pregnant. The day she learnt that was one of the few times that had made Riley happy to be part of the Molbin corporation.

"You don't need to move away from me. I was coming to say hello." His voice was oily.

Riley stood up and started walking away.

"Come on now, let's talk some." He grabbed her wrist and pulled her back. "What's your name?"

"I'm sorry," she managed to say. "My husband doesn't like me talking to other men."

"Well then, your husband shouldn't leave you alone." He pulled her closer, wrapping his arms around her. She screamed. She didn't mean to, but all the anger and frustration built up until she couldn't take it. Yet another man was putting his hands on her, and she didn't have to take it this time. She screamed, and she fought, and she stomped on his foot. He didn't let her go. Instead, he seemed to enjoy the challenge.

A man turned away from a small group standing near the window and watched. Finally, he spoke. "What corporation are you?"

"I'm Molbin," Riley said. "My husband is in our quarters."

The man tapped on the shoulders of his friends and gestured them towards Riley. "She's one of ours." Only then did the group move to help.

"I don't want any trouble," the Segadon man said. "I found her, and now I want her. You can have her when I'm done."

At this, one of the men threw a punch, landing on the Segadon member's chin. He staggered back enough that Riley could move out of his grasp.

A second man came and put himself between Riley and the Segadon man. "There's a group of Segadon breeders aboard," he said. "It would be best if you talked to your boss about privileges. But our women belong to only one man."

Riley turned and ran from the observation room as fast as she could. After that, she only stayed in female-zoned areas. Except the female social clubs were loud. Riley could only handle so much time listening to the women talk about clothing and the virtues of their husbands. They were also decorated in pastel pinks and purples that caused Riley to get headaches. It was next to impossible to get any real work done there, especially since she had to hide that she could read.

However, they were required to do thirty minutes of mandatory exercise each day. It was considered unladylike to sweat, so the women would go into the gym to meet their requirements and leave as fast as possible. Riley found herself staying in the gym longer and longer. She found a new sense of joy in pushing her body to move faster and harder.

Then, when she finished, she found a quiet space and would finally manage to get some work done.

CHAPTER 8

MATTY

PRESENT

MATTY FELT the excitement of First Night in the air as she walked through the community rooms. Each family had gathered together. The adults sat on the cold metal deck plating or their suitcases. Most of the younger children were already comfortable with their new families after quarantining together and were sitting on the laps of the adults. The older children and teenagers who'd quarantined on their own were sitting on their cots, separate from the event but secretly listening.

In each group, the elders told the story of the first days of space travel. They spun tales of how Mars had been colonized and then turned into a free state that wanted to create a world where all were welcome. The story varied slightly with each storyteller. But tonight, it was less about the history and more about bringing the new citizens into Martian traditions.

The mess hall had created a special feast, and the ambassadors passed the meals out to each family. After tonight, retrieving meals would become the family's responsibility. But tonight, it was easier for the ambassadors to handle the task while everyone settled in. Naturally, it had become part of First Night tradition.

Each tray held a collection of hydrated Earthen dishes. As Matty passed out the trays, the elders would tell their family that it was a way of celebrating the planet they were leaving behind. Tonight, they would dine on Earthen food, and gradually the chefs would introduce them to the unprocessed vegan Martian diet. It was tradition, but it was also to help acclimate their body. They had done the same on the voyage to Earth. Most Martians had never eaten the chemicals used to create Earthen food.

There were a lot of changes in travel throughout the last century. When the corporation had first launched their transport ships, they had expected the Martians and Earthens to live next to each other in the small rooms. The community rooms were originally cargo holds. When tensions strained between the cultures during the early voyages, the Martian passengers moved in with the cargo. The Martians never visited their assigned rooms on the next journey. Instead, they headed straight for the cargo holds. Eventually, the corporation gave in, split the ship based on planarity, and doubled its profit.

At the start of each voyage, the Earthens prepared the

room by lining cots arranged with military precision. It was now a tradition on First Night to sleep in the arranged cots. The Martians would store their bags wherever they could fit and sleep apart. It only ever lasted that one night. After that, they made the space their own.

When she had delivered all the meals, Matty returned to her room and collected one of her larger bags. She went into the first community and joined with a family. The family had come to collect a handful of younger orphans, about fifteen. Some children were so young that the emigration paperwork must have started upon conception. The family elder was only in her mid-30s. Families sent who they could; not everyone could handle the Earth's gravity, even with conditioning.

Matty watched the young adults chase the children in a game with few rules beyond not getting caught and laughing a lot. There was a child without legs on one of the cots watching with a smile. On Mars, specialists would provide tools to help navigate without their legs. For the voyage home, the family had brought the child an exoskeleton that required the assistance of someone slightly bigger. Earlier, the child had fearlessly led the chase. Now they sat tired but laughing as they watched.

Matty carefully gauged the child's reaction as she sat on the cot. After spending the quarantine period together, most children were attached to their new caregivers. However, not all were comfortable with unknown adults. When the child did not seem to mind her presence, she relaxed. Then she opened her bag and placed it between her and the child. The child looked; their eyes were wide at all the toys sitting in the bag. Matty knew that at her age, around four years, she would have jumped right into the bag, assuming they were hers. But the child just stopped and stared.

"You can pick one, any one you would like," Matty said. "Don't worry, everyone will have one by the end of tonight, but you can have the first pick."

This was yet another tradition. The new citizens that came to Mars did not have much. Most had struggled with having food, let alone something all their own. In the early missions, ambassadors had seen the new citizens going without and had shared from their luggage. Now, each ambassador planned specifically for this night, selecting something to hand out.

Niko had carried blankets from Mars in vacuum-packed seals, sitting in his quarters on Earth for three years, all specifically for this night. Each blanket was made from the fibrous drought-resistant stalks genetically engineered to survive on Mars. They had been hand-dyed and woven by Niko's family. Then inside each blanket was tucked a letter welcoming the new citizens to Mars.

Matty had chosen to collect toys, specifically Earthen toys. The children would have everything they needed on Mars. But she wanted to give them things they had not had on Earth. When she was young, Matty remembered a new citizen coming to her school and teaching them about Earth. He had taught them about the orphanage where he grew up and how they did not have much. The man had gestured to their classroom and told them that the first thing he had done when he came to Mars was sit and play with the toys, even though he was a teenager when he had made the voyage.

It was something that Matty had always remembered, and she wanted to give that experience to the children on this voyage. So she had stuffed her bag full of every type of toy she could find. There were puzzle games, stuffed animals, toy vehicles, building blocks, and anything small and exciting she could find in the upper-tier toy shops. Every week, she visited at least one shop and spent most of her small allowance and her entire family donation to create this collection.

The child reached in and grabbed a stuffed bunny. They held it to their chest and proudly declared they would name it "Shinit."

"Shinit, what's a shinit?" Matty asked. But the child just continued hugging their stuffed toy. "Do you know what type of animal this is?"

The child looked at Matty blankly.

"Long ago, there were lots of animals that lived on Earth. This one is called a bunny. They would hop all over and wiggle their noses." Matty attempted to wiggle her nose, getting a laugh from the child.

"Does Mars have animals?" the child asked.

"No, there are not many animals on Mars. Unfortunately,

we could not save them. But now you have your bunny to bring there."

The child seemed content with this answer and waved the bunny around for all the children to see. The game stopped abruptly as the children gathered around the toy, stroking its soft fur.

Matty waited, allowing the child the attention before gesturing to the bag and announcing that each child could choose a toy. There was a second of shock, and then the oldest of the children, not more than eight, guided the youngest, not more than two years of age. Matty oversaw their selection a bit, making sure the toy they chose was appropriate for the age, and the child walked away with a rubber duck that Matty had found in an old-fashioned toy shop on one of her expeditions.

"That is a duck. It used to go Quack Quack." At this, all the children laughed and broke out in their version of duck noises. The children took their time picking out their toys. Each one gave homage to the child who had just picked before the next would come to make their selection. The children soon were grouped, showing off their toys. They quickly let another child hold them, but no one did much more than touch them.

"Thank you," one of the older family members said. He was a child himself, no more than nineteen years.

"I need to go visit the other families," Matty said. It was

hard for her to leave them. Only the thought of more toyless children encouraged her to move.

There were plenty of children, more than two hundred of just the younger ones, but Matty had also bought enough toys for the teenagers. Tomorrow they would all be issued pads, which would take up most of their attention for the older kids. But tonight, even teenagers could experience the joy of playing with toys. Seeing a teenager's eyes light up at finally having their own teddy bear or hover ship was nearly as infectious as seeing the joy in the younger children.

This was a night when family bonds began to grow. And this experience would break down the boundaries in a way that nothing else could. Matty saw teenagers playing with their new younger siblings for the first time. One new citizen adult started playing catch with one of his Martian family, tears streaming down his face. One teenager picked out a deck of cards and started a game with her entire household.

But not everyone felt comfortable picking out of her bag. For the younger children, she let their new parents pick for them. The toy would be there for them when they were ready. For the teenagers, Matty let them know that they were welcome to something from her bag as long as there was something in it. A few teenagers slunk towards her later in the evening, away from their new family, and picked out their prize. Some held off, and Matty also respected that choice.

It was a long and festive night, with most families not going to bed until the early hours of the ship morning. Matty slinked off to catch a few hours of sleep of her own. When she left, her people were asleep in cots with bags and items scattered around them. A few still sat gathered together, whispering. She was gone less than four hours, but they had transformed the area by the time she returned.

They had opened suitcases and produced yards of bright fabric. The ambassadors stepped in and helped hang the cloth from the ceiling, allowing it to flow around each family, giving them a home open to all.

By the second night, they had adapted the cargo hold into a colorful community. The room was full of bright reds and oranges with just enough other colors to stop it all blending in together. They brought the cots into the new homes to provide a place for the family to sleep. They created outside gathering places by unpacking electronic fire pits, expanding chairs, and throwing down pillows.

The rooms echoed with the voices of her people. If Matty closed her eyes, she could almost imagine being inside one of the Mars habitats or walking through one of the cave cities. The transformation was essential to help the new citizens acclimate to their new culture. Although, after three years on Earth, Matty realized the most significant difference was not in the noise and community. It was in accepting people for who they were.

. . .

The ambassadors spent most of the first weeks meeting the families and helping when they could. It was a part of the job that Matty loved. People gave her energy that she could not find anywhere else.

Each community had given itself a unique name to help offset the dreary numbering system that the Earthen builders had assigned. Community Three had named theirs after one of the first underground cities, Jezero. It was also Matty's home on Mars, where her mother ran a small supply store in the outer ridges near the observation window. Matty spent most of her childhood playing under that domed sky or running through the maze of city tunnels.

The cargo hold was a different sort of maze. Each family had picked their spot, with walkways created as an afterthought. Children had already started to explore, and whole tribes would come running around a corner with only their screaming as a warning. The sound of singing drifted between the tents, second only to the constant chatter. It was chaos and love. Matty had not felt happier in a long time.

CHAPTER 9

RILEY

PAST

AFTER THE CONVERSATION WITH BUNNY, Riley headed straight home. When she arrived, the house was empty; her son was out, and the staff had left for the evening. It was easy to slip into her son's room and borrow a pair of his clothes that would not stand out in tier-two. Then she bound her chest and pinned her hair up under a cap. She caught her reflection in the mirror and stopped. It wasn't often that she liked how she looked, but Riley felt comfortable in a way she was often not allowed. She liked how the feminine aspect of her face contrasted with the slim masculine build the clothes gave her.

She grabbed her pad and quickly found the restaurant that Bunny had mentioned. It opened a few months ago and already had a reservation list of two years, yet somehow, he'd managed to get in.

Next, she logged into the hacker bar's chat room. She had encrypted it for them years ago. She wanted a way to keep in contact, even when she could not connect in person. These were her people; some she would trust with her life. Some she already had. They had worked on a few projects that could easily have caused them all to disappear in the middle of the night, quietly. Thankfully, the corporations hadn't yet caught them. The project they were working on now made all the rest look like child's play. It only took her a few moments to find the bar's new location and create an acceptable profile to get past the gates. With her face mask in place, even her more feminine features disappeared, allowing her a sense of power.

She slipped out of her house and into the quiet of the evening. It was easier walking around as a boy. No one gave her a second glance or questioned her right to be out at this time at night.

The gates were empty. Most of the workers had already passed. The upper tiers that were slumming it in the middle tiers' bars had already crossed. The bored guard had barely given her a second glance as he scanned her pass, checked her thumbprint, and sent her on her way through the decontamination chamber.

She had crossed into the middle tier a few dozen times since her first crossing. Once, when she was young, she managed to walk through the third-tier gates. The farther she walked, the more the city fell into disrepair. Trash was piled up in the streets, houses crumbled, and stores held lines to purchase necessities.

It was the people that had concerned her the most. They were skinnier than her teenage frame, too poor to buy food or clothing. People ran around without shoes or, worse, face masks. One man was leaning against the side of a building. His chest was red from the sun, and she could see each rib even at a distance. All he had on was a pair of pants riddled with holes. He started coughing, loud wet coughs that echoed in the streets. He couldn't have been more than thirty years old, and his body was already breaking down.

She had stood frozen between her desire to help and her fear of contagion. Her indecision cost the man. He was picked up by a pair of uniformed peace officers during a second coughing fit and put into the back of a motorized pallet. A half a dozen people covered the pallet. Some were as still as death; like the man, others displayed their sickness loudly and publicly.

She was fourteen at the time and just a week away from her marriage. She had planned to run away by crossing through the third tier and heading out to the wilderness until she found a town that would take in a female hacker. But instead, she realized how little of the world she understood. She learned how much no one had ever taught her. No amount of lessons on table manners and social pleasantries had prepared her for the world. So, she headed back to her home and started teaching herself. She had tried to use her status to help the world, but for all her expensive dresses, she had as little control as the man hoisted into the pallet.

Riley pulled herself back from the reminiscing. None of the poverty was visible on this side of town. The area bordering tier one was newly renovated, with just enough grunge that the elite of tier one could pretend that they were risking themselves mingling with a lower class without having to lose any of their privileges.

Even here, her clothing gave her power. This close to the fence, no one knew who was an actual tier-two worker or a young corporate executive having a night on the town. As long as she acted the part, her head held high with an assurance that she was more important than anyone else, everyone moved out of her way.

The restaurant was not far from the gate. It was well-lit, with open windows coming back in fashion. It allowed everyone passing the restaurant to see the faces of those who could dine on fresh food. People stopped and looked like it was a show. The window was the screen into another reality. The onlookers pointed at the famous entertainers and heads of corporate divisions sequestered in their transparent eating pods. They stood transfixed by the food. Most had never seen seafood this far inland. They gossiped about how much it must cost to eat there and fantasized about doing so themselves one day.

Each huddled within their groups, conditioned to put distance between those they knew and strangers, just in case.

It left gaps in the window where Riley was able to look in. She stood back, concerned that she would be recognized if she went too close.

It was easy to identify the man she had been married to for the last 20 years. Her gut clenched, and her palms started sweating at seeing him and the young woman, a girl really, sitting next to him. She smiled sweetly with ruby-red lips, and laughed, her blond curls bobbing up and down, at jokes that Riley knew were not funny.

The comments from Bunny questioning her health now made sense. Her husband needed people to see her. He required the perception that she was not well, which would spread tonight. Now that her son would be collecting his inheritance - the inheritance she currently held in her name as the only adult in the Medici line - her husband would trade her for a younger model. There was only one way for that to happen. Her husband was going to have her killed.

Riley raced off and headed towards the hacker's bar. She had to live long enough to finish her plan. There was still a few months' worth of work to do. The only way to buy herself enough time was for her to leave the planet.

She typed on her pad as she rushed away from the restaurant, double-checking the encryption before sending it. She continued running, her muscles tense until she got the ping. He had read her message and replied that he would meet her there.

Even rushing, it was another ten minutes before she

reached the newest bar location. The area was reasonably nice for being this far into tier-two, but this particular house had fallen on hard times. The chat had mentioned that the previous owner was accused of treason. No one in the area wanted to be associated with it. It was the perfect place to meet, at least for a few nights before the bar moved on.

Riley followed the directions, slipping in from the back alley. The back door was open, half hanging on the hinges from when the corporation must have broken it down. It was easy for Riley to slip in. Locating the basement door took longer. It was cut into the floor of the bedroom closet. Riley was sure she would never have found the button hidden in the wall without the instructions. It must have been how it was missed in the raid, not that it did the inhabitants any good.

The stairs were dark, with bioluminescent tape and the glow from the doorway to help guide the way. As soon as her head cleared the entrance, the door shut, closing her in and leaving darkness. There was just the slight glow of the tape on each step to guide her way down. When she reached the bottom of the stairwell, she had to hunt for the second button. There was nothing to highlight it on the dark walls, and she finally had to use the glow of her pad to see the worn part of the wall. Even then, she would not have been able to locate it if she hadn't known exactly where to look. If they were this good, she wondered how they'd gotten caught.

When the door opened, she could finally see the lights

strobing and hear the music playing. There were only a handful of people set up at the tables. Riley had once asked the chat how they managed to find the locations and move all the furniture undetected. No one was willing to let her in on the secret, not that she blamed them. She was the only tier-one in their group, and they only allowed her in because she had joined them so young.

She looked around and was relieved to see that he had made it before her. She slid into a chair at the table.

"Eliot," she said.

"What was so urgent?" Eliot was about twenty years older than her. His dark hair was cut short and trimmed to the height of masculine fashion. He wore his face clean-shaven, as respectable corporate members should. Even his clothes were the perfect brown suit with polished shoes. Everything about him was tailored, so he would not be remembered.

"Do you still want to get off?" Riley talked fast, having difficulty trying to contain all that had happened.

Eliot looked at his drink, watching the lights reflect off the glass before taking a slow sip. "You know I do. I don't have much choice."

"Neither do I, I'm afraid. There has been a change of plans, and I need to come with you."

"Don't be rash. There is plenty of time to talk things through."

"I'm out of time. I need you to marry me." The words rushed out of Riley without context.

Eliot let out a deep sigh. "If I had any problem marrying a woman, I wouldn't have any reason to leave. No, I have to go alone. He's waiting for me there if he hasn't given up on me already."

"I don't mean to marry me literally. I need you to be my husband on the voyage. They will never let me travel alone, and I need to leave." Riley began tapping her fingers on the table, only noticing when Eliot gave her a pointed look.

"Rushing is how you make mistakes. You need to step back and think things through. You cannot just leave with no preparation." Eliot picked up his drink again, looked at the empty glass, and set it back down.

"My husband is on a date with a young woman tonight." Riley's voice came out louder than expected. She checked around to make sure no one overheard and continued quieter. "He is courting my replacement. My son turns 16 in a month, and he has already decided that I am a liability."

"He would be irresponsible to kill you before your son inherits. It will cause all kinds of complications that would scar the family name. It would be a dumb thing to do."

"No one has accused my husband of being smart. I need to leave tonight. I can't go back there," Riley said.

"The transport doesn't leave for two more months." Eliot turned and snapped his fingers to get the barkeeper's attention. The sound was lost in the thrum of the music, so Eliot raised up his empty glass instead. "What do you plan to do in the meantime?"

"I need to find somewhere to stay. I can pay someone to hide me."

"Money only buys loyalty until someone pays them more." He stopped talking while Eliot's new drink was delivered, even though they both knew the barkeep. "No one would risk keeping you hidden once they start looking for you, and they will start looking for you. He would have no other choice. So, the safest thing is to go back and wait until the night of his inheritance party and slip out. Then I will play your husband until we go to Mars, and I can finally marry my fiancé."

"You love him, don't you?"

"Yes, I do," Eliot's lip curled at one edge in something like a smile. "Is there anyone that you have ever loved like that?"

Riley took a second to think through the question. "I don't think I'm made to love. Do you think I will be safe if I return?"

"I do. It would be prudent for your husband to wait until after your son's party. You have until then. You will need the time to come up with an appropriate plan. If you leave sometime after the party, you should be good. He will need at least a couple of weeks, to be safe. He cannot be too obvious about it, or he will lose the respect of the corporate members."

"What about you? Will you be safe?"

"There have been some questions, but I've managed them. I'm currently engaged to a sweet girl from the second tier. She is a perfect match for someone in my position. We set the wedding for six months from now. Just enough time to call it off and leave for a better opportunity on Mars."

"If I am going back, I should do so now before he gets home." Riley stood up and wrapped her arms around his sitting form. "Be safe."

"Everything will work out all right," Eliot said.

CHAPTER 10

RILEY

PRESENT

LIFE on the Earthen half of the ship was not much different from Earth itself. Riley soon found herself falling back into the same habits she'd had before the ship. She lived her life trying not to do anything to set off Ron while hiding who she was as much as possible. If she left the room, she called him first. He usually yelled at her for disturbing him, but if he forgot to turn off his comm right away, she overheard him bragging to the other men about how he had his woman in line.

It became easier to stay in the room. The compact space was difficult, but she didn't have to worry about people walking in on her. At least she had her pad. She spent hours working on her program. But she always made sure to tidy up first. She had learned that nothing upset a man more than coming home to a dirty place. It was ironic, considering how messy men were.

There were a few more incidents. When they attended a play put on by some other travelers, he grew upset that she was not showing enough enthusiasm for their work. He slapped her, and his new friends laughed and cheered so hard that it was easy for Riley to see how Ron had become so possessive. She glanced at the faces of the other wives. Most refused to meet her gaze. They were probably all relieved it was not them, at least not this time. Riley wondered if all women were as broken.

Riley thought about leaving. It was just that there was nowhere to go. She couldn't confess to the fake marriage. They would throw her in jail and kill her. After putting up with so much to get this far, it didn't seem hard to put up with a little more, except it was. She had spent her entire life trying to be what everyone else wanted her to be. She just wanted a chance to find out who she actually was.

There would be no escape on Earth, and even though she was on a spaceship that was currently hurling through the solar system, it was still considered earth. Yet, just a few floors below her, it was Mars. The Molbin corporation kept strict control over all information about Mars on Earth. Riley had only managed to break into a few government reports. They described the Martian people as uncivilized and uneducated. They called them religious fanatics that disavowed the blessings of consumerism. It also said they allowed deviant behavior, such as allowing women equal rights and promoting a free mingling of society.

In the hacker group, they talked about Mars like a mythical fairytale. People could be whoever or whatever they wanted. Women were the same as men, and anyone could have relations with anyone they chose. She knew a few that had managed to make it to Mars, but they never contacted her on Earth after they left. To do so would have put her at risk.

As Ron's behavior continued to be erratic, Riley felt like she had no other choice. She needed a new plan. To do that, she needed to know more about Mars.

Riley had taken a few glances at the Martian's secure network. Hacking directly was going to be difficult. In all honesty, getting into Earth's systems was easy. Most corporations were so focused on profit that they neglected security. They did not fix known gaps leaving it accessible to enter if you knew what you were doing. Often, it was not even a challenge. However, the Martian network was unknown. Their computer sciences may have started at the same place when the colonies moved to Mars, but now, divided for over a hundred years, it was completely different.

Riley knew a frontal attack rarely worked in a closed system. What she needed was someone to let her in. She needed someone to install a backdoor into the system or find an unaccompanied pad already connected to the secure parts of the network. While she thought of a way in, she kept looking at the entire network. After hours, Riley realized that she had been going about the whole thing wrong.

The Martian network had tiered security. The vast majority of the information was free for the taking. Riley tried to access the information with the tightest security, assuming the available data was propaganda and nonsense. Except Mars was not Earth. Their economy was built on socialism, a vulgar term on earth, and they believed in sharing without profit. So, the available information should tell her everything she needed to know about what kind of society Mars was. If it were the same propaganda as Earth, then she would see that they were not to be trusted.

It only took her a few minutes to connect to Mars' network. It almost felt like they let her in. The signal strength was strong, and Riley was sure that it must run throughout the entire ship.

Riley started searching all the open-access data. There were thousands of free access books, not just Martian literature. There were a few Earth titles that Riley knew only from arrest records she had obtained over the years. Instead of one news station per corporation, there appeared to be hundreds. All the stories were accessible to all the citizens. Some focused on specific topics, others on regions, but they were all there for you to see. The media files alone would take Riley a lifetime to sort through, let alone to watch and listen to them.

Riley went straight for the school textbooks. She figured she could tell a lot about the culture by what they taught their young. Riley lost track of time while reading, and she was engrossed in a history book when Ron stormed into their cabin.

"Why aren't you ready?"

"Ready for what?"

"Dinner. I told you when I left that you needed to clean up for dinner. We are meeting with the McKennins tonight."

Riley tried to remember. This morning seemed so long ago, and she had already traveled through decades of history. There were stories of wars and uprisings and whole civilizations she had never heard about before.

"I'm sorry, I must have forgotten." Riley moved off the bed and towards the wall hangers. She moved her hand over her clothing, trying to decide which of the dresses she would force on herself.

"You're sorry? What have you been doing all day? I am out there trying to build our future on Mars. These are the people we will be living with until we can restore our fortune and return to Earth. Yet here you are lounging around like you don't have a care in the world. You should show more respect for me."

"You do remember that you're not actually my husband? You're pretending." The words that Riley had read were still floating in her brain, causing her to forget to censor her remarks. "Once we get to Mars, you never have to worry about seeing me again. It is great that you are making connections, but make them without me."

When the hand hit her cheek, she expected it. Whenever true words slipped out of her mouth, it always meant that she would get hit. She threw her hand up to her face to check for blood. Thankfully her hand was there to protect her face when he landed a full-on punch. The impact made Riley fall backward onto the bed, and Ron climbed on top of her before she could move.

"You will stop disrespecting me," Ron hissed. "You walked in here as my wife, and you are my wife. I have an image to maintain, and I will not have you leaving me as soon as we get to Mars. This is my chance. You will not ruin this for me."

He pinned her hands above her head with one hand. She tried to move away, but his knees locked in her hips. She wanted to kick him, but her feet couldn't reach him.

"You are not my husband," she screamed. "You're only here because I brought you. You are at my mercy. Imagine if they found out what a loser you are. Imagine if they found out how far you fell, how much you lost. You are the laughing-stock of the Molbin corporation. You will never get back to Earth. Even if you single handedly redefined the Martian business world, they would never see you as more than a joke."

She should have shut up; she tried to shut up. But it was so hard to hold on when the rage washed through her. All the words that she kept bottled up flew out of her mouth. She could see the anger building in his eyes, and she still couldn't stop. All she could think as she continued to call him out as the worthless person he was, was that at least she got off Earth before she died. At least she made it this far.

But he didn't kill her. Instead, he slapped her until her lips were swollen and she couldn't speak anymore. Then he pulled up her skirt, ripped off her underclothes, and entered her, thrusting himself in her dry body and screaming at her, "Who's your husband now?"

When he finished, he wiped himself off on her clothing, adjusted his trousers, and walked out of the cabin. She had thought that it couldn't hurt anymore, that as often as her husband had used her body as his own, she was now immune to the pain. So, while she felt the familiar fractures in herself, like the fissures in the Earth's crust, she was even more surprised to find that she was still capable of breaking even more.

Eventually, after the tears had dried, she stood up. She looked back at the dresses hung on the wall. They all seemed like too much work, so she grabbed a blanket off the bed, not caring about how disgusting it was, and wrapped it around herself. Then she left.

CHAPTER 11

MATTY

PRESENT

A MONTH INTO THE VOYAGE, Matty had yet to reach out to Riley. She had tried, but the Grand Priestex had stopped her. They had told her the couple was being monitored and were not a threat. Her priority needed to be with their planet for now. Every ambassador had to put aside their regular tasks to ensure that all the citizens were settled. Some adults did not connect well with their new families. Some of the Martians were unprepared for the needs of their new citizen children and needed extra hands. It was a lot of adjustment, but Matty loved it.

For the first few weeks, Matty could not walk into a community without a crisis to solve. As time passed, new citizens slowly adjusted, and families gained a routine. Finally, Matty found herself walking through a community before lunchtime. She spent the afternoons going through Riley's files, trying to understand her better.

With things quieting down, Matty had time to develop a plan on the best way to reach out to Riley. She was sitting in the team room trying to create a strategy when one of the tech nerds interrupted her. All the ambassadors had become familiar over the last three years, but Matty wasn't particularly close to any of the tech nerds. Tick was the nerdiest of the bunch. Even on Earth, they'd spent most of their time looking at a screen doing things Matty could not comprehend. So it was surprising that they sat next to her at the long table and started a conversation.

"You're trying to make contact with the Matherson's?" Tick was dressed in the dusty brown jumpsuit all the ambassadors were assigned, but few wore. Their eyes were covered in glasses that let them see screens hovering around the room. It gave the appearance that they were not looking at Matty when they talked.

"Yes, has there been an update?" Matty asked.

"The wife, Riley, has been snooping around our network. It is subtle. I almost didn't catch the pings. It's just not activity we usually see on the ships, so I got curious. It seems like she is trying to figure out what to do." Tick was moving their fingers, typing on a virtual keyboard that Matty could not see.

"I'm not following you."

"She is exploring our network. I'm unsure if she is planning anything specifically or if she's curious."

"Has she gotten in?" Matty watched the tech nerd as they twisted around in their seat. She knew they were seeing something projected in the air, but she could not see it, and all the movement made her head hurt.

"No, but she hasn't tried yet either. She just keeps sending pings to determine the level of security." Tick stopped talking and turned their gaze to one spot.

"What's going on?" Matty asked.

"It looks like she's decided what to do. She is trying to get into the archive."

"The archive? Why would she want to go there?" Matty frowned. "That's all available information. She couldn't get anything useful from there."

"That would depend on what she would consider useful information." The High Priestex's voice joined them from across the room. Walking over, they pulled out their pad, typed, and then flung some information onto one of the wall screens.

"I don't understand." Matty said. "Anyone can access the archives. So why would Riley need to try to break in?" Lines of data displayed across the screen, all of it in computer code that Matty could not make sense of.

"Anyone on Mars can access the archives," the High Priestex said. "But I would hope that you would understand after three years on Earth that Earthens survive through power and control. They do that by limiting access."

"I still don't understand. Why shouldn't she be allowed into the archives?"

"I think allowing her into the archives is exactly what we should do. Tick, can you give her pad access?"

"I can, but she already got in on her own." They touched a few buttons on their virtual keyboard.

"Can we track what she's looking at?" the High Priestex asked.

Tick nodded, typed a few more buttons, and flung another screen onto the wall. This one Matty could understand. It was a simple folder system that sorted public record data based on keywords and topics. Riley was shifting through the folders where she finally opened a set of school textbooks.

"It doesn't look like she is doing much of anything," Matty said. "What is the point of her pulling up textbooks for children?"

"You have seen how they treat women on Earth?" the High Priestex asked.

"I've seen women being controlled by men. I've seen them be talked to like a child and not only take it but also enjoy the attention. The women on Earth are weak. I don't understand why they put up with it. The Earthen men tried the same on us, and it didn't take much before they knew to treat us with more respect."

"Matty, what would happen if Earth stopped working with Mars?" the High Priestex asked.

"Nothing would get done. They know we were the voice of Mars and that Mars respects women." Matty moved her eyes off the screen and focused on the High Priestex.

"Yes, Mars respects women. But we came with power, correct?"

"I see your point. But Earthern women have power also. There are more women in most of the corporations than there are men."

The High Priestex laced their hands together and placed them on their slightly bowed face. "Let me try to explain this differently. On Mars, what would you do if someone were to hit you?"

"It depends. If I needed to defend myself, I would hit them back. If not, then I would report them."

"Would you get in trouble for reporting them for hitting you?"

"Of course not." Matty leaned back in her chair and looked back at the screen. Riley had opened a textbook on early Martian history and was reading through the text.

"On Earth, what happens if a woman reports a man for hitting her?"

Matty reluctantly brought her attention back to the High Priestex. "I assume their peace officers would punish the man who hit them."

"Based upon your experience, that would make sense.

You assaulted one of the highest government officials, and after he stopped hurrahing the female ambassadors," the High Priestex said.

"Exactly."

"Do you know what happens to Earthen women?"

"What do you mean?" Matty finally looked at them with interest.

"On Earth, if a woman reported a man for hitting her, it would be reported to the husband. If it was another man, then the husband could demand justice. Usually, the justice would be financial repercussions given to the husband. The woman would never see justice. If the husband hits her, he may decide to punish his wife for reporting him. I have seen women killed for daring to complain. Do you know the punishment for a husband who kills their wife?"

"I assume they get incarcerated. As barbaric as it is, it would probably qualify them for the death penalty?"

"What would happen if I took this pad and broke it?" The High Priestex held up their pad and slammed it towards the table's edge. They stopped at the last second, a hair's breath from causing the pad to crack.

Matty instinctively flinched away from the pad, causing her seat to turn, the chair leg firmly bolted to the ground. "Besides everyone saying that was a stupid thing to do, nothing."

"Exactly," they smiled grimly. "Because if you destroy your own property, that is your choice. On Earth, women are property. So, why would he be punished if a man justifiably chooses to destroy his property?"

"They can't...they wouldn't," Matty sputtered.

"I fear you spent too much of your time on Earth working on trade deals and not enough time understanding the Earthern situation. Yes, we go there to increase our trade and to represent Mars. However, just as importantly, we go to learn our history. We need to see the Earth's choices so we know not to repeat them. We have to do better than that."

Matty turned and stared at the wall screen, watching what items Riley read. She had just finished reading through the Martian constitution, and was moving on to a political science book. It was a textbook that Matty knew well. She had used it when she had decided to study to become an ambassador.

"She knows nothing about Mars?"

"Very likely," Tick replied.

"Then why did she come?"

"I suppose what she was running away from was worth the risk of being caught forging papers, lying about a marriage, and ending up on a planet that she knows nothing about," the High Priestex said.

"You said before only that the couple is suspicious. It sounds like you have found out more about them."

"We were able to match her to some recent news feeds. We found her obituary."

The High Priestex transferred the news feed to Matty's pad. She read through it quickly.

Riley Medici, the wife of Nisili Medici and sole child of the late Vice-President Benedict Medici, passed away last Friday. The Vice-President's position has been vacant since his passing eight years ago. Many speculate that Vice-President Medici's grandson, Amon Medici, who recently came of age, will inherit the position. Ms. Medici had been suffering from an unknown illness and passed away briefly after Amon's coming of age. Nisili Medici will remarry the daughter of Hermon Simpson, a rising star in the corporation. The couple will keep the Medici name.

"How can that be an obituary?" Matty asked. "It wasn't even about her. It was as if her life was only important when it intersected with men. How can they erase someone from existence like that?"

"I am more curious why they say she is dead if she is traveling aboard the ship," Tick said.

"That's a good point," Matty said. "Do we know who the husband she is traveling with is?"

"I suspect Riley has talents unknown to those in her life," the High Priestex said. "Most women are not even taught to read. Yet, she seems able to navigate a computer system and read a book fluently. It is easy to underestimate people, and I suspect her family may have done just that. Her identity cards are the best I have seen. Either she is a technical genius, or she managed to collect enough money to hire someone who is. Unfortunately, we still don't know who her traveling companion is. However, now that we have her identity, I am confident that Tick will be able to uncover more information."

"I will work on that now," Tick stood up and moved to a different part of the room, already back in their own digital world.

"Tech people are so weird," Matty said. The High Priestex stood still, and their eyes fixed on Matty. Matty looked up at their face, the age lines starting to show, and remembered that they were once one of the tech nerds back in their time. "Don't worry. You're plenty weird as well," she grinned.

"Be careful what you say," they shot back. "That woman you are drooling over seems to be an Earthen version of us tech nerds."

"I'm not drooling over her. I'm just interested in the mystery. She is kind of cute for a short Earthen, though."

The High Priestex walked away, shaking their head.

Matty turned her attention back to her pad. She had downloaded the book Riley was reading and followed along as Riley flipped the pages. Her mind wandered back to all the women Matty had condemned for not fighting back. Maybe she could have done something to help them.

When the pad flicked off, Matty knew Riley must have finished. She looked at the time and realized it was nearing dinner. Matty imagined Riley getting ready to go and get some food. Her stomach rumbled in response.

Yet, she could not get Riley out of her head. She may have failed all the other women on Earth, but this one, she could help.

It was fate that one of the new citizens had gone into labor. When the call came in, Matty asked permission to be the Martian representative. The woman was already in the Medbay, and Matty planned to go to the Earthen levels and access the Medbay from there. On her way, she would stop off at Riley's mess hall. She knew she couldn't talk to her, not openly, but hopefully, she could get her a message.

Matty had written down a communication access code and was sure that Riley could figure out the rest. She thumbed the note in her pocket as she walked, reminding herself that she was only doing her job - nothing more. Except that when Matty went into the mess hall, and Riley was not there, her disappointment felt more personal than professional. Matty did recognize her traveling companion, at least, a man listed as Ron. He looked unsettled.

It concerned her that Riley was not in the mess hall, especially after her pad had gone offline. There had not been any activity on it in the last hour. With no idea what to do, Matty headed off to the Med Bay, eating her portable dinner as she walked.

Visiting the birthing mother was an honor, so this trip was

not a waste of time. It was just that Matty had a sense of dread in her stomach. There were not too many places to go on the ship. You had the rec rooms, the dining rooms, and your quarters. It was likely that Riley was still in her quarters. Maybe she had just turned off her pad to take a nap. Or, perhaps she was devising a way to the Martian side of the ship.

Matty tried to put thoughts of Riley out of her head and focus on the joy of new life.

The mother was a new citizen. She had hidden her pregnancy until she was on the ship. It was a good decision. If the pregnancy had been known, Earth would have denied the removal of her citizenship. She would have had to wait to apply once the child was born, and there was no guarantee they would both be allowed to leave.

Matty was concerned that the Earthen authorities would take the baby away upon their birth. The mother would not be in a fit state to argue for the child's life. Matty would be there as an advocate instead. They had already granted the child Martian citizenship. Thankfully, Earthen citizenship was much harder to come by, even more so since the child was born between planets. Earth did not automatically grant citizenship upon birth. There would only be a problem if the father wanted to press the issue. Then it would become a diplomatic matter. The child would not be allowed to leave the ship until they settled the case.

Matty had always thought that the rules that Mars had

created were to protect the child from the long voyages. Children would spend many years of their lives being shuttled back and forth between planets if there was shared custody, which could be detrimental to their growing figure. The children could end up like the Spacers, the individuals who ran the space ships. Most had been born and died on the ship. They could not go to a planet if they wanted to. Instead, they lived in the center of the vessel, where there was no gravity.

Now Matty realized the rules were more political. Matty had condemned Earthen women for not fighting back, yet she realized she was going to see a woman who had risked her life so that her child would have a better future on Mars. Matty finally started to understand how much this woman had already sacrificed.

The Med Bay was mainly an open floor. The nurses had drawn curtains around some of the beds, but overall, the room seemed pretty empty. An Earthen child was getting fitted for a cast. It was common for Earthens to forget that even though gravity was reduced, it still existed. Although, it was rare to see an Earthen child. Most parents left them behind in corporate boarding schools.

There were also two beds near the back with curtains pulled around them. Matty peeked behind one of the curtains, uncertain of which way to go. The face looking back at her did not belong to a pregnant woman, but it was familiar. Only now, bruises covered Riley's face. There was one arm outside the blanket with a purple mark in the place of a handprint. The two women made eye contact, and Matty was about to take advantage of the situation when a nurse grabbed her shoulder.

"You must be the Martian representative."

"Yes, I am." Matty kept her eyes on Riley, hoping she would know she could get help from her.

"Your patient is right over here. You made it at the perfect time. Her contractions are starting to come closer together."

Matty let the medic move her over to the other curtained bed. Beads of sweat covered a woman's swarthy skin. Matty moved and picked up a cloth.

"Do you mind?" Matty asked. The woman shook her head. Matty dampened the cloth and wiped the woman's face.

"Do you need anything?"

"Just to not be alone."

"Of course. I'm here for you and your baby. You are our family, and I will ensure that nothing happens to either of you." Matty focused on the woman in front of her, not the one in the curtain next to them.

Matty saw the woman's body relax, bringing her into the moment. She picked up the woman's hand as she tensed up with a contraction.

"Did you learn breathing techniques?"

"This is not my first child," the woman said. Matty saw the pain that came with those words.

"Ok. You've got this. They're going to be ok. Breathe with me."

This was the third birth that Matty had assisted. Once again, she was grateful for the mandatory midwife training all ambassadors had to take.

Matty stayed with the woman, helping her to breathe, supporting her when the pain became too much. She even cried tears of joy when the doctor and nurse pulled out a beautiful, healthy baby into the world.

"It's a girl," the doctor said.

"It's a girl," the woman cried with relief.

Matty waited while they put the child on the mother's stomach and cut the umbilical cord. Then she slipped past the curtain and met the Earth representative. He was dressed in a brown suit that had started to pull on his frame, filled out from the availability of food. He was balding, but his dark hair was combed over in a failed attempt to hide his lack of hair. He stood stooped over, hunching in on himself.

"It's a girl?" he asked in a quite voice.

Matty nodded, feeling uncomfortable with the gender assignment at birth. Martian children were seen as gender-neutral. They were spoken about with gender-neutral pronouns until a child announced their gender. Then everyone respected that announcement. Calling an infant a girl felt like a violation to Matty.

"Yes. Is the father going to leave them alone?"

"It's not worth all the hassle for a girl," the representative shrugged. "Just make sure the mother doesn't give her his name."

The man turned to go, but Matty called him back. "Where is the paperwork?"

He stared at her, then pulled out his pad and added his thumbprint.

"There. It's in the records. Earth officially acknowledges that the child does not belong to our planet."

She watched him walk off. That was it; a brief visual glance at an infant's sex organs, and they lost all interest. Earth's binary obsession with gender had always confused Matty. It didn't even hold up to science, let alone lived experiences.

She knew some Martian families still followed these old Earthen traditions, especially those who had recently come from Earth. Yet, she preferred her own experience. Around the age of six, she declared she was female, and that was that. It wasn't even questioned when she first had a crush on another girl. Even at a young age, she knew this wasn't the case on Earth. She had seen too many new Martian citizens come to Mars seeking acceptance for who they are, whether that is because they loved someone who was the same gender as themselves or because Earth didn't value their gender. However, it wasn't until Matty replayed the image of Riley in her hospital bed that she realized how dangerous Earth was.

The curtain to Riley's bed was still closed, and Matty peeked around the partition, relieved to find she was still there. The woman seemed to be sleeping, but Matty had to try to make contact now. Unfortunately, there may not be a second chance.

"I'm sorry to bother you. My name is Matty, and I represent the Martian Council."

Riley kept her eyes closed, but she answered quietly. "I can't be seen talking to you. He is coming to pick me up."

Matty leaned down closer to her ear. "We know he isn't your husband. We saw your obituary and know you faked your death to come on board."

Riley's eyes flew open. Then she paused and thought about what was said. "They said I'm dead?"

"Yes, there was an obituary in the corporate news feed."

A smile spread across her face, and Matty's stomach fluttered. In the brief glimpses of photos, she had never once seen the woman smile. It lit up her face and gave her a beauty that was only hinted at prior.

"If he's reported I'm dead, that means he won't chase after me. I am going to make it." She seemed to remember Matty then, and the smile slipped from her face. Matty couldn't help but mourn the loss.

"We are not going to report you. We want to help. We want to protect you from this."

Brought back to her injuries, Riley seemed to slip away into herself. "You can't stop this," she said, her voice barely audible.

"Excuse me. I heard my wife had an accident. Can you

please help me find her?" Riley pulled up the covers and went back to pretending to be asleep. Matty recoiled at the fake sympathy in the man's voice. It was apparent that he caused her injuries, yet no one seemed to care.

"We can help; we can bring you over." Matty leaned over and whispered in Riley's ear, slipping the access code into her palm. Then she walked out of the curtained room and right into Ron.

"Hello, I'm the Mars representative." She held out her hand, prepared to shake. Ron sidestepped her, avoiding her hand and peering at it in disgust.

"We are from Earth," he said.

"Yes, yes, my mistake. The woman I came to see must be behind the other curtain. Take care." Matty walked away with a massive grin on her face and slipped behind the other curtain.

The woman looked up at her, her eyes narrowed. Matty pointed with her finger outside the curtain, hoping the woman understood. She was recently from Earth, after all. Then she continued in her bright voice. "You do not have a thing to worry about, Ms. Walker. Everything is going to be just fine with your child." The woman's whole body relaxed with the news, but she did not press further as Matty sat beside her and held her hand. Together, they listened as Ron escorted Riley out of the Med Bay. Matty just hoped that she hadn't made it worse for her.

"Was it bad?" the woman asked.

"I'll find a way to help her. But, for now, we can celebrate that you and your child will be fine. The paperwork was signed and filed. The corporations have given away any legal right to your child."

"I knew she was a girl," the woman said. "There was a healer in the middle levels that would see you discretely. She had something called an ultrasound machine that let you see black and white pictures. I knew we had to leave. I couldn't let her grow up like that."

Matty continued to hold the woman's hand, and for the first time, she finally understood.

CHAPTER 12

RILEY

PAST

RILEY'S FATHER had told her that she was not allowed to listen to adult conversations. It was a rule that she was supposed to remember. She was never allowed to break it. Except, sometimes, her father got angry when she wasn't listening. He would scream and sometimes hit her for being a bad girl who didn't listen. When she didn't listen, she got in trouble. When she did listen, she got in trouble if he caught her. So, the rule was to listen to adults but only talk about it if her father asked her.

Although, sometimes, he even got angry when she answered. He once asked her, "How many times have I told you, 'Good Girls do not listen to adult conversations?'"

"Two hundred and sixty-three times," Riley answered. "However, that is only when you have said it exactly that way. Sometimes you say it differently, but it means the same thing. If you want this number, it is six hundred and seventy-eight." Riley was proud of herself, learning that words arranged differently could still mean the same thing. She thought her father would notice and be proud too.

Instead, the blow knocked her to the ground. Then the yelling started. It was loud, and her head hurt. She moved her hands up to her ears and scrunched up into a ball while he finished yelling. She stared at the clock on the wall, watching the time tick away. It was thirty-three and a half minutes until he finished. It ended as abruptly as it began. One second it was loud, and the next, it was quiet, and he was walking out the door.

But if she didn't answer him, it made him yell also. She hadn't figured out that rule yet, so she tried to stay away from him. If he couldn't see her, then he usually ignored her.

Her favorite spot was a small space under the built-in window bench she had found in her father's office. She was only allowed in his office when he was there. She was also only allowed to use her data pad in his office. But if she came into the room to use her pad, he would scream. He would tell her she was disturbing him while trying to get work done.

She found that she could remove her pad from his drawer and then slip into the loose paneling if she came into the office before him. Then she could stay there for hours working on her projects while he was doing his important work, and she didn't disturb him at all. She was proud that she had found a way to follow the rules and not hear scream-ing. However, she decided it was best not to tell him.

She was in her secret space when the doctor came into the office. Riley liked the doctor. He let her do lots of tests. Usually, only boys got to do tests at school. Girls had to go to school to learn how to put makeup on and cook, while boys learned about math and computers. When Riley told the school that she wasn't a girl, so she should learn how to read also, they called her father. He yelled so much at the teacher he forgot to yell at her. She still had to be a girl, at least at school. At home, she decided girl rules and boy rules didn't matter, so she informed her pad she was not a girl and learned how to read.

Riley had told all of this to the doctor after he promised not to yell.

"She has what?" her father yelled. Riley put her hands over her ears, but then removed them so she could hear what the doctor had to say.

"It's not that bad. She's is quite brilliant. You could send her to the TKR corporation and let her go to one of their schools. She can grow up to be an engineer, helping the men design a better future. I hear they're working on a new space-ship that can travel at twice the current speed capacities."

Riley put down her pad at the mention of spaceships and tried to listen harder to the conversation.

"No child of mine is going to another corporation. She is

my only child. You told me yourself I cannot have another. Now you tell me she is worthless."

"I wouldn't call her worthless. On the contrary, her math and logic skills are off the charts."

"Which would be of use if she was a son. No, the only hope I had was to marry her off and get me a son-in-law to carry on the family name. Who would want her? She can't do anything. She barely even talks, and when she does, it's nonsense. There has to be a way to fix her. I will pay anything."

"There is no fixing her. This is who she is. Some of our society's greatest achievements have come from individuals on the autism spectrum."

They had stopped talking about spaceships, so Riley picked up her pad and continued working, making sure to keep quiet so she could still hear.

"Were they women?"

"Some of them, yes. As I said, the TKR Corporation has a school."

"There is an entire school for worthless children?"

"She's not worthless. She is different. You could use her. You could teach her how to work the stock market with her skills. I bet she would easily learn how to handle the economics of your company. She may never have the social graces, but a husband would benefit from her help. Behind the scenes, of course."

Riley had heard of the stock market. She knew it was

something to do with her father's work. His work seemed boring, but maybe if she learned more about it, he would start to like her.

"I swear, Matthew, if you were not a close family friend, I would have thrown you out on your ass by now. So, what can I do?"

"Do you know Robert Glass?" the doctor asked.

"Yes, what does he have to do with anything?"

"I'm not supposed to divulge this, but he sent his youngest son to a Reaper school. Unfortunately, it isn't an option for Riley. They do not accept women, but the TKR corporation does."

"Robert only has one son," her father said.

"He had another, a few years younger. When he was three, he sent him away after he found out his boy was autistic. No one talks about it. Even you have forgotten that he exists."

Riley knew they were talking about her. She wanted to go to the school to learn how to build spaceships, but she knew the doctor didn't have a chance of convincing her father. No one convinced her father of anything except the corporation president. Her legs were scrunched up against her chest so that she fit in the space. She adjusted her food, twisting it against the wood panelling, causing it to make a slight squeaking noise. She hated squeaking noises, so she stopped moving and waited for them to talk again.

"It won't work. She's too old. She's already been at school."

"You could tell them you're pulling her out to send her to a private school. No, not to the TKR school. You can tell them you are sending her to a corporate school for difficult children to help straighten her out. They would applaud your dedication to making sure your child has discipline. When she's older, she could even come back home. They do teach the children how to be more socially adept there. Imagine what she could do for your family name."

"Are you suggesting that my family name needs saving by a woman?"

"No, not at all. I am only saying it's no wonder that any child of yours would be brilliant, even a girl."

A loud banging noise caused Riley to move her hands back up to her ears. She knew that sound. Her father liked to hit his desk when he became angry.

"My child would have the good grace to do what needs to be done. That child takes after her mother. You're sure it is me who is infertile?"

"It's so hard for anyone to get pregnant. The population is declining. It is no fault of your own you cannot have another child. At least, not naturally."

"What are you saying?"

"We could use a close relative to help conceive a child. No one would have to know, and the child would still be your genetic line."

"You want me to go find an imbecile cousin to help me produce a son? Others in the corporation may be selling out, but my line will remain pure, no matter how damaged it is."

"Then what do you plan to do?"

Her father signed, deep and heavy. "You're right; I should take her out of the corporate school, but I'm not handing her over to another corporation. Instead, she will have private tutors who will train her to be a proper woman. Then I will find a son-in-law that can take on our name. Then, the line will be pure, and I can have a true son I can be proud of."

"I could recommend some tutors that have experience with children such as herself. They are very discrete."

"I thank you for your advice, friend, but I think I know what my daughter needs."

Riley stared at the diagrams on her pad. It was a manual explaining the parts of the engine of a transport. It wasn't a spaceship, not yet, but if she didn't have to go back to school, maybe she could study enough to learn how to build one of those, eventually.

CHAPTER 13

RILEY

PRESENT

FOR THREE DAYS, Riley lay on the bed. Ron would come in at random intervals, smelling like alcohol and sex. Then he would change clothes and head back out again. Riley had no idea how he'd found someone to sleep with him. She was just glad it wasn't her.

Then, on the fourth day, he told her that she stank and needed to get cleaned up because they were meeting someone for dinner. Riley didn't question it. She pulled her aching body out of bed, cleaned herself off, and threw on her nicest dress. It rubbed against her sore skin, but nothing else would have felt any better. She went to put on her face mask, but the lines seemed to rest right where he had held her jaw with his hand. Everyone else had given up wearing theirs long ago, but she had resisted. With a deep sigh, she put her mask back on the counter and turned towards Ron.

"Good," he said, apparently fine with having his handiwork on full display. Then they walked to the mess hall.

Riley didn't register the people. They did not matter to her. They all knew what had happened; they all did the same or had the same done to them, and Riley was sick of hiding her head in shame. So she walked in and grabbed her food like it was any other day. Riley sat down next to Ron and stared at her untouched food while he talked on and on. When people peeked at her, she looked up and acknowledged them. More people stared, so she sat straight, placed her hands under the table, and let them look. She was done hiding.

Ron saw the gazes and assumed he had engaged the entire mess hall in his over-the-top story. His voice and gesturing became more dramatic until the people were drawn away from her open defiance and listened to what he had to say. It occurred to Riley how ingrained it was in these people to be okay with a man freely abusing a woman, but not a woman freely showing that hurt. The people were damaged, and flying to another planet wouldn't change that. It wasn't just Earth she needed to get away from; it was also the Earthern people. There were still months left on their voyage, which meant there was only one choice. She was going to have to cross over to the Mars side of the ship.

While he finished reciting the made-up story, Riley repeated the communication code in her head. She had destroyed the original paper before they had left the medical bay. Over the last few days, she had been reciting the code to herself to keep it memorized. The string of numbers running through her head provided comfort.

After dinner, she went with her fake husband to the co-ed lounge. They had never gone together before, and he enjoyed showing her off. They went to every table where he seemed to know everyone. He introduced her as his lovely wife, who was finally well enough to join them. She didn't return their greetings, but she did meet their gaze as much as possible. She watched them see the bruises on her chin and neck, then watched their eyes take in the bruises on her arms. Then they returned their gaze to Ron and continued the conversation as if they had seen nothing.

He seemed to be enjoying himself until an hour in, when his hands twitched. The co-ed lounge did not serve alcohol, and Ron missed his after-dinner drinks. Riley knew she could use this to her advantage. She just wasn't sure how to do so without upsetting him even more. In the past, she had tried manipulating situations with her husband, and they had never turned out well. The rules for people did not make any sense. She sat next to him, quiet and unmoving, as people started to come to them. She waited as he told his stories and watched as his hands began to shake more and more.

He told them about their childhood romance, the children of two equal corporate members thrown together while their mothers gossiped and fathers worked. He told them how he'd worked his way up to ask for her hand in marriage, only to have it given to another. The decision broke his heart, but he put his energy into the corporation. On the very day his company offered him a manager position in the Martian division, he had also heard about the passing of her first husband. When he came to call on Riley, he found her parents had passed on. Riley was penniless and due to be turned out. Her fictional first husband had not been as good a businessman as her father had hoped, and lost all his money before his death. So he had offered her his hand in marriage. They had said their vows as soon as the formal mourning period was over. Then he brought his bride to start a new life together on Mars.

The gathered crowd was hanging on to every word. The women were sighing and saying how romantic it was. The men all made comments about having similar reasons for traveling to Mars. Each of them held their women a little tighter. Riley thought it was pathetic dribble. The men were not doing this for their wives, but for themselves. This whole social gathering was all performative. It was all a means to an end, and the women were objects to help them reach their goals. The women were trying their hardest to ignore this. After all, what other choice did they have?

The evening drew long. After Ron's story, the men grew nostalgic, and they all shared their version of how they ended up on this ship, headed to a planet that was not their own. They told how they were using the time to move ahead, or how misunderstandings led to their exile or coworkers out for their positions had framed them. With each tale, they confirmed how pathetic they all were. No one took responsibility for what had truly led them here.

Eventually, the parties drifted away. Ron began talking about them heading back to their quarters, but Riley hesitated. He was caught up in the moment, and Riley was afraid that he had forgotten, once again, that they were not actually married. She was still hurt, and she did not want to try to fight him off again.

"There has to be somewhere else to go," Riley said. "Maybe somewhere we could get a nightcap. It would help take the edge off."

Ron seemed to see her bruises again. His face was etched with concern, and Riley was sure he'd conveniently forgotten that he had given them to her.

"Yes, I can't have my baby in any more pain. You need to be nice and relaxed." He winked at her, and Riley became nauseous. She had to concentrate on not visibly reacting. "Unfortunately, the only place with something to take the edge off is a man's place. We can't have women being tempted. You know how easy it is for you all to be led astray."

"Yes, of course. We wouldn't want that." Riley tried to make her face as passive as possible, but she was afraid she didn't manage it. Once upon a time, she could have pulled it off well. Now she was just done with all of it. "What if you went and brought some back for me? That way, there's no temptation, just what would be proper." Riley knew she had succeeded when he got that glint in his eye.

"How about you head back to the quarters and get cleaned up? I will drop into the men's club and get us something."

"That is a brilliant idea." It was. Riley did not doubt that he would probably stay the entire night. She would become a forgotten thought. Either way, it was enough time and space for her to at least send a message.

She walked back, replaying what she would say in her head.

As soon as she got to her room, she took out her pad and put in the communication code. A secure text channel opened, and Riley began to type.

Are you there? She waited, afraid the channel wasn't being monitored, that no one would see her message until after Ron returned. When the reply showed up on her screen, her body relaxed for the first time in four days.

Yes, I'm here. We met in the Medbay.

I want to formally request Martian citizenship.

Unfortunately, there are laws limiting the granting of citizenship while between planets. What we can do is offer you sanctuary until we arrive. You need to come to us.

How?

I can help you.

CHAPTER 14

MATTY

PRESENT

MATTY GLANCED down at her pad, thinking that she'd heard a ping. There was nothing. It had only been a day since she had seen Riley leave the med center, yet she could not get the vision of her bruises out of her head. The medical staff looked the other way, sending her back to her abuser without a thought.

It was her role to help Riley to safety. The thought hit Matty with a clarity that she had never felt before. Matty was struck with theia mania, a Martian term that meant that her destiny was forever intertwined with another. Riley would contact her; she had to. Then Matty would help her to escape. She had to be prepared for when that moment came.

Matty planned on keeping the woman close to make sure that she was safe. However, she would still need a family.

Matty scanned through the files of families. She discarded any that did not have prior experience adopting adult women. Then she began to shift through the remainders, categorizing them based on her interactions with them. She worked for hours, unable to focus on anything else until she found a family that would be the best fit.

It was late when Matty went down to the community room. Dinner had passed, and the family was gathered together around the electronic fire pit, listening to a story. Mama and Papa Hapots talked, their hands as animated as their voices. They were both in their early fifties and short, even for Earthen-born. Papa Hapots had a pointed grey beard that he insisted made him look younger. The rest of his head was bald. Mama Hapots had long, flowing red hair that had just started graying.

Matty was close enough to hear that they were giving a history lesson. The adults sat in just as rapt attention as the children as Mama and Papa told the story, their bodies saying as much as their words as they flung their hands and acted out the scenes. From the tidbits Matty could hear, they were telling the story of Martian independence.

"As the Earthen corporations started taking away more and more rights from anyone different," Mama Hapots said. "The corporations started closing themselves off until you could tell what corporation a member belonged to just by how they looked. But universally, corporations took rights away from women, they redefined gender under stringent guidelines, and those guidelines guided relationships. To be different was punishable by death. Corporate members were expected to conform and devote their life to the betterment of the corporation."

The Earthen corporation officials knew this history. They were proud of it. The few times Matty had walked around the lower tiers, she was appalled that the people would support a structure built upon their oppression. Yet, as Matty watched the new citizen adults, they hung on every word as if it was the first time hearing their history. They sat as enthralled with the storytelling as the children, and Matty felt shame at her assumptions.

"When Earth tried to impose these viewpoints on Mars, the great revolution happened," Papa Hapots took over the story with practiced ease, his cheery voice at odd with the topic. "Mars had only survived because every member depended on the others to survive on such a barren planet. By appreciating everyone's differences, great innovation happened, and the people thrived. The revolution was not all that dramatic. The people gathered together and decided that one of the covens would represent Mars. They sent a message to Earth declaring independence and shut down all communication with the corporations."

"What is a coven?" one of the younger children asked.

"When Mars was first being settled," Mama Hapots answered, "People went there to stop from being hurt. A lot of these people were Pagan or Wiccan. They believed that nature was sacred and had tried fighting the corporations' treatment of the planet. People would gather together in covens to talk about their beliefs. When the rebellion happened, the people turned to these covens for guidance, as they were the most organized groups at the time. Now we call our government a coven, and each ambassador makes a pledge to the planet as well as to the people, to keep it safe."

"Why didn't the Earth send more transport ships when they shut down communication?" one of the teenagers asked.

"It was before the Reapers had created their large transports," Mama Hapots answered. "Earth still sent out a few ambassadors, but it was a one-way trip, and they always stayed and benefited from Martian prosperity."

"Once a generation had passed, Mars reopened communication," Papa Hapots continued, "and Earth recognized Mars as an independent planet. The coven were now our politicians and devoted their lives in service to the people and the planet, not their greed. Each citizen over the age of thirteen is given a vote with no voice greater than the other. When given a chance to thrive, most people choose to do so."

"Here is one of those politicians in training," Mama Hapots said. "Do you all remember Ambassador Matty?"

The group turned and looked at Matty. With that invitation, she moved forward and sat down at their fire. The children became restless soon after and were sent to bed. The adults and teenagers sat and asked questions. Eventually, they also wandered off. Finally, it was just Matty and the parents left.

Matty studied the couple. They were in their mid-fifties, earthborn and adopted at a young age, but they both kept the ability to transport between worlds. Unable to have their own children, they'd decided to become an adoptive couple for their family. This was their eighth trip between worlds.

Mama Hapots was two heads shorter than Matty, with long red hair that hung in waves down her back. She still had a youthful presence despite the lines showing on the corner of her eyes and mouth. Papa Hapots was only a few years older and a few inches taller. He was completely bald, and his beard was completely gray. He radiated a presence of joy that lit Matty up no matter what difficulties were ongoing.

"What can we help you with?" Mama Hapots asked.

Matty hesitated, unsure of how to begin.

"Oh, this must be serious," Papa Hapots said. "I don't believe I have ever seen Ambassador Matty speechless. I think we will need some tea."

He sat a teakettle of water atop the electric fire pit while they all sat quietly watching. Matty finally let out a sigh and began. "I would like to ask a favor of you. I am looking for a family to adopt an adult, someone in a precarious position."

"Oh, Matty dear," Mama Hapots began, "You know we will gladly help, but we're not sure we will be cleared for another trip. However, upon our return, we will talk to our family and convince them to sponsor her."

"I need someone who is already aboard to adopt her."

"I'm not sure that we understand." Papa Hapots sat down next to his wife, and they naturally reached for each other's hands. Matty loved watching how they seemed to know what each other needed without communicating it.

"There is a woman I hope will defect from the Earthen side of the ship. I don't know her complete story, and I cannot tell you everything I know. But she is not safe."

"What can you tell us?" Mama Hapots asked.

"She left a marriage on Earth; one we believe was very abusive. She is traveling with a man posing as her husband. He has sent her to the medical center at least once." At this, Mama Hapots had a sharp intake. "She is smart, brilliant, but she needs our help. I am waiting for her to request asylum. She will need a family when she does."

"I don't think I have ever heard of anyone requesting asylum mid-transport. Once we are in orbit of the planet, sure, but on the ship? Is the High Priestex aware of this situation?"

"They are. We intended to wait until we reached the planet to help her, but I'm afraid she won't make it alive. You should have seen her. He left handprints of where he grabbed her."

Mama Hapots gave a brief look to Papa Hapots, and he stood up, taking the teakettle into the sleeping area.

"Who is she to you?" Mama Hapots moved closer to Matty, wrapping her arm around her.

Matty settled her head on her shoulder, trying to stop the tears from leaking out of her eyes. "I don't know her, not really. I've only seen her twice. It's just that I know."

"You know what?" Mama Hapots encouraged.

"I know our lives are interconnected somehow. I'm an ambassador. I have heard all about fate and destiny. I know what it means to devote your life to a cause, but this was more than that. She is my theia mania."

"Oh, dear. You love her."

"It's not that. I don't know her, so how could I love her? Maybe I'm destined to love her? I know everyone we rescue deserves to be saved, but she is special. There is something about her that is unique."

Mama Hapots held her as they both pretended that she wasn't crying. When Papa Hapots returned with two teacups, she threw him another look. He gave her a slight nod and waited until Matty righted herself before handing them a cup. Then he sat down with them again. "We need to talk to the family before making an official decision, but knowing them, I doubt any will turn her away. Do you expect any harm to come to our family?"

"No," Matty paused, "I don't anticipate any harm. However, there have been so few midship asylum cases that we are unsure how Earth will respond. I can't imagine her fake husband will give any problems. If they found out he smuggled another man's wife, it would have dire consequences for him."

They sat and drank their tea, trying to talk about what was happening in the community. But when Matty could not stop looking at her pad for communication from Riley, they finally sent her on her way, telling her they had preparations of their own to make.

CHAPTER 15

RILEY

PAST

THE WALLS ARE WHITE. The walls are white. Riley kept this mantra going through her head even when she saw the patterns.

The walls are white. There was a stampede of horses in the far-right corner. She knew them, even though she had only seen pictures of the animals. Watching their strong, muscular bodies run was hypnotizing. *The walls are white.*

Behind her was a woman. The woman had shown up first. In the beginning, she had hidden in the shadows, whispering words of comfort. As time passed, she crept closer until she hovered behind her like a guardian angel. The woman protected her from the monsters, the ones with claws that reached out, demanding Riley to pay attention to their squeals.

The walls are white. The walls are white.

Riley held her hands to her eyes and leaned her head into her bent knees.

"The walls are white. There is nothing here. It is all your imagination, brought on by extended sensory deprivation." She removed her hands from her eyes, balling them into fists and pounding them against the back of her head.

Pound. *The walls are white.* Pound. *The walls are white.* Pound. *The walls are white.* Pound. *There is nothing here that can hurt you.* Pound. *None of it's real.*

She just needed to hold on until she was let out. *Let out where? What else was there except for this room?* The horses ran straight at one of the demons. The demon's hands reached out and plucked the horses off the wall...one by one... dropping them into its gaping mouth. The demon went for her next. Riley hid her head between her knees and begged the woman to protect her.

There was screaming. There were footsteps. They had broken free. They were coming to get her. Riley screamed. She felt hands on her, and she screamed louder.

"Ms. Medici." The words were nice and sweet. They must belong to the woman. The woman wouldn't hurt her. Riley removed her head from her knees and tentatively glanced up. There was the woman. She had broken free. She had long black hair and ruby lips. Her face was friendly, not like the sharp-toothed monsters. Riley chanced a glance at the far side. The monsters were gone, and the walls were quiet.

"You banished them."

"You've been in here a long time. I got worried. I brought you some more food and water." The woman pointed to a pile on the ground. She had forgotten about food. How long had it been since she had eaten? But then she saw the bags of water and forgot all about the food again. She grabbed one, poked the attached straw into the pouch, and started to drink.

"Not so fast." The woman tried to grab the water from her, and Riley growled. The woman flinched back away from her. "You can't drink so fast; you will make yourself sick."

Riley remembered that the woman was there to protect her. Without the woman, she would be lost.

"It's all that I could manage. Hopefully, he will let you out soon." The woman started to walk away, and Riley reached toward her.

"Don't leave me. Please don't leave me."

"I'm sorry, I must go now. I will come back when I can. Just remember to take your time. I'll be back if he doesn't let you out. But I don't think it will be long now."

The woman closed the door. The woman returned to the wall. She would watch over her. She would protect her. Riley looked at the pile of food and water. She had to keep it safe. She had to keep it from the monsters. Riley separated it into little piles. She hid one pile under her blanket. She hid one pile under the waste bucket. The bucket smelled so bad that Riley knew even she would avoid that food unless she were desperate. Then she placed the third pile under her legs, carefully ensuring her skirt covered it all. Her food would be safe.

She ate slowly. She drank slowly. She never took a swallow unless the thirst became unbearable. She never ate a bite unless her stomach had cramped in pain. Yet, the food still disappeared. The water was gone, and the woman didn't come out. Instead, the monsters taunted her until she lay on the ground, ready to let them take her.

Then, a the screech. And Riley cracked open one eye hoping the woman had returned. Instead, it was the monster. He looked at her.

"You're alive then? We better get you cleaned up for your son's inheritance ball. Everyone knows you've been sick, but that is no excuse for you to stink so bad."

He left the door open, and another man came and lifted her.

"The woman," she muttered.

"Gone," the monster said. "There will be no more women working here. They have too much of a bleeding heart. You were supposed to be left alone. We couldn't have anyone catching what you had, could we?"

An illness. She had an infection. But she remembered coming home and finding him waiting for her at the dining room table. She had stopped in the entryway to the condo and changed out of her son's clothes. To be safe, she had left them hidden behind the giant carved lions guarding the main entrance. And when she had seen him, she pretended like nothing had happened as she moved to clean up the liquor bottles he had splayed out over the counter.

He hadn't said anything. He watched her put on the lids and move the bottles back to their shelf. She finished and walked back to her bedroom to get ready for bed. Except her husband had stopped her. He had grabbed her hand and led her to the back of the unit to the servant's quarters. They no longer had live-in staff. It was not cost efficient, so they had turned the room into storage. Only now, it was empty. He shoved her into the room and locked the door behind her.

There had been meals, at first. She used their occurrence to help count the days. Her son had visited her once. He stood in the doorway and looked at her sitting on the floor.

"You could stop this," she said. "I may be his wife, but you will inherit the family."

"I could," he finally had said. "But if I do, then I would leave him with nothing. I am not giving him part of my inheritance. So, the least I could do is not stand in his way while he betters his fortune." Then he threw a blanket at her and turned and left.

She had known her fate then and had done her best to prepare for the inevitable. She could never have prepared for the madness. Her husband must be so upset that she had survived.

CHAPTER 16

RILEY

PRESENT

RILEY SHUT her eyes and pretended to sleep as soon as she heard the door open. Ron was loud, bumping into the wall and yelling at the light switch when he couldn't find it. Riley concentrated on staying still and calming her rapid heartbeat. She heard the struggle as he maneuvered out of his shirt and felt the bed move with his weight as he sat down. Then there was angry muttering, and Ron stood back up to shut off the lights, forgetting that he could have just vocalized the command.

Then he was around her. His arms reached and held her to his bare chest. His face nuzzled against the back of her neck. Riley's whole body tensed, and she had to focus on relaxing. She couldn't do anything to upset him, not tonight. Then she heard his soft snores, and she felt trapped beneath his weight. But she had survived this long because she had learned patience, so she waited until his arms unwrapped from hers, and she moved slowly from the bed.

She picked up her pad and put on her facemask, something she had not done in weeks. Then she left, leaving everything else behind. It was best if he had no idea what had happened. Hopefully, he would forget her soon enough, anyway. He would use his money and connections to make a great life on Mars. A life that did not involve her.

Riley looked back down at the data pad. She had hacked into the ship and downloaded the schematics. Then she'd marked the entrance and coded a simple program to help track her progress. Unfortunately, she did not have time to program the ad hoc app to give her actual directions. She was sure that she was lost. The corridors did not look familiar, and the doors were too far apart. This had to be where much higher-ranking corporate members were housed.

Riley heard voices from down the hall, so she turned into a corridor and pressed herself against the wall. Her heart was pounding, and she hoped they would not turn down and see her.

It was just two crew members complaining about their next shift. Still, Riley stayed pressed against the wall until she could no longer hear them. Then she looked back at her map, trying to orient herself. When she was confident that she knew where she was, she continued on her way.

Riley walked for about fifteen more minutes before she

saw the door. It had a keypad next to it, and the words "For Official Use Only" were stenciled in bright yellow. Riley checked the code that she'd been given and typed it in. To her relief, the door opened. Riley took a deep breath and stepped over the threshold. She had managed to make it to Mars.

The relief was short-lived. The corridor was empty; Matty was supposed to be here to meet her. Riley had even given her access to her pad so that they could track her progress. She searched down the empty corridors trying to calculate where she'd gone wrong. Riley felt exposed at this nexus between two planets, but there was nothing to do but shut the door and start walking forward.

A few minutes later, she finally saw a figure walking toward her. The figure was farther down the hallway and nearly cast in shadows. Still, Riley tried to match it with the woman she had seen in the medical clinic. Riley was uncertain. She had only seen her once, and then when she was on pain medication. As they walked toward each other, the figure took on a familiar shape, and finally, Riley relaxed. A huge grin spread across her face. A matching smile spread across Matty's face. Riley walked fast with a leap in her step that had nothing to do with the reduced gravity.

She was less than six feet away when she felt someone ram into her, tackling her to the ground. Her arms were pulled behind her and were secured in a set of magnetic cuffs. The man stayed on top of her pressing his weight on her. Then he leaned down and spoke to her ear.

"You are in violation of border crossing. No Earthen citizen is allowed to cross into Martian territory. You are in violation of attendance laws; all women must be accompanied by a man for travel or be given special permission. You have been granted no such permission."

Riley felt the joy drain from her body. She hardened herself and didn't struggle. There was no longer any use. She had tried to change her fate and had failed. Riley felt her body going limp. The officer's body pressed on her own until she could not breathe. *Maybe it would be easier if it all ended now.* The thought flitted through her as her vision clouded over.

"Excuse me." Riley remembered that voice from the hospital. "This individual has requested and been granted sanctuary from the Martian consulate. Please unhand her now. She will remain here, and an ambassador will meet with your delegation to negotiate."

"Women cannot enter into legal agreements, meaning that she cannot claim sanctuary," one of the guards said.

"We are on sanctioned Martian territory. Here our laws are the rules, not yours. She has requested sanctuary, and it has been granted. Let her go."

As the officer's hold loosened, Riley managed to move her head. There were a handful of officers in tactical gear holding weapons trained on her. But when she saw Matty, she couldn't look away. Like a typical Martian, she was taller than the Earthen-born officers. Yet she was so slight of build. It almost looked like you could push her, and she would blow over. Yet here she was, standing up to this group of men. *I thought weapons weren't allowed on ships.* The thought came and went, and Riley realized how ridiculous it was. They were officers. They could do whatever they wanted.

The man holding her stood up, and Riley took a full breath of air. Then the officer grabbed the cuffs around her wrist and pulled her up. The man kept one hand on her cuffs, and with the other, he pulled out a weapon and aimed it at the Martian woman.

"You can go file whatever forms and petitions that you would like. But you will do it while she sits in an Earth cell."

Matty walked straight up to the officer, putting her face right in front of the energy gun. "If you take her past those doors, you will violate the 2314 Earth-Mars pact. It could mean war between our two planets."

The man snickered at her. "Good luck getting to Earth to fight."

Matty's face filled with a giant grin. "This must be your first trip." Then she turned and looked at some of the other officers.

Riley moved her head and noticed that some of the officers were looking at each other. There was something that they were not willing to talk about. But before she could think on it, she felt herself being pulled backward. And it was all she could do not to fall. However, she thought she heard the Martian mutter, "Don't worry; we can."

Chapter 17

Matty

Present

Matty had devoted her life to creating laws for both planets to follow. It was what had kept the peace for the last generations. And to see the Earthens violate the most basic treaty caused her anger to flare. If they didn't have Riley, she would have lashed out, daring them to start an incident so they could respond in force. It was time Earthens knew that they didn't have the upper hand. But there was Riley. And if Matty started anything, she knew that Riley would bear the consequences. So, she clutched her hands into fists, tightened her jaw, and watched the men drag Riley away. Her eyes never left the woman's face; Matty needed to let her know she wasn't alone. But the fear that shone in Riley's eyes nearly broke her. Matty had failed her again.

Never once had she heard of officers entering Martian territory to arrest someone. While on-ship crossings were rare, once the person had crossed over, they were considered under Martian sanctuary. There had to be more going on with this Riley Medici.

Right now, Matty was Riley's only chance of making it through this, which meant that Riley needed the entire team. Once the Earthens were out of sight, Matty pulled out her pad, put out an alert, and asked everyone to meet her in the conference room. Matty started to run as if making it there a few minutes faster might be the difference between Riley making it out of this alive.

She made it to the room before half the team arrived and paced anxiously, even though there was not enough room to move around the table and chairs. When the High Priestex asked her to take a seat, Matty just looked at them in disbelief and went back to pacing.

Finally, the last team member entered the room. Matty shot him a glare and started narrating the night's events. When Matty had finished speaking, everyone remained silent. Concern floated through the air.

"You were on the Martian side?" the High Priestex asked. They were sitting at the head of the table, their head lowered in thought.

"Yes."

"You can prove it?"

"Yes, Riley had created a map that identified her location." Matty threw the information from her pad onto one of the wall screens. "Since we could track her pad, I could follow along with where she was."

"You're sure they were corporation?" The High Priestex had a desperation to their voice that Matty had never heard.

"Yes, they were Earthen," Matty said. "I don't understand how they even knew that she was crossing. The only people who could have known were on our side."

"We will have to figure that out later. We must now determine how to get her out of an Earthen jail. She's in serious trouble if they are willing to break interplanetary law."

The High Priestex turned to their screen and started opening channels. The ambassadors stayed frozen in their seats, remaining silent so they could hear what was said.

First, they called the ship's captain to inform him about the breach. The Reapers were a corporation, but they tended to be more neutral since they had a better understanding of Martian culture.

The captain's face filled up the screen. He had the dark skin of the reaper corporation with white hair cut short to his head. He had been on a ship most of his life and was usually quick to laugh with the High Priestex, but today his expression was reserved.

"I have no knowledge of any illegal crossing," he said. "If such a thing were to happen, it would be above the station of a captain."

"Who would be able to authorize such an action?" The High Priestex asked.

"No one aboard this ship. Such a call would have had to come from Earth."

"This far away, someone local must have been put in charge of such an action."

"No one would need to be in charge of an action that did not happen." His voice was curt, and his hand moved to disconnect the call, but his face remained on the screen. "If there were any Earthen criminals on board, they would need to go before the judge." Then the screen flickered off.

The High Priestex attempted to call the assigned judge, but it did not connect, so they reached out to Earth. The communication was delayed and kept being routed through low-level officials. The ambassadors lost their attention. Some left to do their assigned work or to sleep, but most moved over to track the situation in their own ways. Matty flittered between stations answering questions. She tried sitting down and reaching out on her own, but no one picked up her calls.

Finally, the com panel went dark and did not start up again. Matty turned expectantly, but the High Priestex's face said it all. Diplomatic channels had failed.

"We've got nothing?" Matty asked.

"We don't have Riley back, but it wasn't entirely a waste. We know where she is."

"What good is that if she's dead by the time we get anyone to negotiate with us?"

"I taught you better than that. Information will often win, or stop, a war far better than guns and missiles."

"Is she safe?" Matty fell in the chair closest to the High Priestex.

"I think she is, for now. But we are going to have to figure out a plan fast."

"They aren't going to let her go easily," Matty said. "Not if they were willing to risk a war to pick her up."

"No, they won't. But Riley officially requested sanctuary, and on Martian soil, it was granted. She is officially one of our own, one that was taken by force. It gives us a little more flexibility in handling the situation."

"You have a plan?"

"Yes. We need to reach the main Mars coven."

CHAPTER 18

RILEY

PAST

RILEY WAS HUNGRY. Her stomach was growling, but every time she moved to grab some food, the teacher hit her hand with a thin, flexible wand. Riley stared at the marks across her hand. Most were red, but a few were slightly purple. One had cut through the skin and had started bleeding. Riley reached up to the table, grabbed the napkin, and used it to clean off the blood.

"Riley Medici, napkins are for your lap. You pick them up, fold them, and place them on your thighs. You do not grab them and bunch them up in your hands." The teacher stood with her arms folded across her chest. She was so close that Riley could smell the old person's stench off her. The smell bothered her, but not as much as her empty stomach.

"I needed it."

"What you need is to learn manners. Your job is to sit quietly and not be noticed."

"That is not possible with you standing there looking at me." Riley shuffled in her seat, her eyes fixed on the biscuits in the middle of the table.

"You should be as invisible as possible at all times, but especially when people are looking at you." The teacher's voice was a shrill whine that seemed to drill into Riley's head.

"If someone looks at you, you can't be invisible. If you were invisible, they wouldn't be able to look at you." Riley heaved a sigh and slunk down in her chair. Her stomach let out a loud gurgle. Suddenly, she reached up, grabbed some biscuits, and slid under the table.

"Get out of there right now, young lady."

This teacher had just started last week. Riley wasn't sure if she was the kind of teacher that would reach under the table and grab her out or just the lazy type that would yell at her. She was older, so Riley hoped she could at least get some eating in before the teacher decided one way or another. Riley put the first bite of biscuit in her mouth when the teacher yanked her from behind. The woman held her up by the collar of her dress, causing the biscuit to stick in her throat and cut off her air.

"Your father warned me that you would be a tough case. He asked me to come out of retirement to whip you into shape. He warned me that you had gone through everyone else, and he needed the best. The vice-president of the corporation asked for my help, and I'll be damned if you are going to get the best of me."

The teacher put Riley down on the ground. When she noticed the wide eyes and tiny hands clawing at her throat, she pounded on Riley's back several times. The biscuit came flying out of her mouth, and Riley pulled in a gasp of air.

"Now, sit in that chair until you remember all the steps to a proper teatime."

Riley stood unmoving. Her feet had disconnected from her brain, and she was stuck, not knowing if she should run away as far as possible or walk over to the chair and try again. She had been trying, even if the teacher didn't think so.

"I think perhaps she may benefit from a break first." The voice was new. It came from a child much like herself but with confidence older than the voice. A young boy walked into the room.

"Young Lord Bishop, I did not know you would visit us today."

Riley turned and looked at the boy. He was dressed in a black business suit with a maroon vest and shiny black shoes. His brown hair was short and flat, like it was trying to break free, but knew better. He was staring straight at her as he spoke.

"My father thought it might be a good idea for me to spend some time with Ms. Medici. He had something to discuss with her father."

"Of course. Is there anything I can do for you?"

"Would you mind bringing us some punch and maybe a light lunch? I know it is late, but we didn't have a chance to eat before we came."

"Right away, sir."

The teacher swept out of the room, leaving Riley forgotten.

"How did you do that?" she said.

"People are easy. You must act like you have power over the situation, and they will do anything you ask. I figured you might want some different food than these cold biscuits." He picked one off the tray and held it out to examine. He tentatively put it in his mouth and then put it down uneaten. "These are dreadful. They make you eat these?"

"They are from yesterday."

"Why do they make you eat day-old biscuits?"

Riley emptied the crumbled biscuit pieces from her hands onto the table. She wiped her hands together to get off all the crumbs. Then she picked up a new biscuit from the tray and happily started eating. While still chewing, she began to talk. "They aren't that bad. They were better yesterday when we started, but I didn't get to eat one then."

"Why not?"

"I kept getting in trouble. So, I had to start over until I got all the rules right."

"You've been sitting at this table since yesterday, and she wouldn't let you eat? I'm glad I don't have your teachers. How come you don't just do it right the first time?"

"I don't know. I don't know how I guess."

The teacher returned with two plates full of a creamy nut sandwich and a side of sautéed vegetables. There was even a small sweet cake and an entire pitcher of punch. The teacher looked at the table full of crumbs and opened her mouth to say something. She looked at the young man and closed her mouth. She took out a towel and brushed most of the crumbs off the table onto a tray. Then she removed two place settings and reset them with all new silverware and plates full of food. She turned and left them.

Riley turned to her food and started grabbing it. It had been a while since she had been allowed to eat so well. A whole serving of fresh vegetables was rare and reserved for special occasions.

The boy watched her start eating. Then he picked up his fork and knife and started cutting his sandwich. "I see why your teachers get upset."

"Why?" Riley asked, her mouth full of sandwich. The boy shook his head and finished eating.

Riley finished all the food on her plate, plus her sweet cake. She then picked up the biscuits, wrapped a few in a towel, and shoved them under her dress. There were no pockets, so they just sat on her lap for now. Then she took the remaining biscuits and began to eat them.

"Why do you do that?" the boy asked.

"What?" Riley looked at him, confused.

"Why did you just put food under your dress?"

"Why wouldn't I? How will I have something to eat later if I don't?"

"I would just ask for food when I get hungry."

"That doesn't work for me. They tell me I need to ask nicer or that food will make me fat, and I need to fit into a new dress, even though someone comes in and makes the dresses fit just right no matter what size I am. She says I should be bigger, so I figure I can eat more. I hate being hungry. Besides, I don't want the dresses, anyway. Although the woman is nice, I like when she visits."

"My father said you were strange. But that's OK. When you are my wife, I'll help you to know what to do." The boy finished eating and laid out his utensils across his plate.

"I'm not going to be anyone's wife."

"You will. You must. That is what women do." The boys spoke with absolute certainty. "They get married and give their husband a son. Then they help their husband to do better in the company. My father is third, but when I marry you, I will get to be second. We will almost be as powerful as the president."

"What if I don't want to marry you?" Riley looked at the strange little boy. His suit seemed to fit him in a way that Riley knew her dresses would never fit her.

"You might as well marry me. At least I will make sure you will get food. However, you are going to have to try a little harder. You will have a very important job as my wife.

You will need to make sure that all the other wives are talking nice about me and that everyone loves us."

"Why would we want people to love us?" Riley asked.

"People treat you better when they love you. What's your teacher's name?"

"I don't know."

"You don't know your teacher's name?" The boy threw up his hands in exasperation.

"Names are hard to remember, and there are so many of them I can't remember them all." Riley looked down and stared at the table while eating more of the biscuit.

"Names are important. When you remember someone's name, it makes them feel special. Even if you do not think about them, they think you remember them just because you could call them by their name. My father says it is one of the keys to success."

"What's your name?" Food slipped out of Riley's mouth as she spoke.

The boy's face held a look of disgust as he spoke. "Everyone knows my name. I am Ronald Bishop the Third."

"If you are the third, does that mean I am the second? Riley Medici the Second. I like that." Riley carefully put her packet of biscuits on the table as she stood up and started spinning. Pieces of biscuit fell off her dress.

"No, sit down. Names don't work like that. I am the third because my dad's name is Ronald Bishop, and his dad is Ronald Bishop. So, I am the third Ronald Bishop. Besides, you are not the second because you are a girl. Only a boy can become the second."

"I hate being a girl." Riley sat down in a huff putting her elbows on the table and rested her head on her hands. Now that her stomach was full, she started noticing how much her dress itched.

"You don't have a choice. Besides, if you weren't a girl, then you couldn't marry me. It's good that you will marry me because I will teach you all you need to know. I will do a lot better job than your teachers have. They haven't taught you well at all."

"Well, I can teach you lots of stuff, also. I am going to build a spaceship one day."

"No, my wife cannot build spaceships. You must go to parties and wear pretty dresses."

"Then I don't want to be your wife." Riley got up from the table clutching the packet of biscuits, ready to escape the talk about parties and dresses.

"It doesn't matter what you want. My father and your father are talking right now. They are signing the contract. So, you have no choice but to marry me."

CHAPTER 19

RILEY

PRESENT

WHEN THEY OPENED the door and threw her into the cell, she screamed and screamed. They yelled back, telling her to shut up, but still, she screamed. Eventually, her voice left her, and her scream was more of a squeak, but still, she tried to scream.

Exhaustion overtook her, and she curled up in a fetal position on the ground. It was then that she noticed the walls were gray. There was a bed with a thin mattress and blanket. Next to the bed was a sink. Only then did it hit her that this was not the room that haunted her.

Riley ran to the sink and turned it on. She sighed in relief as water poured out and then cupped her hands, filling them, drinking until she could not drink anymore. It wasn't that she was thirsty, but you never knew when the water would disappear. Then she sat and took in the rest of the room. All that was left was the toilet and the door. It wasn't so different from their quarters if you didn't think about the door being locked.

Riley went over to the door and tried to open it. It didn't open. Of course, it didn't open, but she had to try. She sunk back onto the bed. This was not as bad. They were not going to leave her here to die. No, they would take her out and deliver her to her husband or kill her quietly. Riley couldn't help wondering how they would do it. She was so tired of fighting. Every time she thought she could outsmart them, she kept losing. Maybe it was just time to give up. Perhaps death would at least give her a chance to rest.

Riley laid down on the bed and stared at the ceiling. She did not know how long she was there before the door opened again. She did not move.

"Get up," the guard shouted.

Before Riley could consider if she should listen or stay, the guard, dressed in Segadon colors and not much older than her own son, had reached her and yanked her up.

"Your husband is here." He said the words like they were a curse. "Get out of here and don't trouble us again."

Riley started when she saw Ron at the door. She looked back at the guard in confusion and then remembered that he was her husband on this ship.

"Come on, Sweetie. Let's get out of their way." His voice had a fake quality, and Riley knew that more would be coming when they were alone.

He began walking away to their quarters. She followed him as she longed for her data pad, the one that had the map to the Martian door. Then she sat down on their bed and waited for him to do whatever he planned.

Riley expected him to start shouting. She expected his fist to hit her face or for him to decide to take her again. She closed her mind and went far away. Yet nothing happened. He was there. She could smell him. She could hear his body moving. Finally, she looked up. He wasn't looking at her. Instead, he was staring at the wall, his hands rubbing his face, then straightening his shirt. She realized he was nervous.

"I called him," Ron said. "When I was at the bar, I decided it was about time to get some money out of you, and I called him."

Riley stared at him in confusion. Ron wiped his face again, then turned and hit the wall.

"Shit, fuck, shit." He held his hand to his chest. The idiot had probably broken his fingers.

"He laughed at me. When I asked him for money, he laughed at me. He told me that the people on Earth thought you were dead. They even had a funeral. He buried an empty coffin and is already remarried to the daughter of a director. He gave them your family name, and he got their money. It was a pretty good deal; all he needed was you gone."

"I know," Riley managed to say.

"According to Earth, Riley Medici is dead. So, he laughed and said that he wouldn't give me any money for a dead woman. When I woke up and you were gone, I knew he would kill you. Then I realized he was going to kill me. I had to make some noise to get you out to ensure they would know I would be noticed if I was removed. But, I got them to release you. Now we need a better plan. We need allies to make it to Mars."

"You idiot." Riley found the rage that had slipped away from her. "You fucking idiot. He had let me go. He had officially acknowledged that I was dead. We could have been on Mars living our lives, and you called him."

"I needed money," Ron said.

"I have money. I told you I have money." Riley realized she was screaming but didn't stop.

"You're a woman. You lie. And..." he stopped talking then and looked at her bruises.

"You thought I wouldn't pay you after you raped me."

He didn't bother answering. Instead, he went to the desk and laid his head down.

"It's ok," he said. "We're fine now. They let you go."

"They let me go so I didn't die in their custody. Now it will be some accident. Some hazard of space travel. No one to blame, but we will be just as dead. Had I realized you were this stupid, I wouldn't have picked you."

Riley wanted to hit him. She wanted to lash out and inflict on this man everything that had ever been done to her. She had been free and could have made it, but he got greedy and ruined everything.

The bell on their door beeped, and they both froze. Would they do it now, or would they wait a few days? It was easy to give up when she knew she had failed, but she hadn't. She had managed it. Now she would have to find a way to get out of this. Riley walked up and answered the door.

CHAPTER 20

MATTY

PRESENT

MATTY DIDN'T THINK Riley could look any worse, yet she did. In less than a day, her eyes had sunk in and filled with despair. Matty took one look at Ron and dismissed him.

"Come with me," she said. Matty watched Riley pause and assess the situation. *Does she not trust me?* "I didn't have anything to do with them finding you, but the High Priestex tried to use their pull to get you out. It didn't work. We don't know why they let you out, but they did. I am taking you back to Mars, immediately. We need to be quiet about it. We still don't know why they came after you."

"I do," Riley said and then looked back at her fake husband.

"We can talk about it later. Pack your stuff and let's go," Matty said.

"I don't need anything." Riley walked towards the door.

Before she could reach it, Ron jumped up and grabbed her arm. Matty flew into the room and pushed him against the wall, her hand against his neck. She knew how to fight, and she had already lost Riley once. This man was not going to make it happen again.

"I'm going to walk out this door. Riley is coming with me. You will not get in the way, do you understand?" Matty's voice came out in a snarl.

"If you take her, I'm dead." He barely managed to spit out the words with his throat being pressed.

"Well, that's your problem."

He tried to speak again, but the words didn't come.

"He's right. The idiot told my husband I was alive and on this ship. He's already remarried; he has no choice now but to get rid of me. If we leave Ron here, the only chance of bargaining for his life would be to help them find me. They'd kill him after, but he would still try."

"So, we can save him the trouble and kill him now."

"As satisfying as that may be," Riley sighed, "I am guessing it would not make for very good political relations."

"What do you want me to do with him?" Matty tried not to show the jealousy that flared up in her. This man had sent Riley to medical, and she was still defending him.

"We could take him with us. He could be a prisoner or something. There must be something about holding someone for questioning."

"Yeah, but what for?" Matty loosened her arm slightly,

allowing him to get air. When he went to speak, she applied pressure again.

"I have some sort of legal rights on Mars?" Riley asked.

"Yes, but this isn't Martian territory."

"But it was last night when I was taken, and he was involved. So could he be held in relation to that?"

"That depends," Matty loosed her hold again, "are you going to come willingly?"

Ron stood there, not saying anything. The color was returning to his face, but he kept looking at her as if afraid to speak. Matty threw her hands up in the air, letting him go completely. She didn't want to, but the man needed all the oxygen his brain could get.

Matty watched Riley walk up to him. It was like she was transformed. The fear was gone from her eyes, and Matty could see how she had survived so long.

"You want to live?" Riley asked. Ron nodded his head. "You know if you stay here, you will die. You come with us, and you can live. If you're nice and show them you can play by the rules, they may keep you safe once we land on Mars."

Ron looked at Matty then. She just glared back at him. Yeah, they probably would. But Matty didn't want him thinking that her people were pushovers.

"Fine," he said.

"Fine? It is more than fine," Riley said. "You should be grateful. You got greedy, and you screwed up. You could have just gone for the ride taking the money and lived a good life.

Maybe you could have even done well enough to return to Earth someday. But you wanted power too fast. You wanted it without the work, so you got drunk, and you forgot that I was the one financing this trip." Riley moved towards Ron, and he moved back against the wall. "Then you got stupid. Now we will both die unless this nice Martian lady helps us. So, you better say it's more than fine. You better agree to walk nicely down to the door leading to Mars. When we are there, you will not cause any trouble, or I am sure they will have no problem sending you back over the Mars/Earth boundary."

Matty looked at her with awe. She saw the fear on Ron's face, but even Riley seemed slightly taken aback by what she had done.

"Are you ready?" Matty asked.

They both nodded in agreement.

"Ron, you first," Matty said.

The man moved without complaint. Riley walked after him like she was trying to keep up. Matty walked a few steps behind them, pretending to focus on her pad. Having a Martian walking through the halls would be noticed, but most had probably seen it. Having a Martian walk with Earthlings would have caused too much attention.

When they made it to the doorway that connected the planets, Matty let out a sigh of relief. She glanced at Riley, hoping to share the joy, but Riley's eyes were filled with fear. Flashes of the night before went through Matty's head. Then she slipped past them, typed in the updated code, and opened the door.

Ron slipped through first, not bothering to wait for Riley. It surprised Matty how much it bothered her, how he was treating the woman, or maybe it bothered here more that Riley accepted it as normal. There was no sign of the fierce independence she had shown earlier.

Once they had all gone through the door, Matty sealed it behind them. "Follow me," she said.

She led them directly to the ambassador's conference room. It wasn't until they were sitting across from the High Priestex that Matty finally relaxed.

CHAPTER 21

RILEY

PAST

THE SIXTEENTH BIRTHDAY was the most significant event of every young man's life. On this day, they would be given an investment from their father to go out into the world to make their way. It was an idyllic tradition that claimed a young man's hard work gave him his station in the corporation. But, in truth, the more powerful your father, the more opportunities you had open to you. If only the same had been true of girls.

There was a weird energy in their household. Riley's son, Amon, was excited. He was hardly home, too busy picking out his new lodging and having dinner invitations from his grandfather's friends. When he did come home, he was utterly oblivious to the mood of the rest of the household. All that concerned him was that he was set to inherit his grandfather's estate when he came of age in just a few short days.

Without a male heir, the estate had been given to Riley to hold until her son came of age, at least on paper. In truth, a lawyer managed the estate, and Nesili made frequent financial requests on it, all in the best interest of their son. Their house, vehicle, and even a large portion of the monthly budget had come from her son's accounts. Her husband would go to her each month with a new set of requests to sign before taking them to the lawyer.

All that was coming to an end. Now Riley sequestered herself in her room, trying to stay out of everyone's way. It had only been a few days since her husband had let her out of the white room, and she had not yet recovered. Mostly, Riley did not want to set her husband off again. She was currently too weak to survive and she had plans to make. There was no choice but to leave during the party. Her husband wouldn't let her last the night. Even if he didn't have it planned, his temper would get the best of him when their son had officially left with all the money.

Nesili was so sure that their son would stay around, that he would allow his father to mentor him, and that the money would continue to pay for his lifestyle. However, each day, as it became more apparent that their son was out the door, her husband became moodier.

Her son's name day was going to be an extravagant event. Nesili had spared no expense, mainly because it was entirely funded by their son's trust. Riley knew it was a desperate plan to use the party somehow to move his way up in the world before the rest of the payments came due.

It was the first time Riley had been given a party dress in quite some time. She hated the thing. It was built more for the enjoyment of men than for her comfort and compressed her already flat stomach, pushing up what little cleavage she had. It was made to accentuate her frame, now gaunt from the month in solitude. Her husband had picked a pale blue color to make her look even more flush. She felt like a skeleton put on display at a holiday event.

The guests had poured into the rented hall, the corporation's best. Even the corporation president had made an appearance, and Riley could see the excitement on her husband's face as he moved her from one couple to another. She smiled and greeted each in turn. Then she stood back and let the men talk while the wives tried not to be bored. This, at least, she could manage well.

The night dragged on, and Riley focused all her attention on not watching the clock. The people were drunk when her husband went on stage to command everyone's attention.

"I would like to thank you all for attending." The conversations continued, and Riley could see the lines of frustration on her husband's face. "There is no more important day in a man's life than his name day, except one." The crowd quieted slightly, and Nesili became bolstered by the attention. "The only day more important than your name day is that of your sons. It is the day you remember your child so small in your hands and know that you helped him to this point. You know that your time, patience, and money have created the ultimate investment." The crowd chuckled slightly at this old joke. "I know I am sending my son off into the world. I know he will take the name of Medici and do it proudly."

He had said the last of this with a slightly bitter tone that most of the crowd did not pick up on. When Nisili had taken on her family name, he had been so proud. The name was a legend in the corporate world, and he would forever be part of that legacy. However, as the years went on, he became bitter. Every time he said it, he knew he had only made it at the grace of his wife; that without her, he would no longer be a Medici. Now, as the money was leaving, his son would continue his grandfather's legacy and not his father's. It was a bitter wound he had yelled about quite often. However, there was just a brief grimace before he motioned for his son to take the stage.

"Thank you, Father," Amon took to the stage. He filled it in a way that his father hadn't, like he was made to be the center of attention. Yet, even under his control, Riley saw a little self-doubt and uncertainty. Sixteen seemed so young to make someone a man. "The Medici line is a long one. Our family has a proud history of serving the corporation. My grandfather was a great man. He served at the president's side for many years before his death. I remember when I was six years old and he took me on his knee and told me that one day my job would be to advise the greatest man alive." Her son took his drink and held it up towards the president. The room broke out in applause.

"I intend to make my grandfather proud. I hope to one day be worthy of being the president's advisor. Yet, I know that I still have a lot to learn. There is only so much that books and tests can teach a man. I need to be in the field. I need to lead and learn how to make the decisions that are so crucial to business success. It is why I have the honor of announcing my plans to work under Mr. Stevenson in the northeast branch as his mentee. I will be moving immediately and starting after the quarantine period."

The room broke out in explosive applause. Mr. Stevenson was one of the most respected regional leads. Even Riley was impressed that her son had landed such a role. Her husband seemed less so. Their son had not mentioned him once. Even after his speech, he walked away and went to shake the hands of the crowd. His son had abandoned him, and he had no more cards to play.

As the men came to the front to congratulate the young man, Riley moved slowly to the back of the crowd. It was not unexpected. Women had no part in the ceremony. When the president himself stood up to give a toast, Riley slipped away completely.

Riley went into a small room she had found while helping to set up the ceremony. She locked the door. She tried to take off her dress but could not reach the zipper. It had been created to be taken off by another, trapping her in. Instead, she took the fabric in her hand and pulled it as hard as possible. The stitching of the zipper gave way, and she tore it enough to slip it off. She took the dress in her hands, balled it up, and hid it in the corner behind some extra tables.

She reached into the same area and pulled out a bag. Inside was a male server's outfit that she slipped on. Next, she took out her cap, the same one she had been given at the hacker club many years ago. Afterward, she gathered up her hair and tucked it under so no strand was visible. Then she took out the last item, a smaller bag that held the last untraceable remnants of her past life. She took one last glance to ensure nothing was visible and left the room. She walked straight to the server's entrance and slipped out unnoticed.

CHAPTER 22

RILEY

PRESENT

RILEY WOKE UP DISORIENTED. A foot above her head was a metallic wall decorated with pictures of people she had never seen. The night came back to her in flashes. They had crossed the boundaries between planets unhindered. The room was full of people of all genders, talking like they each had an equal voice. Hours later, Matty had brought her to her quarters, a room built to sleep eight. Riley had been lent the bed of an ambassador that worked a different shift and had fallen asleep as soon as she laid down.

She turned over and looked at the shuffling of bodies. Some, like herself, were waking. Others were ending their shift and preparing to sleep. Matty was sitting on the floor, leaning against the bunks. There was a figure leaning over, talking to her in a language that Riley did not understand. The figure stood up and turned around, and Riley realized he was a man. She looked around the room and saw men and women wearing informal clothing. Riley was startled at the realization, her head hitting the top of the bunk. The noise drew everyone's attention toward her. She pulled up the bedsheet and wrapped it around herself. The bunk was too shallow to sit up, so she pushed as far to the wall as possible.

"What's wrong?" Matty asked. She moved the few feet from her bunk to the one Riley was using.

"There are men in here," Riley managed.

"Yes." Matty tilted her head in confusion.

"There are men and women all in the same sleeping room. Do all couples sleep together in the same space?" Riley could not help wondering if her father was right to think Martians were savages.

"No one here's a couple. Everyone shares the room, each with their own bunk."

"Why would you want to sleep in the same room as men?" Riley whispered to Matty.

"Why should rooms be separated by gender?" Matty asked.

"To be safe." Riley's answer was instantaneous. "Women should only have to share a space with a man when married."

"Things don't work that way here. You would be safe no matter who was in the room. But we also understand," Matty's voice picked up so that everyone in the room could hear, "that you feel safer around women. I found a family for you to stay with; however, we think you will be more secure with us for now. I promise that no one here will hurt you. But we can talk to the High Priestex to see about getting you your own quarters. Once you get more comfortable with how things work on Mars, you will better understand why we arrange things the way we do."

The room seemed to empty as Matty talked. Soon, there were only the two of them left. Matty handed Riley the dress that she had worn the day before. Riley clenched it to her chest.

"I'm going to go grab us some breakfast. You don't need to worry about anyone coming inside. They will give you some time to get dressed."

Riley slipped off the bed after Matty had left, still holding the blanket tight around her. She looked over the room. The bunks were in various states of disarray. The floor was covered in containers taken out of the storage areas and left abandoned. Riley finally let the blanket go and slipped her dress over her underclothing.

Without the people to distract her, Riley noticed how close the bunks were. You could only walk a few paces before you hit another wall. The walls seemed to be getting closer together. Riley's breath caught, and her heart raced. She was alone in another room, locked and forgotten. She slipped to the floor, pulled her legs to her chest, and started screaming.

The door opened, and unfamiliar hands touched her. Riley screamed louder. Then there was Matty, next to her.

She crouched down close enough for Riley to feel her presence, but not touching.

"I'm right here. No one will lock you in here." Matty kept repeating her words until they sunk in, and Riley began to calm down. "I think it may be best if we go for a walk."

When Matty stood up, Riley followed. They moved out of the room. The other room's occupants, having returned when Riley screamed, moved to let them through. They walked quietly until they arrived at a viewing port, not unlike the one Riley had seen that first day. The area was empty except for the two of them. They sat staring at the darkness of space in silence.

"Will you be alright if I get us some food?" Matty asked.

Riley looked up at the woman and nodded her head in assent, still too tired to speak.

Matty came back quickly, carrying two trays of food.

Riley instinctively took one of the trays and looked down at the unfamiliar food. When she noticed Matty watching her, she picked up the fork and began picking at the food.

"It's good, I promise. We are working on shifting back over to Martian food, but I tried to get something you would be familiar with. The red cubes are potatoes. I think it has something to do with the soil. Then there are some ham and eggs. We don't have animals on Mars, so those will disappear from the menu soon. I will miss being able to eat meat. I begged my mother for a chicken when I was younger after I read about them in a storybook. Did you have one as a pet?"

"I've never seen a chicken," Riley said. "Once, when I was young, I attended a party where they served a pig. I wasn't allowed to try it; such novelties are forbidden for children."

"I thought you ate this stuff for breakfast. There's an Earthen book I read as a child, Green Eggs and Ham. "

"I've never heard of it." Riley put a bite of eggs in her mouth and immediately spat it out.

"I'm sorry. I thought it would be nice to have something that reminded you of home."

"Did you eat like this when you were on Earth?" Riley asked.

"There is a chef at the consulate that made us Martian food. We weren't encouraged to go out unescorted. It isn't safe for us on Earth."

"You mean being a woman?" Riley picked up one of the potatoes and put it in her mouth. It looked weird but tasted delicious.

"Yes, but being Martian in general. We are a bit more offbeat than Earthens are. It's easy to notice us, and the corporations do not like us drawing attention. We learned about Earthen culture by studying the literature and meeting with the government. We met with the heads of every corporation and saw what they wanted us to see. There were luncheons and stuff, but they tended to serve Martian fair. I did try some lamb one time."

"You lived a very different life than the rest of the population. I was born into an influential family, a woman, but still, a rich woman, and I haven't even seen half the things that you are talking about." Riley stabbed through another piece of potato. "Wealthy Earthens tend to eat a lot of vegetables or occasionally lab-grown meat. Lower tiers tend to eat many packaged meals made with whatever is the cheapest ingredient at the time. Animals are mostly extinct. There are farms somewhere, but it is only shipped in for special events. Animals bred viruses, and most people do not want them around."

Matty picked up her own food, a bowl full of beans and red potatoes, and started to eat while she talked. "I searched for animals when we went out and was always disappointed not to see them. I assumed they were keeping them from us, so we didn't try to take them back to Mars." Matty laughed, but Riley could not understand what was funny about her statement. "It is so different on Earth. Especially how you separate people into different tiers so you can quickly lock down if there is an illness."

"I think that's how it started. Now, it's just a way of separating people based upon how much money they have." Riley finished off all the potatoes and eyed the ham wearily.

"I visited a few shops to pick up toys for the children on the ship. There was always an earthen representative with me, guiding me where to go. I would have liked to have seen more of the city and had a chance to talk to the people."

"If you want to learn more about the third tier, you should talk to Ron. He spent the last five years living in a place he pieced together from discarded materials. It was not a place the corporations would have wanted you to see. I've only seen it twice."

"Why would he want to do that?" Matty asked. She had finished her food and put her tray off to the side.

"He didn't have a choice. He lost all his family's money and was cast out to live poor." Riley put a small bite of ham into her mouth. She swallowed it, but not without her face scrunching up in disgust.

"Is that why you picked him to come with you?" Matty had already finished her food and was watching Riley as she ate.

"I didn't have a lot of time." Riley looked at her tray, her mind playing back all the times she did not have enough to eat. But that was not now, and the contents of her tray were not edible. Finally, she put the tray down next to her. "I made plans to get out, but my husband may have found out, or maybe he didn't trust me. He locked me away until my son's coming of age party."

"You have a kid, an adult kid?" Matty's eyes widened in shock. "You can't be much older than me."

"I was a difficult child. My father thought it was best to marry me off young."

"Oh. . ." Matty trailed off, uncertain how to continue.

"I love my son. I tried to teach him to be better, but I wasn't allowed to be around him much. It is the father's job to raise the son. My husband hoped my son would keep his inheritance with the family. But even my husband wasn't sure. He already had a side plan. I saw him eating dinner with a young woman and knew he planned to marry her. I knew I was in the way."

"Couldn't you just have gotten unmarried?"

"There is no divorce on Earth." Riley stood up and moved closer to the observation window. "It's believed that when a woman and a man are joined, the woman becomes a part of the man. He becomes responsible for her, and she becomes his burden. I suppose it is supposed to be romantic, but all it does is burden a man with someone he doesn't want and make the woman be less than human. I have heard that it is not the same in other corporations, at least not to the same extremes that we have."

Matty stood up but did not approach Riley. "If he wasn't going to divorce you, how could he remarry?"

Riley did not respond. She looked at Matty until Matty took a deep breath. "Oh....oh. That is why you risked forging documents."

"Someone else was supposed to go with me. He was engaged to a man who had already made the trip to Mars. We lost contact, and he was gone when I could reach out again."

"They imprisoned him for being with a man?" Matty's body tensed up, and her face flushed.

"No, they killed him and only by association." Tears pooled in the corners of Riley's eyes. She turned away from Matty and quickly wiped them away.

"You cared for him?" Matty moved towards Riley, tentatively placing a hand on her shoulder.

"He was a friend. I did not have many of them."

"And they killed him." They stood silently staring at the window, Matty's hand resting lightly on Riley.

"With everything that happened on Earth," Riley broke the silence, "I don't understand why they would even care about two men being together. It is not as if it were two women together."

Matty froze at the statement. "You dreamed of being with another woman?" The words came out so quiet that Riley could barely understand them.

"No, I dreamed of having a choice. I dreamed of being in a relationship that was equal or choosing not to be in a relationship at all."

"Oh," Matty's voice sounded disappointed, and Riley did not understand what would have caused it, so she continued.

"Ron was the only other person I could think of. My social circle is not very big. I found him, and he agreed right away. The ticket alone should have been enough for him, but men are greedy." Riley jerked away, breaking their contact.

"So, what happens now? Could you ever go back to Earth?"

"Why would I want to do that?" Riley looked up in confusion.

"It's your home, and I just thought maybe you would want to go back someday."

"There was nothing for me on earth. I never fit; it wasn't just that I was a woman. I wasn't even a good woman. I taught myself to read, I learned to code, I would put on my son's clothing and pretend to be a man." Riley expected Matty to move away from her in horror. She had never spoken the words out loud. Her fellow hackers knew, but even they didn't mention it.

"Are you a man?"

Matty spoke so evenly that it took Riley some time to process the sentence and even more time to find an answer. "I'm not a man." She paused, considering how much to say, and decided to continue. "I'm not sure I'm a woman either." It had been so long since she had spoken those words that she felt like a weight had been lifted off her. "I know I'm a woman because I have their anatomy and can bear a child. But having a child growing inside of me never felt natural; it felt like an invasion. If I had a choice, I would never have gotten pregnant. After my son was born, I found someone, a doctor; he made it so I would never have to do that again. I'm probably not making any sense."

"What you are saying makes perfect sense. I have some people that I want you to meet." Matty looked at Riley in her

Earthen dress. "But first, what do you think about getting some new clothes?"

Riley had braced herself for condemnation and ridicule, but the offer of clothing not connected to Earth caused the tension to leave her body. "That would be nice." She said.

CHAPTER 23

MATTY

PRESENT

"**THERE IS** a makeshift market on one of the lower levels," Matty said. "We'll go down there and talk with the seamstress. She can help get you set up with some new clothes." Riley looked stricken at the suggestion, and Matty faltered, uncertain what had upset the woman who had seemed so happy just a few minutes earlier. "I just thought it would be nice to have more than the dress you are wearing."

"Clothes hurt me." Riley's voice came out almost apologetic.

Matty paused, trying to understand what that meant. "You mean the textures hurt you?"

"Yes, I have used the same seamstress since I was a child. She is extremely kind and makes my dresses, so they don't irritate my skin."

"Trust me. Micha will be able to create what you need, and she can make you more than dresses."

"All my money is in Molbin credits. They took my pad when they arrested me. I don't have any way to transfer my funds."

"Oh, don't worry about that." Matty started walking down the corridor, looking back once to ensure Riley was with her. "There is no currency on Mars. We work more on a barter system. I think your planet would call it socialism, but it's not that."

"Socialism?" Riley said. "My father said that socialists were evil."

"Your father? And that means that you should listen? Do you even know what socialism is?"

"It's where people do not have to work for what they get. They can ask the government for it, and everything is handed to them. Some people work very hard, and others do not have to work hard at all." The words sounded robotic to Matty, like they were quoted word by word from something Riley had heard.

"Well, that is one way to twist it, I guess." Matty continued walking, trying to keep her anger out of her voice. "You said that on Earth, there are different tiers. The people on the bottom tier have less than those on the top."

"Yes."

"Do they work?"

"Some of them would go into the second tier to do jobs. I don't know that all of them work, but at least some do."

"Do you think they choose to be poor?" Matty asked.

"I think that would depend on whom you ask."

Matty turned at looked directly at the other woman. "What do you think, Riley? Does it sound fair to you?"

"When I was young, a doctor came to our house. He told my parents that there was something wrong with me."

"There is nothing wrong with not fitting into gender roles."

"Not that. They said that I had something called autism. I could never figure out what it was. But if my father wasn't as high in the corporation as he was, I would have been sent to an orphanage in tier three. I would have still gone there if my father had not found a husband for me. It is where everyone who is defective goes."

Matty stopped suddenly. She waited until Riley looked in the general direction of her face before she started talking. "There is nothing wrong with you, Riley, nothing. To say that there is anything wrong with people just because they are different is evil. There is a boy I know on Mars. He owns a small market in one of the colony towns. Everyone there knows him and relies on him to make sure that they have what they need for the season. Once, one of his customers didn't come in for their regular visit. It was an older gentleman, and the boy knew it wasn't like this man to break his pattern. So, he put a note on the door and visited the man.

The man had fallen and had been lying on the ground since the night before. The boy didn't want to leave the grandpa alone, so he stayed with him. He was like you."

"What do you mean?" Riley asked.

"He also has autism. It wasn't something that meant he would be thrown away. Instead, the city that he grew up in helped him find a job that he was good at. He was happy, and he made other people's lives better."

"He just stayed with the old man forever?"

"No, the mayor saw the note on the store door and went to the old man's house. He saw the situation and went and got the doctor. The older man had to spend a few weeks in a hospital center in the nearest city, but the townspeople took turns visiting him. Even the boy went to visit, though he did not like cities. Once the gentleman healed, he went to live with the doctor's family. The couple had young children that called him grandfather and got to learn from his wisdom."

"They didn't get rid of him?"

They stood in the middle of the empty hallway. The words echoing off of the metal walls.

Matty was filled with hurt for everything that Riley had been made to go through. She could not have imagined how anyone could have made this intelligent and beautiful woman feel as if she were worthless. "No, everyone has value."

"He was old. He had no value to the corporation anymore; once you can't work, you must retire. There are centers for that."

"So, Earth just locked all their elders away?" Matty turned away and started walking again, afraid to show Riley the anger displayed on her face.

"Yes, I don't think people like being reminded of death."

"Well, maybe Earth is so screwed up because you do not have the wisdom of those older than you. Either way, I think you missed the point of my story."

"What was the point?" Riley hurried to keep up. Matty was walking fast, her long legs outpacing those of the shorter Earthen woman.

"That just because people are different does not mean that they are of less worth. Look at you, you have amazing skills. Did you know it took our entire programming team to keep you out of the Martian computer system? Two of the programs are considered some of the best."

"No wonder I couldn't get in. Do you think I could meet them later?"

Matty could not stop the smile on her face and the light chuckle. Riley had sounded like a child about to be given a new toy. "I'm sure that can be arranged."

They arrived at a large room. Like all the communities, the doors were left continually open. The room was full of people in bright clothing walking between various booths. The people walked without face masks, greeting each other by touching hands or wrapping their arms around each other.

Riley stared at the scene, a look of horror on her face. "Everyone's touching. What if someone is sick?"

"We don't have the same problems with sickness as you do on Earth. It isn't that we never get sick; it just hasn't become as widespread. We quarantine when needed and follow hygiene protocols, which all seem to work well. People like being connected."

"They are together all the time, and they enjoy it?"

"If you want privacy, you can close your walls, but most people don't bother. There is someone I want you to meet before we get your clothes." Matty grabbed Riley's hand, oblivious to the shudder that went through the other woman at the contact. Then she dragged her into the swarm of people. "I want you to meet Jackson. They do electronic repairs and are here to pick up some distant cousins that were dropped off in the orphanage. No one in their family could make the trip, so they came alone to bring them back."

Jackson was sitting on a rug placed on the bulkhead. They were a hulking figure with the darker skin of the Reaper corporation. They were dressed in a simple shirt and pants that were bright purple. Surrounding them were containers full of electronic pieces and a scattering of data pads. There was a child that looked to be about ten years old, with slightly lighter skin, watching over their shoulder as they worked on soldering the open back panel of a data pad.

"Jackson, there is someone that I would like you to meet." Matty saw Riley looking at Jackson with confusion. She wondered if she should have explained why she was bringing Riley to meet them, but she wasn't sure that Riley would understand. "Riley, this is Jackson, and this is their assistant Baston. Where are the other cousins?"

"Alicia, the baby, was getting bored watching me work, so Mama Tilly took them and Elly to play with the children in their family." Jackson seemed to be at a pausing point and finally looked up from their work.

"This is Riley," Matty said. "She just came over from Earth yesterday. She gave Tick and the High Priestex a hard time trying to keep her out of our systems."

Jackson released a low whistle and then focused on Riley for the first time. "That is very impressive. They are two of the best specialists."

"She lost her data pad when she came over. I could give her a standard pad, but I'm guessing she would appreciate something with a bit more power."

"I have just the thing, back at our camp. Where are you staying? I'll bring it over."

"I, um, I'm staying with Matty," Riley said.

"She's staying in the ambassador's quarters for now. She has a family assigned, but we want to make sure everything is safe before she moves in with them. We have some errands to run, and maybe we could stop by your camp after. We could help you wrangle your cousins for dinner."

"That would be lovely. I'm sure Baston would appreciate the help. Poor kid gets stuck feeding the baby every night."

"I don't mind." Baston kept tinkering with the electronics.

"She's - I mean they, are kind of cute. Besides, she isn't much of a baby. They're almost four."

"Why do you call her they?" Riley asked.

"That was the other reason I stopped by. Do you mind if we sit for a minute?"

Jackson gestured at their blanket filled with electronics. Matty took it as an invitation, cleaned off two containers, and sat on one of them. Riley, hesitantly, sat on the other.

"Riley has lived on Earth all her life," Matty said. "We are just going around meeting people, helping Riley to see that the world doesn't have to be the way she was taught."

"Oh, anything, in particular, you wanted to show her?" Jackson asked.

"We will head to the Market and probably stop by the Marshes community. But earlier, we talked, and while she does need a new pad, I thought it also might be helpful if she met you."

"Ah," Jackson's smile filled their face. "You want her to see that the world is more than male and female."

"What do you mean?" Riley asked. "How can there be more than male and female?"

"When babies are born on Earth, someone tells them what their gender is." Matty paused, and when Riley didn't respond, she continued. "On Mars, all babies are called they. When they are old enough, they tell us their gender."

"When they're old enough? When is someone old enough to tell you their gender?"

"It depends on the person," Matty continued. "Some know when they are very young. Others never decide they are one gender. Sometimes they feel male one day and female the next, male and female at the same time, or sometimes something else entirely."

"My parents were both new Martians," Jackson's voice was deep and rich. "My parents followed Earthen traditions and declared my gender at birth. When I was young, I knew the gender they had given me was wrong. I knew I was not male and not female. I am curious what conversation you had to think to come and talk to me."

"We were talking about gender roles," Matty said. "Riley, would you like to tell them more?"

"I don't understand how you cannot be male or female," Riley said.

"What is gender?" Jackson asked.

Riley thought before answering. "It is the anatomy that you are born with."

"Many people would like to believe that it's that simple. The sex people are born with is much more than what is found between their legs. Physically there are more markers of biological sex, and in some people, their biology cannot give a simple answer to if they are male or female. Gender, however, is defined by the society in which a person lives. On Earth, you are considered either male or female. Then there are a firm set of rules that you must follow determined by your gender."

"Isn't it the same way on Mars?" Riley asked.

"To a point," Jackson said, "it still means something to be male and female. We also understand that people's gender may not match their genitalia and that gender goes beyond these two choices."

"And that sometimes," Matty said, "there are people who have no gender identity at all."

"I didn't know that was an option," Riley said, her voice nearly a whisper.

Matty looked at Riley, who was sitting there blankly. "Are you OK?"

"Yeah, sorry. It's just, how do you know?"

"Know what?" Jackson asked.

"Know if you are different."

"You must figure it out for yourself. In the meantime, just be yourself. Knowing your gender gives you a better idea of who you are, but it's also ok to take the time to explore. It is like when you were a teenager and tried all sorts of jobs to see which one you wanted to do."

"I didn't have much choice when I was a teenager," Riley said. "But thank you. You have given me a lot to think about."

CHAPTER 24

RILEY

PAST

RONALD DID NOT COME OVER OFTEN at first. When he did visit, he would rebuke Riley for her lack of progress and admonish her for not trying harder. He expected more from his future wife. Yet, the rebukes came with sugar cakes and respite rather than a solid strike or days of confinement. She began to look forward to his visits.

As they grew older, the visits became more frequent. When Ronald was fourteen and she was twelve, he was at her house nearly monthly. At times he even attended without his father. Except, as he grew taller and started to fill out, he also lost his easy childhood rebukes. Riley found her behavior being criticized more harshly.

One afternoon, they sat together playing stones, an ancient game that had come back in fashion, in the family living room. Riley's newest tutor sat on a nearby chair. Her tutor had told her earlier that her role as an attendant was only a formality. If Ronald wished to take liberties with her, then as his betrothed, it was his right if there was no permanent damage. Riley was uncertain what her teacher was going on about, so she ignored it. Not speaking had become her most successful strategy against getting in trouble.

Stones was a boring game. All you did was move your stones from one end of the board to the next by jumping over and capturing your opponent's pieces as you went. If you reached the other side, your piece would be promoted to president and gain control over the board. Riley had found a most effective strategy; she didn't move the pieces nearest her. Then her opponent could never be promoted. All she had to do was make sure that she had at least one other piece that could keep moving. They had been playing this game for the last three months during Ronald's visits. It was their eleventh game, and Ronald had yet to win. So, each visit, they set back up the board and played some more.

Riley was bored. She wished he would move on to a game requiring more skill. Although, it was at his insistence that she was allowed to play at all.

"This is my game. Luck cannot keep with you forever. So, this time, I will win." Ronald had taken the green pieces again, leaving her to play with the blue.

"Luck is a series of actions brought on by chance and not by one's skill." Riley's voice was even-toned.

"Yes, I know what luck is." Ronald picked up a piece and set it down carelessly.

"Then why say I am winning because of luck and not my skill in the game?"

"Because you are a girl. Girls are not supposed to win games. They are supposed to lose badly and then marvel at the intelligence of men." Ronald picked up another piece and grinned as he went to place it down.

"Then I would suggest that you start to make intelligent choices. If you move your stone there, I will be able to jump three pieces."

"You don't need to tell me how to play." Ronald paused, glanced at the board, and then placed his piece where he had originally selected. "I know this game better than you. I've never lost at it. I would say that you cheat, but such behavior would be unladylike."

"Apparently, winning is unladylike as well." Riley picked up her piece and used it to take out three of Ronald's stones.

"Women should not win because men are smarter," Ronald grumbled. Then he refocused on the board.

"I can let you win if that would make you feel better. Then maybe we can move on and play something else." Riley moved her feet against the legs of the chair. Her eyes darted around the room, looking for something exciting to see.

"I don't need you to let me win. I am destined to be the second hand of the president and can handle the logistical challenge of a stone's board. Just stop making so much noise so I can concentrate." He picked up another piece and moved it.

"Are you sure that you would like your piece there?"

"Do not try to outmaneuver me with your women's logic. My hand is off the piece, so that is where I want it to go."

Riley gave him one last look, unsure of how best to proceed. However, ultimately, she just wanted the game to end. So, Riley picked up one of her presidents and jumped his last four pieces. Before she finished moving her piece, the board and all the pieces flew off the table.

"I told you to stop cheating. I will not have a wife who cheats."

"It's just a game. Why would I cheat at a game?"

"Right, it is just a silly game." His temper cooled down as suddenly as it sprung up. "Of course, you are good at such trivial things as stones. You wouldn't be able to handle real company work. I need to go."

He got up and walked out of the room, not giving her a second glance. Her tutor yelled at her that night, telling her everything she had done wrong. But if men were supposed to be so much more intelligent than women, how come they didn't act like it?

Ronald showed up for a visit two weeks later. He brought with him his pad full of information on stock market predictions.

"My father has given me an assignment to invest in the

market. It is a training exercise. I have already managed to double my profits."

"I hate the stock market," Riley said.

"Of course you do. Women do not understand it. It has complexities and nuance, and takes nerves of steel to play."

"I wouldn't say it is all that complex. It is just so easily manipulated and is controlled by those at the top," Riley said. They were sitting in the parlor, a tray of tea on a small table between them.

"Anyone can play in the stock market. It is the ultimate liberator. It can make a poor man rich and a rich man poor. All that is required is a fine business sense."

"Insider knowledge helps also," Riley said as she nibbled on one of the honey cakes, Ron's data pad in her other hand.

"What do you mean? Having insider knowledge ruins the game."

"Then why did you invest in Chintar two weeks before they bought Tinex? Since they are both under the management of your father, you would have been aware of their intentions. But a man in the third tier is most likely not aware of either corporation as they create parts for transports only available to those in the first tier."

"What do you know of the third tier?" Ronald stood up and yanked the pad away from Riley. "You have never left your privileged apartment except to go to parties in your lace and silks. I've been to the third tier. I have walked among them."

"Then you know that they do not have transports." Riley reached for another honey cake. "You have invested most of your money in a cloning facility on the west side of the corporation. The stock should go up for three more days, but then you should sell it."

"How dare you tell me how to manage my portfolio. The stock market is not a game of stones." Ronald started pacing in front of the chairs.

Riley eyed her Tutor standing a few yards away, appearing to be looking at one of the paintings on the wall to give the couple the illusion of privacy. She was in her mid-twenties, a new hire from tier two who didn't know how hard to be on Riley, so she fluctuated from letting her get away with anything and then locking her in her room for days at a time. It seemed like a good day. Maybe Riley would be able to eat all the cakes on the plate.

"No, but it is not all that much different either," Riley said. "The eastern district manager created the company to provide a position for a favored nephew. The nephew is not very bright; this way, he gets prestige, and the district manager gets a company to funnel money through. Only the nephew seems to think it is a legitimate company, and he has scheduled a press conference for late this week, unbeknownst to his uncle. At that point, everyone will know the company is a sham, and stock prices will plummet."

Ronald stared at her in disgust. "How would you know

such a thing? You never attend the women's lunch to have such gossip reach back to you."

"I don't need to attend lunches to see what is happening in the corporation. All I need to do is read the reports." She reached for another honey cake.

"Read? Are you telling me your father taught you how to read?"

"I taught myself when I was younger."

"Well, that needs to stop right now. No wonder you are incorrigible."

"I can't just stop knowing how to read."

"You are fortunate that you are the daughter of Medici. If you were anything less, you would have quietly been gotten rid of by now."

"I wish I had. Did you know in the Reaper corporation, they let women work? In the TKR corporation, they have women in science divisions. They can even build starships." She went to reach for the last honey cake, but Ronald ripped it off the plate and threw it on the ground.

"I will not stay and tolerate this kind of conversation." He turned and faced the tutor. "You are not prepared for this position. You are dismissed. I think I will work with my father to find someone who can properly train her on how to be a woman."

The tutor fled with tears rolling down her eyes.

"There is no one else," Riley said, her eyes drifting to the cake on the floor. "My father has already gone through every tutor in the corporation. He is not going to be happy that you fired her."

Riley saw the hand lift and knew to expect the strike. Still, she stood frozen in shock. She was used to being slapped by her father, but Ronald had never lifted a hand to her before.

"If the tutors cannot help you find your place, then I will. Your audacity has grown over the years, and I will not have you think you are better than me."

Riley held her hand up to her cheek, tears leaking from her eyes. "Wouldn't it make more sense for us to work together? Isn't that what you had always said we would do when we were married? We would be a team. First, I would help you with information, and then you would act upon it. I just gave you information, and you are upset. I don't understand why you are mad if this is what you have always wanted to happen."

"You should gather information like a woman, not a man. You want to make a fool of me, and I will no longer allow that to happen." He turned and walked off. Riley hoped that he thought to sell the stocks before they lost value, or he would be even angrier.

He did not return to visit for four months. Riley was confident then that he had not listened to her and had lost the bulk of his investment. The company scandal was all over the news feeds. The nephew was a laughingstock of the family. Even confined to her home, Riley could hear everyone talking about the story. The nephew was stripped of his rank and banished from the first tier. The uncle had disowned him, leaving him little chance of ever finding work in the corporation again. People seemed to be happy about this. Whenever the servants spoke about it in their whispers, they had huge smiles. Riley found it confusing.

Riley decided to hack into the nephew's finances to give him some money so he was not destitute. However, when she saw how he had managed his money prior, she realized that she could do nothing to help. So instead, Riley took the funds she had acquired from his uncle and used them to help sponsor some Martian citizenship applications. She couldn't help but feel jealous thinking of others going on a spaceship.

When Riley next saw Ronald, it was on his 15th birthday. As is traditional, the party was as elaborate as the family could afford. Of course, Ronald's family could afford a lot. They had rented out an entire auditorium and invited every child in the first tier. There were games, activities, and music everywhere. The birthday was a symbol of the end of childhood. It was the last time to act like a child, as the next year would be a bridge to adulthood, leading to his finally being a man.

Riley had been stuffed in the itchiest and fluffiest dress yet. She could barely breathe, and every part of her skin felt on fire. They had placed her on a stage in a pair of mock thrones. Next to her was Ronald's throne, except he was not there. He was allowed to go off and enjoy all the fun. They expected her to stay, as someone had to be present to accept the birthday wishes.

There was a line of first-tier female children holding gifts and waiting to present themselves to her. Mixed in was a scattering of young male children, accompanied by a nurse and not significant enough to greet Ronald himself. She had been sitting on the chair for the last three hours. Her head hurt, and she was thirsty and hungry, but there were still so many children waiting to greet her betrothed.

They came up one by one, placing their gift in a pile and giving her a curtsy. They introduced themselves and told her their family name, but she no longer heard what they said. She greeted them all the same way, having said it so many times that it had lost all meaning to her.

"Thank you for calling on my beloved on his special day. Your gift is most appreciated. Please enjoy his gift to you."

Then they would turn and leave, with their duty done, and went to enjoy the party. It wasn't that Riley wanted to be on the packed floor with all the noise. She just wanted to be done, back in her quiet room where no one remembered her existence. At least they had turned off the music streaming into the speakers above her head when she had refused to remove her hands from her ears.

When Ronald finally came and joined her, she thought she would at least get a break. She needed to stretch her legs and get some water. But instead of releasing her, he picked up a present and started talking to her.

"You know I'm 15 now. I will be a man in one more year, and then we will be wed." Riley sat quietly, letting him continue. Her thoughts were on how to excuse herself to get some water. "My father was not too happy about the stock market incident. He nearly told your father I lost all that money and would have called off the whole engagement. I fixed it, though."

The present he had picked up was small enough to be palmed in his hand. Most were the same size, containing data coins. He took off the lid, picked up the data coin, and held it to his pad. "Only 50 credits." He turned over the box and looked at the label. "It is from the Matter kid. I guess they couldn't afford much more. I guess she can stay." He took the box and coin and threw them over his shoulder. As he stood up to grab another box, he kept talking.

"I told him how you had told me to hold onto the stocks, how you had heard at one of your lunches about how successful the announcement was going to be, and that the stock prices were to rise." Riley put her lips between her teeth and bit down hard, focusing on the pain rather than the inaccuracies. *Men do not like to be corrected* ran on a repeated thought through her brain.

When the next child walked up to hand over her gift, Ronald took it directly from her hands. He opened it on the spot, another data coin, and scanned it into his pad. "250 credits, not bad considering how small your family is." He tossed the box and coin behind him and sat back down, with a third gift, in his chair.

"My father gave me quite a lecture. He told me not to listen to women too closely, that we men needed to be the ones making the decisions. Also, he reminded me that I could listen to you less than the others, that your true value was moving me closer to the president and joining our families together. He is right, of course. I just lost myself for a moment. My father granted me one foolishness of youth, and thankfully didn't tell your father. But he is concerned; I can see it in his face. So I have come up with my own assignment. I am going to invest in a new company. It should take off in a few months, just before my name day. Imagine starting as an adult already with my own company."

He opened up the third box and pulled out a small flying drone. It was one of the new ones with an updated security camera and 15 petabytes of data. The battery life was over a month. Riley had seen the commercials for them and had wanted one so bad. Ronald rolled his eyes and threw it over his shoulder with the other discarded boxes.

He stood up and handed her his pad. With Ronald in attendance, more elite children had gathered, moving ahead of those already in line. No one thought to object; it was their right. Even Riley knew how to categorize the families by importance. Finally, Ronald faced them, and a young man stepped forward.

Ronald no longer needed Riley, so she escaped into the data on his pad. The information was random and didn't make any sense. She wasn't sure what to do. The last time she said something, he didn't believe her and got upset. So, she decided it was best to say nothing at all.

Ronald was so absorbed in the attention of the other children that he didn't notice when Riley got up and walked behind the throne. He didn't see when she pretended to fix her shoe and picked up the discarded drone or as she slipped off the stage to find some water and a quiet place to rest.

Ronald visited her twice a month after his birthday. They had a wedding to plan and arrangements to make. Each time he visited, he stressed his company's success, and Riley started to hope that she had been wrong about the data. Until he no longer paid her visits, and she noticed the servants whispering and continually looking at her. Then she found it on the feeds. Ronald Bishop the Third had lost not only his own money but had accessed his trust early and lost it all. He was taken in by a simple con and left destitute. His father disowned him and cast him out of the corporation. A few months later, Riley's father introduced her to her new husband-to-be.

CHAPTER 25

RILEY

PRESENT

As they moved deeper into the market, Riley thought about what Jackson had said. She had always known that she wasn't a woman in the same way other women were. The times when she shed her gender were the only moments she had ever felt like herself. She was buried under the expectations of feminine roles. She didn't want them. Until now, she didn't know there was another choice.

"Where are we going next?" Riley asked. The symphony of voices in the market knocked her out of her contemplation. The clatter was so loud that she had to raise her voice for Matty to hear her. People were walking so close that she could reach out and touch them. Her face felt naked, missing the protection of her facemask.

"The seamstress is near the back wall. It shouldn't be long before we reach her," Matty said.

A young child raced through the stalls, nearly knocking into Riley. Three other children came barreling after. No one seemed to pay them any mind.

"Did you enjoy talking to Jackson?" Matty asked.

"I quite enjoyed talking to..." Riley trailed off, uncertain how to continue.

"Them," Matty supplied.

"Right, I quite enjoyed talking to them." Riley began to fall behind Matty, letting the taller woman create a path she could follow.

"I wasn't sure. I know that Martian customs are very different from Earth. It can be hard for Earthens to adjust." Matty had to turn her head to talk to Riley.

"There's a lot to adjust to." Riley tried not to think about the people pressing into her, or hear the sounds pressing into her skull. The colors swirled all around her, causing her head to hurt. But she couldn't return to Earth, so she had to cope with Martian customs...somehow. Riley tried to focus and remember what she was saying. "I like the idea of allowing people to be themselves, and it would be quite nice to have been born on Mars. I hope I get to see it. It seems like a wonderful place." But as she looked around the market, she wondered if that was true.

"Why wouldn't you be able to see it? You're safe now. You are here on Martian soil under sanctuary. They can't harm you."

"I've thought I was safe before," Riley muttered.

Matty turned and faced her.

"Are you sad?" Riley asked.

"I just want to make things better for you." The Martian had stopped in the middle of the path, causing a torrent of people to walk around them. The people pressed in on Riley; all she wanted to do was move again.

"You already have. As you said, I'm safe."

Matty stood looking at Riley. Riley wasn't sure what was expected of her, so she tried to look like she was enjoying herself in the mesh of people. Finally, Matty broke the silence. "It's not much further." She turned back around and continued walking.

The stall that Matty brought Riley to belonged to a middle-aged woman with various fabrics and equipment.

"Hello, Momma Micha," Matty said.

"Why, hello, Ms. Matty. What do I have the pleasure?" The two women embraced, causing Riley to flinch at witnessing the direct contact.

"Can't I just stop by and say hi and introduce you to my new friend?"

"Oh, I love new friends." Momma Micha turned her attention to Riley. The woman was near Riley's height and most likely Earthen born. Her skin was a light olive shade, and her dark brown curls were tied back with a bright purple cloth. The woman moved as if to hug Riley, but when Riley moved back, Momma Micha pulled back immediately. "It's nice to meet you. Any friend of Matty's is bound to be a friend of mine as well."

"I'm Riley," the words came out awkwardly. There was so much going on to filter out that she could not control herself as much as she usually did.

Someone strummed a musical instrument a few stalls over. A child started screaming long, tired cries. Nearly a hundred people were talking, all so close that she could feel their germs leaking off them. Riley's hands shot up to her ears, and her breathing became short rapid breaths.

"Riley, are you ok?" Matty asked. She reached her hand out and placed it on Riley's shoulder. At the contact, Riley let out a squeal and dropped down to the ground. When she was younger, Riley had had meltdowns like these regularly. As an adult, she learned to control them or hold them off until she was alone. But this world was so different from the one she knew, and it was too much for her to take in.

"I think I know what will help," Momma Micha's voice sang into the noise.

Riley felt a heavy weight covering her body. It started at her feet and then covered her head, causing her to fall into darkness. The music stopped, the hum of voices dimmed, and Riley came back to herself slightly.

"Is that a bit better?" Momma Micha's voice broke through the silence.

"I'm sorry," Riley muttered, safe in the darkness.

"No need to be sorry." Momma Micha had started

rubbing Riley's back through the safety of the blanket. Without direct physical contact, Riley found the motion surprisingly soothing. "This bunch is a lot to take in right from the stiffness of Earth. Matty should have known better, but don't be too hard on her. She was only trying to look after you."

"I am sorry to have caused so much trouble." Riley moved the blanket off of her head. There was still noise. People still went about their business. But, much to Riley's amazement, people were not paying attention to her.

"I think it is best if you two head off. I'll stop by the ambassador's quarters after I finish up some work here."

Riley stood up and lifted the blanket off herself to return it to Momma Micha.

"You should keep it. I think it was meant for you."

"Thank you," Riley managed. The blanket was heavy in a comforting way. It was made of finely woven material dyed in reds and purples that almost looked like a sunset over a canyon. It was beautiful.

"Come on." Matty placed her hand on Riley's back and helped to guide her back towards the exit. The hand felt safe and even though the blanket provided warmth. They were silent as they walked out of the room. It wasn't until they had walked far down the corridor, the market's noise fading into a distant hum, that Matty spoke again. "I should have realized that would be difficult for you. I shouldn't have put you in that situation."

Riley stood frozen, unsure how to respond to the concern. She kept waiting to be yelled at and punished for her lack of control. An awkward silence settled around them.

"Well, should we go get lunch?" Matty moved, and when she noticed Riley did not follow, she paused again.

"I'm sorry...the germs...I need to get clean," Riley said.

Matty looked from the market to Riley, the blanket still wrapped around her. "Right, how about a trip to the sonic showers instead?"

CHAPTER 26

MATTY

PRESENT

THE MARKET HAD BEEN A MISTAKE. Matty realized that looking back. Riley had told her, but Matty hadn't thought about what that would mean. It was probably much worse since Riley had never been exposed to a Martian market. Shopping on Earth was so dull. Most items were ordered and brought to your house. Specially item stores usually required an appointment so that the store was never crowded. Even the stores holding everyday items were places to go to get what you needed, not areas to be enjoyed. Earthen society was all about separation. Matty knew it was necessary for their world, but she also knew that it was caused because they hadn't taken care of their planet. Matty mostly found it sad. Some of her greatest memories as a kid were going to a market with her mother.

Riley had looked so overwhelmed. Matty wasn't sure she had ever seen anyone so freaked out, and there was nothing she could do. She wanted to reach out and hug her, but she knew it was a selfish desire. Riley would not have welcomed her touch.

But now she had showered, and they had eaten lunch and were sitting in their quarters waiting for Mamma Micha.

"I'm sorry," Riley said for the hundredth time.

"I told you it's ok. You don't need to keep apologizing."

"I know that behavior is not acceptable. I will do better."

"Riley, this isn't Earth. I'm not upset. No one is upset. You are not going to get punished, and we are not sending you back. This was my mistake, not yours." Matty had told her this at least a handful of times. If anything, it seemed to confuse Riley more. Matty wanted to hop on another ship back to Earth to punch everyone who had ever hurt her.

The door dinged, and Matty stood up to admit Mamma Micha.

"How are you doing?" she asked Riley.

"I'm fine, thank you. I'm sorry if I did anything to your store."

Mamma Micha walked up to Riley and got close to her face without touching it. "You listen to me. You don't need to worry. Nothing got broken, and even if it did, it would be ok. You were overwhelmed; it happens. And Matty here is a sweet girl. She isn't going to get upset by something like that.

If anything, she will consider it another grand adventure. So don't you worry none."

"Ok, I won't." Somehow Mamma Micha had said just the right thing. Matty watched Riley go from the meek, childlike person to someone almost herself, or at least the self that Matty enjoyed. The take no shit badass woman even though she was pretty sure that Riley did not see herself that way.

"Let's make you some clothes then," Mamma Micha said. "There are only so many times you can clean those before they are just going to stink, anyway." This elicited a slight giggle out of Riley; it was the most beautiful thing Matty had heard. "Now, I will have to touch you to get your measurements. If it becomes too much, feel free to go ahead and climb into your bunk until you're ready again."

Matty watched with joy as Momma Micha guided Riley to move as she measured her and held out fabrics for her to sample. Riley looked so free and comfortable, and it occurred to Matty that this was probably something familiar to Riley. She may have had a shitty life back on Earth, but it was still a life full of money. Every article of clothing was probably tailored directly for her. It made Matty sad that she had left it all behind. But the sadness didn't last long.

"What was your favorite outfit back home?" Momma Micha asked.

"Anything without seams and with soft fabrics will be just fine."

Momma Micha stopped measuring and stood up and looked at Riley. "If you wanted, fine, you could have gone to anyone. Matty brought you to me because she wanted you to have the best. I want you to think back to the outfit that made you the happiest you have ever been. Picture it in your head and describe it to me."

Riley hesitated at first, then she began to open up about what it was like to slip on her son's clothing and walk around with people thinking she was a man. Then she faltered, as if confessing the most heinous part of all. She told them about what it was like before she transformed when she was this combination of feminine and masculine. How, looking in the mirror, even she could not tell. As she spoke, Matty watched her eyes sparkle. Her body stopped fidgeting, and she looked genuinely alive for the first time.

By the time Momma Micha had finished her measurements, it was nearing dinner time. They packed up Momma Micha's supplies, and the trio decided they would go and eat at the closest mess hall.

They were talking, Momma Micha telling about the first time she arrived on Mars, when Riley froze. Matty saw her face fall and followed her gaze. Ron was sitting at a far table sandwiched between two Martians.

Matty reached out and put a tentative hand on Riley's arm. "Are you ok? We can go to another mess hall, or I can bring back food."

"No, I'm good." Riley looked down at Matty's hand in confusion, but she did not seem upset by it. To be safe, Matty removed it. She was so used to touching people that she forgot how unusual it was for Riley.

When Riley started moving towards the food line, Matty and Mamma Micha followed. "Don't worry too much. Just give her time." Mamma Micha whispered.

Riley paused at the start of the food line. Up until now, Matty had always grabbed their food so they could eat elsewhere. Before coming, Matty had prepped Riley to expect to see people dishing out the food instead of having the food transferred through dispensaries. Matty watched as Riley looked at the gloves on the people and then the masks on their faces before picking up a plate and proceeding through the line.

Riley sat with her back to Ron, so Matty sat across from her. Matty made a point not to look at him directly to allow Riley to forget. But Ron did not offer the same courtesy. He stared directly at the back of Riley's head, not even bothering to touch his food. Riley must have felt his gaze. Halfway finished with her meal, she stopped eating and turned around. Matty watched the side of Riley's face. She kept her expression neutral, barely glancing at him before dismissing him and returning to her food.

Ron scowled, picked up his utensils, and started jabbing at his food. He shoveled it into his mouth and ate with a rage that Matty had never seen before. Matty glanced at Riley and saw a blank expression on her face. Then suddenly, she seemed to come back to herself. Riley's eyes flickered back to life, and her mouth slid into a practiced grin. She leaned towards Momma Micha slightly and responded to the older woman's comment like nothing had happened.

CHAPTER 27

RILEY

PAST

AFTER HER SON'S name day, Riley checked into a boarding house in second-tier that was owned by one of her husband's friends. He had often boasted that he would rent to anyone because he could charge more when he kicked them out than when he let them in. A horrible landlord was precisely what she was looking for. She had paid upfront for a month using a fake profile. This profile was more intricate than most of the ones she'd created, as it was tied to her actual biometrics. She had to ensure that in two weeks, all records would cease to exist in any files. She had two weeks to fix the next part of her plan.

Riley followed the location on her pad until she arrived at an old-fashioned wooden building. The exterior was brown, but from paint or dirt, she could not decide. The windows were covered in rusty bars, and most still used glass as a covering. Riley stepped over a sleeping figure as she climbed the chipped concrete steps to the main entrance. The door was made of thin metal bars that looked like they would fall apart if pulled too tightly. Riley waved her hand above the biometric scanner and noticed that there was no light indicating that it was functioning. She tried pulling on the door, and it opened at her touch.

Inside the building, there were more huddled figures in the hallway. They watched her as she walked past them to the stairs. These stairs were wooden and creaked under her slight frame. She stepped on them carefully, grateful when she reached the top. She located her room quickly, not far from the stairs. Riley let out a breath of relief to see the steady red light of the biometric lock on the door. She waved her hand over it and relaxed when the door opened.

Her room was compact with a plastic bed frame with a thin foam mattress covered in unknown stains pushed up against the largest wall. A small black plastic table was pushed up against the wall. One of the legs had been broken and melted back together; a wad of paper was shoved under the leg to stabilize the table. The chair was a continuous piece of white plastic. It looked fragile like it would bend under any weight. But at least it was in one piece. The walls were bare, missing even a basic screen. Riley waited for the panic to overtake her, but the cracks and dirt covering the walls were nothing like the room she had been trapped in. And above the bed was a window looking out into the dirt-covered walking street below.

There were no biofilters in the room, and it was evident that the room had not been cleaned in some time. Riley backed out, checking to make sure the lock reset itself, and then headed down the rickety steps and back past the unmoving huddled figures. She continued to the nearest convenience center.

Riley had had years to perfect her skill of being a man, but only for short distances. Usually, she only donned the clothing long enough to make it from the gate to the newest location of the hacker bar. She had heard about life in the second tier from the chatter in the online forum. They had teased her relentlessly whenever she asked questions about something they saw as an everyday occurrence, but it didn't stop her from asking. But hearing about this other world was very different from experiencing it.

There were only novelty stores in first-tier. Most items were ordered and delivered directly to your house, and Riley had never been to a shopping center before. She wasn't sure what she was expecting, but it was not a screen displayed on the front of a building. Riley moved to the back of the line. People stood uncomfortably close, only a few feet between each other. A few people did not have face masks on at all, and most only had a basic filter to use. She knew her filtration system stood out but couldn't bring herself to remove it.

Some people stood outside the line, typing on pads. Riley

thought about pulling out her pad and locating the shopping application, but she did not want to call any more attention to herself. So, she waited until a screen opened up.

The interface was simple. It was a touch screen with all the items available in the shop. Thankfully, the store was stocked with a variety of cleaning products. They even had a portable purifier that would work well enough for the room. She also ordered enough food so she did not have to go out again for the entire two weeks. She waved her hand to pay, and a large red number 82 flashed on the screen before it reset itself.

Riley moved out of the way, allowing the next person in line to order. She looked around as discreetly as possible and noticed a scattering of people, mostly males, waiting at the other end of the building. She made her way over and tried to stand casually while she took in the situation. There were three openings covered in plexiglass. Above each opening was a screen. A number would flash on the screen, and someone would walk over and wave their arm over the biolock. The door would slide open, and the person would take out their bagged items. It seemed simple enough.

Riley waited as the numbers continued to flash. When the screen flashed with her number, she approached the opening. Everything she'd ordered was contained in two large bags sealed at the top with a long strap down each side. She put one bag on each shoulder and made her way back to her temporary shelter.

As soon as Riley arrived back, she started to clean. She scrubbed down the walls and floor with decontaminate. She wiped down the furniture, taking off the mattress completely. She opened the door and set the mattress in the hallway, hoping someone would get some use out of it. Once that was done, she sprayed down the air with decontaminating spray and set up the purifier. Only after it had cycled the air a few times did she finally take off her face mask.

She had to find Elliott. There had been no activity on their private chat. His public profile was inactive. He hadn't been marked as dead, but he also wasn't using it. He'd either gone to ground, or someone was quietly covering up something. She hoped it was the former. Usually, the corporation liked to be as vocal as possible against what they saw as deviant behavior. They claimed it was to stop others from exhibiting the same behavior. However, it was evident that most corporate members enjoyed hurting others. Nice people did not stay in power for long.

Riley worked until she could not hold her eyes open anymore. She put down her pad and laid back down on the hard bed. Her body refused to relax. She was back in a room, the walls pressing into her. Without the task at hand to focus on, her mind went right back to being trapped. She sat up and looked out the window, reminding herself that she could leave anytime.

The streets were dark. In tier one and the start of tier two, lights lined the walkways. Here they were completely absent.

The only illumination came from lamps glowing in the windows of some of the houses. Most of them were dark. But, the streetlights and most of the housing ran entirely on solar power. So, there should have been more than enough to provide all citizens with electricity.

When she paid for her room, Riley saw that electricity was an optional charge. It was just another way of hiking up the rent, squeezing money for something that should have been provided for free. It wasn't until now that she realized the implications for everyone who couldn't afford the extra expense.

The streets were also dirty. Without the flow of people, it was easy to see the trash that had filtered and piled up on the side of the sidewalk. The packaging was now required to be compostable, but without compost stations on the streets, it left decomposing garbage everywhere. She noticed piles of it in spaces between buildings.

Riley knew she had grown up wealthy, but money had always been such an abstract concept to her. It was easy to log in and move around the bits of data. She had thought she understood pain and suffering, and she had suffered. Only now she realized she grew up more sheltered than she could imagine. Guilt crashed into her. The project she had been working on for the last several years took on new meaning. However, none of that would mean anything if she did not get out, and for that, she needed Elliot.

The first few days of searching were frustratingly unsuccessful. All traces of Elliot seemed to be removed. He left his house one evening and just never came back. It gave her hope that he was out there waiting for her to contact him. Except he had not been active in their personal chat or the hacker chat since he had gone missing. Both were secure channels he could access from even a public terminal without being traced. Elliot was one of the best, and she knew that he would have reached out if he were able.

It wasn't until the third day that she devised a new solution. Instead of searching directly for Elliot, she looked for any other public condemnation of deviant behavior. It only took her a few moments to find what she needed, and then she had to face the sinking realization that her friend was gone.

Riley spent the next day finding the files she needed to piece together the entire story. Elliot had gone out to his friend's house for dinner. They were a couple, Riley knew from Elliot's conversations with her, but there was nothing damming about the dinner itself. The three of them were sitting down for a meal. They weren't even alone; there was a servant that had cooked and served the meal. Yet someone had put in a report against the two men, and peace officers had shown up.

Elliot wasn't even put up for arrest. He could have gone home. However, he stayed and stepped in to stop one of the peace officer's fists from hitting his friend's head. She watched the video of them stomping the life out of him, then they turned and shot both the other men. There was a brief conversation, and the gun was turned on the servant, eliminating any witnesses. They must not have known a camera was hidden, recording the entire thing.

Next, Riley found a series of interviews with the father of Elliot's fiancé. Some money was exchanged, and his presence at the dinner was covered up. He was missing, with no one left to look for him. No one except her. Riley backed up all the files, securing them away with the others she had been collecting. One day, everyone involved would pay. She would make sure of it.

A part of her had already known he was dead, but it did not stop the pain from coursing through her. She curled up in a ball and cried silently until no tears were left. Then she stayed unmoving, frozen from the pain. It was hours before she felt herself start to climb out of the grief. There was only one way to avenge her friend, and it required her to get off the planet.

CHAPTER 28

RILEY

PRESENT

RILEY WAS asleep in her borrowed bunk when the lights flicked on to full brightness, and an alarm started ringing in the room. The ambassadors had jumped out of their beds and were nearly dressed by the time Riley had turned around in the bunk to face the room. Before she had managed to sit up, the room was almost empty. The only person left was Matty.

Matty was standing in the middle of the room, looking at her pad. She was dressed in just a long t-shirt that barely covered her ass. Riley couldn't help noticing her long legs, toned from the years on Earth's gravity. Or the way the t-shirt clung around her frame. She felt an unfamiliar fluttering as she took in the Martian. It disappeared as she looked at her face. It was etched in concern, and a bit of fear, as she typed viciously.

"What's wrong?" Riley asked.

"They can't find him." Matty's voice was so quiet that Riley could barely hear.

"Who? Who can't they find?" Riley wanted to go and comfort the woman, but she didn't know how. So, she stayed sitting in the bunk, her hands clinging to each other.

"They can't find Ron. The night guard was doing a bunk check, and he wasn't there. He couldn't have gotten out; he must be somewhere in the room. The door was locked, and there was a guard inside and outside."

Riley sat up and started putting her clothes on. The familiar fluttering of anxiety flared through her. "If you are so sure he is in the room, why did everyone leave in such a hurry?"

"It's just a precaution. The others will go help check the common areas to make sure everything is safe."

"They should check the bar," Riley muttered.

"That's not a bad idea." Matty opened the door and spoke briefly to someone standing right outside the room.

Riley tried to slow her breathing and get her anxiety under control. She had slept next to the man for months, and he was probably more dangerous then than he was now. Now he knew he needed the Martian's help, or someone else would get to him. *What a stupid man.*

But why did he leave if it didn't have something to do with her? He had it made. All he had to do was behave, and he would get Martian citizenship. Riley got up and started pacing before the thoughts started looping in her brain, causing more anxiety.

"Did you give him access to a pad?" Riley asked.

"He didn't have his own, but they probably let him use one."

Riley walked over to her new pad and left the corporeal world behind for the digital one. This was a place that she had understood since she was young. If Ron had made any plans, it would leave a trace. It was just a matter of being good enough to find it. And the one thing that Riley was confident about was her ability to find the unfindable.

The world around her became lost as she kept searching. At one point, Matty brought over food. Riley knew it was there, but she was so close she didn't want to stop. "I know, I know. I will be out soon; just let me finish this."

By the time Riley surfaced, nearly everyone was back in the room. Most of them were passed out asleep on the bed. Riley walked over to Matty. She was now dressed and sitting on the floor, working on her pad.

"What happened? Why is everyone back?" Riley asked.

"It's over. They found him. One of the guards fell asleep, and he took the opportunity to leave when the other became distracted. He was hiding. They moved him to a private room and doubled his guard. No need to worry."

"Except that there is." Riley held the pad out to Matty and let her look at it.

"Does that mean what I think it means?" Matty asked.

Riley looked at Matty, uncertain what she thought it meant. "I'm not sure. But we need a new plan."

CHAPTER 29

MATTY

PRESENT

SHE HADN'T AGREED to this. When Riley first told Matty her intentions, Matty completely turned her down. Then when Riley accompanied her to meet with the High Priestex, Riley interrupted to lay out her plan. The High Priestex had thought it was a great idea. Matty was upset at Riley for going around her, but also weirdly impressed.

Then there had been other conversations. Riley had been pulled in to talk to the High Priestex, and then met with various ambassadors, all without Matty. They had told her it was to iron out the details, but there were so many hidden meetings for what was supposed to be a simple conversation, a ploy to get more information. Now Matty sat uneasy, unable to protect the one person she had sworn to protect, as she watched the interaction behind hidden cameras.

Riley looked confident, but Matty was beginning to see

her tells. They were subtle, but there was the flicking of one finger that Matty knew meant that she was nervous. Matty was worried for her. It wasn't that she thought Riley couldn't protect herself. It was just that she wasn't there to help protect her. And this man had hurt her. She wanted to hit him, not give him a pardon.

"I heard you tried to escape," Riley's voice filtered through the screen.

"Why are you here?" Ron snarled.

"They thought I might be able to help you to reform." Matty hated her tone of voice. It was demure and halting, so different from the woman she had come to know.

"Martians are weak." Ron stood up and started pacing the room.

"Too weak to protect you?" Matty tensed as she saw Ron approach Riley. He leaned over her until Riley flinched. It took everything Matty had to stay in the room and not interfere.

"They aren't even trying to protect me. They are keeping me prisoner. Even then, they aren't doing such a great job. I mean, they let me get out." He hadn't moved back, and his words flew in Riley's face. Little pieces of spittle broke off and clung to her cheek. Matty could see Riley's revulsion. She could see her trying to reign in the panic until she was out of danger.

"You decided you would try to cash in on me instead?

You tried to use my location as a bargaining chip to buy your freedom from Earth."

Ron pulled back at the accusation. He began to pace again, now just walking the short span in front of where Riley was sitting. "What are you talking about? We came here to get away from all of that."

"Except when you escaped, I investigated what you did. You may be able to slip away from people who are just trying to keep you away from me, but you can't hide what you do online, at least not from me."

"You think you are so smart, always going on about how much better you are than me. You don't know anything," he sneered, his eyes wide and dark, his voice rising in pitch. As he spoke, his arms moved as if searching for something to hit.

"The corporation contacted you." Ron's face lost all pigment at Riley's words. He stared at her, afraid to speak. "They wanted you to meet. Telling you that you could trade your life for mine. And they even told you they would hook you up with a nice job once you got to Mars."

"I wouldn't turn you in. We have a deal." But his words were barely a whisper.

"They know you. They know how desperate you are, how you like to bet big, and how you like to drink. And they know that you are an idiot that will fall for anything."

"Don't call me an idiot," he screamed spittle flinging out of his mouth.

"You honestly think that you would have met up with them, told them where I was, and then they would let you walk away?" Riley's voice was steadier now. It had gained back the confidence that Matty recognized. "Why? They don't need you anymore after that. They would have gotten rid of you. It wouldn't even be hard. Who would notice if you went missing? And if they noticed, who would care? They probably would figure that you were passed out drunk or slept with the wrong man's wife and got what's coming to you."

"All I have to do is give them your location." His voice was almost like a lost little boy. Matty felt her head spinning with how fast his emotions changed during the conversation. "I figured the Martians would protect you. I would get to go back to Earth, back with regular people, and you would get to stay here. It seemed like the best solution for everyone."

"You believe that? Maybe I should ask the Martians to let you go. You can meet with your contacts and see if everything turns out the way you want. I mean, what is the worst that could happen?" Riley got up and went to walk out the door.

Ron grabbed her arm, and Matty jumped, ready to protect Riley.

"No, wait," the High Priestex said.

Matty stopped and turned back to the screen. Ron had let go, and Matty felt herself relax slightly.

"No, don't," Ron pleaded. He shifted on his feet, agitated. Then he searched forward pushing Riley against the wall. "It was a mistake. I wasn't thinking."

Matty's heart leapt into her throat. She glanced at the High Priestex, but they were still watching serenely, unconcerned.

When she glanced back, Matty saw that Ron had found the knife that Riley was carrying for protection. He pulled it out of the sheath and held it up with one hand, using his other hand to keep her against the wall. "What is this? Were you planning on killing me?"

"No." Tears were falling down Riley's face. The High Priestex held onto Matty's arm, keeping her from running off. "They gave it to me to keep myself safe."

"Why would you need to be safe from me? I'm your husband. It's my duty to protect you. I would have kept you safe, but you keep betraying me."

Matty felt her breath leave her as she watched Ron lift the knife and go to stab Riley in the chest. Riley moved out of his grip and tried to run, but the blade caught her right in her abdomen. Matty screamed as the blood seeped through Riley's shirt, soaking on the floor where she fell. Only then did the High Priestex let Matty go. By the time she arrived in the room, Ron was already being held down by two people, and Riley lay dead on the floor.

CHAPTER 30

RILEY

PAST

IT HAD BEEN six months of thrown dishes, screaming, and the entire household hiding whenever her father had come home. Her mother, in a rare act of independence, had ventured to ask if it may be best to send Riley to one of the Reaper schools after all. Riley had been banished to her room, but the screaming could be heard throughout the entire house. The doctor was summoned, and Riley's mother spent a month on bedrest healing. Every day, when her father left, Riley snuck into her mother's bed. They watched forbidden videos, and Riley read her mother stories. Her latest tutor, no more than a companion until she wed, would usher her out of the room shortly before her father came home.

Riley found herself content in a way she had not been before. She had never spent much time with her mother. Her mother was usually scheduled with social events to help her father in the corporation, while Riley's days were spent with tutors. Now that they could spend time together, she found she quite liked the older woman. She understood Riley in a way that no one else did. They found themselves drawn into conversations about the state of business that would have rivaled the corporate boardroom. It was the first time that Riley realized that she wasn't the only one that suffered under the expectations of gender.

The relationship was short-lived. Only days after her mother had been released from bed rest, her father arrived home in a good mood. He ordered a set of dresses to be made for Riley. They all itched and were made of bright colors that hurt her eyes. When the tutor put her in them, they squeezed her chest so tight that she could not breathe. But it was the first time in a long time that her father smiled at her, so she tried to do what was expected. Riley sat in her room rehearsing all the rules when she was called to dinner.

At the table, there was an extra person. Riley knew it must be one of her father's business associates. Even she knew that this was not just any other meal. There was something her father expected her to do. She just wished that he would have told her. During dinner, her father and the man kept talking. Usually, Riley would try to follow the conversation. She made a game out of predicting what strategies of her fathers would fail and which would succeed, although she knew not to tell her father about them ever again.

This time, however, she was too nervous to follow the

conversation. The man kept looking at her. He would randomly take her hand off the table and hold it in his own. His hands were cold and sweaty and covered in germs. It took all of Riley's attention not to wipe her hand on her dress when he let it go. Riley's father caught them holding hands. He took it in without comment, and Riley understood she was meant to be given away to him.

Midway through the meal, Riley finally focused enough to look at him. The man was old, although probably not as old as her father. His hair had not started to gray, but he had been out of school for years. He was nothing like Ronald with his youthful ignorance. This man glared at her so intently that she did not look up from her plate again. She focused on her table manners, hoping to get through the evening without upsetting her father. Except in the middle of picking up the proper silverware or cutting her food into small enough pieces, the man would retake her hand. Riley glanced at her mother, hoping for some help from her new friend, but recognized that the brief period of their lives was over. Finally, Riley gave up trying to eat. She stared at the food growing cold on her plate as the man took and released her hand through the rest of the meal.

The man started visiting more and more frequently, and Riley dreaded his coming. Even though each visit also meant that her father looked at her with approval.

One night after dinner, her father suggested the two go

for a walk. The man watched her put on her face mask and helped her into her coat. She grabbed her gloves, planning on putting them on like normal, but he took them from her hands and put them back. Instead, his hand held hers, flesh touching flesh, as they walked outside.

Once they had walked a few buildings down from their residence, he pushed her up against a fence, tore off her face mask, and kissed her. It was her first kiss, and she was torn between fear of her missing face mask and the revulsion of his lips pressed against her. She tried to pull away, but he held on to her. A piercing scream erupted from her, and he laughed and held her tighter until finally letting her go. She stood uncertain about what to do. Then, with trembling fingers, she reached down and picked her mask off the ground where it had dropped. She fastened it back to her face, and she waited.

"You're not very pretty or smart." He moved closer to her putting his mouth inches away from the side of her face; his hand was wrapped around her chin. "I do like that you don't talk much. And you squirm so perfectly when I touch you. I love that you still scream, even as much as he has beaten you." He let go of her and moved his mouth to her ear like he was whispering a secret. "I'm glad you were born broken. I do not need you, but I do need your name. No matter how high I have managed to crawl my way up in the corporation, you can only go so high without a proper name."

He picked back up her hand and walked with her back to the house.

The walks turned into dates where he took her to the theater or out to dinner. Riley had never been allowed to leave the house much, and she was amazed by all the world had to offer. Yet, she had to discover it with him at her side.

They would be listening to a concert, and he would suddenly pinch her to see her jump. When he noticed she found clothing uncomfortable, he asked for extra lace to be added to her dresses. He took her out to fancy restaurants and had the kitchen cover her food in maggots.

She held on, hoping that her father would take notice. She knew he would not have a problem with how she was treated, but he had to notice that the man, Nesili, was not much of a businessman. Yet somehow, her father was taken in by his confidence and lack of significant losses.

Riley hacked into his profile, determined to find something she could use to derail their relationship. There was nothing. He had attached himself to the right people, using them to connect to someone higher. He may not have been great at running a business, but he was a master at making connections. She felt stuck and hopeless in a way that she never had before. Her future loomed before her, and it was more of the past. There would be no spaceship or lasting contribution. It would just be endless corporate parties and horrible dresses.

Then on her fourteenth birthday, her father announced he was throwing her a party. She was instantly suspicious.

Not once had a party been thrown in her honor. The people arrived, music played, lights flashed, and Riley refused to leave her room. It was too loud and too bright. There were too many people. Her dress was too tight. Her father marched into her room, grabbed her wrist, and dragged her out to the center of the living room.

There he announced her engagement to the young up-and-coming Nesili, soon to be a Medici and future father of the heir to their family name. The man's arm snaked around her waist, and she stood too afraid to move. But she was soon forgotten, an afterthought at her own birthday party as everyone gathered around Nesili to congratulate him. Riley slipped back to her room and knew she would have to fix the situation.

Nesili took her to the newest trendy restaurant across the tier checkpoint on their next date. It was the type of restaurant where food was piled onto plates and cleared with only a few bites taken. Nesili made her pause in front of the gossip reporters while he smiled adoringly at her in her bright pink dress that fit tight around her top and fluffed in layers of tule in the bottom. In her hands she clutched a large black purse she had received as an engagement present. As they watched from the outside window, Nesili put on the ultimate performance. He held his chair out for her while he told her to sit up and smile, making it look like flirting. Then he whispered descriptive and violent things he planned to do to her once they were married.

After the first course, Riley excused herself to go to the restroom. In one of the stalls, she took off her dress, bound a cloth strip across her emerging chest, and slipped on her shirt and trousers. She piled her hair under her cap. It felt like a familiar second skin. She pulled out her pad, which she had smuggled in her handbag, and loaded up her fake id. Then she took her dress and shoved it into the trash can.

She waited at the door, making sure it was silent before she slipped out. There was a servant exit near the back of the building. Since she was leaving, she did not have to wait for the decontamination sequence. She walked through the door and out to the freedom of the second tier.

Chapter 31

Riley

Present

THE ROOM WAS HOT. It didn't help that the vest she wore under her shirt seemed to restrict her breathing. Or maybe it was just the nerves. Ron was screaming. It was a familiar scene, but Riley could not focus. She was too worried about making sure the plan went right. She didn't want to die.

"Don't call me an idiot."

Riley tried to remember the words that had come out of her mouth. She knew better than to call him an idiot. Except, she knew he would be upset. It was all part of the plan.

"You honestly think that you would have met up with them, told them where I was, and then they would let you walk away?" The words flowed out of her. She was transported back to the little girl who did not know to keep her thoughts to herself. "Why? They don't need you anymore after that. They would have gotten rid of you. It wouldn't even be hard. Who would notice if you went missing? And if they noticed, who would care? They probably would figure that you were passed out drunk or slept with the wrong man's wife and got what's coming to you."

Ron was so close to her now. His eyes were wide, and his lip went into the same pouting face he'd made as a child. He had always expected to have to show a smidgen of remorse and have everyone instantly forgive him for whatever he had done. "They said that I must give them your location. I figured the Martians would protect you. I would get to go back to Earth, back with regular people, and you would get to stay here. It seemed like the best solution for everyone."

"You believe that?" Riley knew he was not very good at strategy, but even he couldn't have thought that plan would work. He really was deluded with his own importance. "Maybe I should ask the Martians to let you go. You can meet with your contacts and see if everything turns out the way you want. I mean, what's the worst that could happen?"

Riley stood up and pretended to walk towards the door. For a brief second, she thought Ron would let her go, that he would be reasonable, and this would all work out. But then she felt his hand wrap around her arm and pull her back to the center of the room.

"No, don't." Riley's breath caught and her heart pounded as he pushed her against the wall. She struggled, the terror of what happened the last time he held her coming back.

"It was a mistake. I wasn't thinking," Ron said.

Then Riley remembered Matty waiting on the other side of the camera. She was not alone, and she could do this. Her hands were pressed against the wall, but she tried to maneuver one so that she could reach the knife hidden in the sheath under the waistband of her pants. He saw the movement of her arms and reached around to pull the knife out of the sheath.

"What is this? Were you planning on killing me?" He pressed into her, the knife pushed against her face as he screamed the words.

"No." She couldn't stop the fear that overcame her. One slip and the knife could slit her throat and their plan would be ruined. The tears came unbidden down her face. "They gave it to me to keep myself safe."

"Why would you need to be safe from me?" He kept in close to her, his words now a dangerous whisper. "I'm your husband. It's my duty to protect you. I would have kept you safe, but you keep betraying me."

Riley could tell the moment he was going to attack. He pulled back slightly; the knife angled at her chest. *No, no, no,* she thought, *that isn't the right way.* She moved, just enough that the knife bit into the vest she wore. She felt the pressure of the blade as it burst open the sacks of fake blood. It was supposed to collapse, and it must have, but the tip of the blade sliced through the back fabric of the vest, and into her skin. Her chest burned with the raw fire of pain, and then a cooling sensation spread fast through her body. Her legs lost the ability to hold herself upright, and she felt herself falling into Ron's arms.

Chapter 32

Matty

Present

THERE WAS BLOOD EVERYWHERE. The bed held smeared handprints that were already dried. The wall was decorated in reddish dots outlining where Riley had stood. A giant pool on the floor had been stepped in and tracked around the room.

Matty tried to avoid the body next to the blood. Once she saw it, everything would become real.

"She can't be dead," Matty said.

Tamiqa stood right next to her, holding on to her shoulders as if keeping her from floating away. Her presence gave Matty enough courage to focus on Riley. The skin was too pale, and her body was too still. Her fingers, which had constantly been rubbing together or tapping on surfaces, were now lifeless. *Lifeless.* Matty collapsed at the thought. Her knees dropped into the puddle of blood next to Riley's chest. The chest that wasn't moving.

"She needs air." Matty moved to Riley's head and then braced her body as she turned it over. She held her ear to Riley's mouth and then tipped back her head. Her lips found hers in their first kiss, their last kiss, as she tried to breathe air into her lungs.

Matty felt hands grabbing her from behind, pulling her away. "No, no, no," she screamed until it became a sob. Then she turned and buried her head into the shoulder of her ex-lover. "I need to save her."

"You need to let her go. The Earthen representatives will be here soon, and you need to be ready for them."

Matty heard the words, but she let them pass straight through her. Her eyes had found something more important. Ron was sitting against the far wall, as far away from the crime scene as he could be in the cramped quarters. By his side were two Martians making sure he didn't try to leave before the authorities arrived.

"You." Matty slipped out of Tamiqa's arms and ran straight at the man. He flinched back as if hoping to be able to sink through the wall. "You did this. You no good excuse for a human being."

Ron had stood up as if facing her on his feet would somehow be a better situation. The Martian towered over him, her tall frame nearly a foot higher than his own. All it did was make it easier for her fist to reach him. His head flew back against the wall from the impact, but not much damage was done. Matty was more than happy to fix that. She pulled back for another punch, but arms wrapped around her, and the other Martians moved in front of Ron.

"That's enough." At the High Priestex's voice, everyone froze except Ron.

"That crazy bitch. How dare a woman hit me? You wait until I get your ass locked up. I'll ask to pull the trigger myself."

"I said that is enough." The High Priestex moved towards Ron. They towered over him. Their pale, hairless face and flowing brown robe did not connect in Ron's head. But he recognized the authority and decided to keep his mouth shut. "The officials are here. They wish to examine the body."

Two figures walked into the room. Matty recognized the doctor. He was earthen born but had officially moved to Mars to live with his husband, whom he had met during one of his trips. He knelt next to Riley, taking care to avoid the blood, and put a small electronic instrument on her chest. Then he looked at his pad.

"There are no signs of life," he said.

Tears fell from Matty's eyes, but the second person spoke up before she could do more. "Let's get this over with then." He was a short, balding man who had enough girth to suggest a lifetime of adequate eating. "Where do I sign?"

"No." The words came out of Matty involuntarily. "She had Martian sanctuary. I will sign."

"This girl," the man sneered, "was a member of one of the most important earthen corporate families. It will not do for a Martian to sign for her death." He nearly ripped the pad out from the doctor's hand and placed his thumbprint on the screen. Then he turned to walk away.

"I believe there is one more matter to discuss," the High Priestex said.

"Oh yes, the third tier. Guards bring him this way." The Earthen man took off without looking back.

The two Martian guards looked at each other. One rolled their eyes, and the other shrugged. Then they put their hands under Ron's arms and started walking him towards the door.

When they left, a medical technician came in with a large plastic slab. They moved the body onto the plastic piece and strapped her in place. Then they lifted Riley and carried her out of the room.

Matty watched it all, her eyes never leaving the body. Her tears never stopped falling. She waited until she could no longer hear their footsteps and then turned to Tamiqa and the High Priestex and asked in a quiet voice. "How could I let her die?"

CHAPTER 33

RILEY

RILEY

RILEY HAD REACHED out to the hacker group first. She uploaded all the files she had found on Elliot to the group chat. No one was shocked to hear of his death. No one else wanted to leave, though, either. Earth wasn't so bad if you had money and the skills to stay undetected. Especially when you hid no major secrets. Riley paid them all well, funneling money from various accounts to keep them all working on her project. So, all the men wanted to stay, and all the women couldn't help her.

She paced the small room, uncertain what to do. If she stayed, she knew she wouldn't survive, not long enough to finish her project. But she also could not leave Earth alone.

Riley was monitoring the news networks when they started playing a tribute to the president. He was about to celebrate his fortieth year in power. The video showed clips of the corporation under his control. It wasn't surprising to see a clip of the president and her father talking. But in the background was a young Riley fidgeting with her dress, and next to her was Ronald.

Someone had messed up. Any mention of Ronald had been banned with his exile to the third tier. Riley had nearly forgotten that she was ever supposed to marry another. Now, confronted with his existence, he seemed like the perfect solution. If he'd survived.

It took longer than she would have liked to locate him. He had lost his last name when he lost his family. First, she had to find the corporate city they had relocated him to. It was a small town that focused on agriculture. He only lasted six months before he was banished for refusing to work in the fields.

He was moved a few more times, mostly for refusing to work, before he finally was made to do time in a forced labor camp. There, his trail became cold, and Riley was worried that he had died nameless because someone did not want to bother with the paperwork. She sorted through years of files before she found an employment record of a guard who was prosecuted and eventually executed for being a member of an anti-labor union that smuggled out prisoners. With no other leads, she decided to research the group.

It was easy to find their headquarters and their meticulously kept records. It didn't take long to cross-reference the time Ron spent in the camp and find their notes. They had managed to forge new documents and move him to a large city where he was living in an unemployment camp. The anti-labor union still checked in with him once a week. He took their food, listened to their spiel about unionizing, and sent them on their way.

It wasn't easy to find a way to travel to him. She had to fake bereavement papers, which allowed her to travel unattended through cities. The documents told others she was a widow returning to her family after the death of her husband. It was one of the few reasons women were allowed to travel, and she had to pull in favors from the hacker's group to get a proper mourning outfit. Then, dressed head to toe in black, with a veil covering her face and a pin memorializing her dead husband attached to her chest, she made her way between the cities.

There was a thrill at leaving the city gates at last. But outside the walls was a desolate area full of dead, barren Earth. She imagined what her fourteen-year-old self would have done if she had reached the walls and realized this was all that awaited her. The land was flat dirt. Occasionally, there were wisps of grass and a lone tree. Once she spotted a bird, but mostly there was just a dead shell of what should have been.

She traveled by hovercraft, one that did not service families. Each adult sat in their seat, pulled their curtain, and ignored each other for the next four hours. When they landed in the city, they gave each other space making sure never to make eye contact or acknowledge that the other travelers existed.

It was easy to find the unemployment camp. The transportation agency was on the far end of tier two, the annoyance kept far away from all the tier one aristocrats. It was a quick walk to the tier three gates. She had pulled the hidden location she had found to the anti-labor union. It was barely a building and had probably been condemned long ago.

Riley was not particularly good with people, but it was not hard to convince one of the activists that she was looking for her brother. The mourning garb probably helped. She led him right to Ronald. His home was barely more than an old corporate crate. Inside were a few blankets and a chair that was missing its legs. If the organizer had not insisted that it was Ronald, Riley would not have recognized him. He was no longer the lanky teenager she had last seen. His face had filled out and was covered by an ungroomed beard. His frame was wiry but fed, and his skin was a deep tan from long hours in the sun.

He did not have any problem recognizing Riley. He rushed from the chair, the seat sitting flush with the bottom of the crate, and straight at her. "You have come at last," he said. "You've finally come to take me home."

The union member left them. Riley felt unsettled, the type that made the inside of her skin crawl. She couldn't tell if it was from the unemployment camp or the man that now held on to her hands as if no time had passed.

She looked away from him and analyzed the world so unlike her own. There were adults laid out in a drug-induced haze, but there were also adults cleaning their makeshift housing and doing their best to prepare a meal. Around her were children running and playing, all maskless and nearly naked. The odor was so strong that she could smell it through her face mask, the smell of urine and too many unwashed bodies. Finally, she decided it must be the unfamiliar area that had her on edge. There was a shame in her privileged upbringing of clean sheets and clean air, even if it had its challenges. She found solace in knowing that soon she would be able to fix things for everyone, but first, she had to get off-planet.

Riley turned her attention back to her childhood betrothed. "How would you like to go to Mars?"

CHAPTER 34

RILEY

PRESENT

RILEY LOOKED DOWN at the bio downloaded to her new pad. *Sinta Talik.* It had been hard enough to remember Riley Matherson, and now she had to remember an entirely new name. Riley had pushed back at first. She knew the best lie was one that stuck close to the truth. But the High Priestex had pointed out how easy it would be for the Earthens to notice a passenger being added to the manifest in the middle of space.

Sinta Talik had passed decontamination and boarded the ship with her twelve-year-old son. Except she was never anything more than the product of a boy desperate to survive and a social worker willing to help him. Riley couldn't help but wonder how much of the money she had funneled to the orphanages had gone towards bribes to hide this exact situation. At least now she knew why getting children off the planet was so expensive.

She had yet to meet her pretend son. Last night she had woken up to the faces of the High Priestex and medical personnel. Riley was lying in a coffin, and before fully waking up, she was helped out and hidden behind crates of medical supplies. She heard the Earthen representative impatient to get the launch over with. She listened to the long sobs of Matty and felt a pang of guilt over not telling her the complete plan, but the High Priestex had been adamant about leaving Matty in the dark. Then she heard the soft wush of the coffin launched out into space, and she wondered how many funerals she would have until she was truly dead.

It had been hours before the medical personnel returned and smuggled Riley into the Martian corridors. When Matty saw her, she rushed and hugged her, tears still falling down her cheeks.

"You're alive. You're alive," she had said continuously while touching her face, as if not convinced.

"It was all part of the plan," Riley had said.

"Not like that. Never like that." But before Riley could understand what she had meant, the High Priestex had encouraged them to move.

Riley had been given a new pad, even though there was no way her old one could be traced, and deposited with a middle-aged Earth-born Martian. She had been led into a space barely covered by draping material, past cots of sleeping forms. When they arrived at an empty cot, the woman had pointed at it and told her to go to sleep.

Riley couldn't sleep. She could hear the bodies shifting in their cots. Some were snoring. Others let out gas, and others just shifted their body. It was loud and intrusive to a person who was used to sleeping alone. Her mind focused on all the germs festering in the populated space. She finally tore off part of the fabric from the funeral garb she was still wearing, careful not to make noise, and wrapped it around her mouth and nose. It was nothing more than a psychological gesture, but that was at least something.

The family had woken up hours ago, but Riley had stayed hidden with a blanket covering her head. She had read through her new profile several times and became familiar with the sounds of her new family before she finally ventured off the cot.

Riley tried to calm her breathing as she walked out of the sleeping area and into the large community. The colors were bright, and the room echoed with noise. It was nearly as overwhelming as the market. Someone was playing some drums, and a few people joined in the singing. There were people everywhere. A child was running, nearly running her over.

Riley stopped to watch the family. There were so many of them. An older couple, probably not more than their 50s, was gathering laundry. A group of younger children was sitting in a circle playing games with a woman who seemed slightly younger than Riley. There was a young man was doing some sewing, and a young woman getting taught to read by a male adult. One of the other adults was setting the table provided by the ship. Matty had explained that many of the Martians communities didn't go to the mess hall, preferring to eat in their houses. Riley realized it would be challenging to navigate the mess hall with so many young children. She did not remember seeing a single child traveling on the Earthen side of the ship.

They were all so different. Most of the children seemed to be from Earth with their shorter, stockier statures, although at least one looked like they were from Mars. The adults were mostly Martian, but at least one seemed to be from earth. Riley spotted a male child that looked to be about twelve. He had dark skin and dark, curly hair. She recognized him from the bio as her son.

Riley was amazed how everyone could be so happy with everything they had faced. She knew what it was like to starve and struggle to survive, but she felt broken, and she marveled that these people had adapted and found joy in life.

One of the children noticed her and ran over. She was a cute child, probably around seven or eight. Her brown curly hair was held together in bright pink bows, and her clothing was a bright pink that contrasted with the bright blues, reds, and oranges that surrounded her.

"Hi," she said, her words almost running together. "Are you my new sister, Sinta? Mama said that you would be coming today. I'm so excited to meet you. I've never had a sister before, and now I have lots. Have you had a sister before?"

Riley looked at the child, took a deep breath, and kneeled. "No, I have never had a sister, but I am excited to have some now."

The child smiled, then it slowly slipped off her face into a quizzical glance. Riley looked down and remembered that she was dressed in a thin white robe used to bury the dead. A long strip was missing and now tied around her face, causing a part of her leg to show.

"Don't worry. Mama will fix you up." The child reached out her hand. Riley reluctantly grabbed the child's hand. Together, they walked toward the rest of the family.

Immediately, Riley was surrounded by people. They were all hugging her and asking her questions. It was flashes of sound and color, and Riley let go of the child's hand and put her hands up to her face to try to block it out.

"Enough, give her some space. We talked about this." The voice was loud, demanding to be heard over all the chatter. The family members backed off, and Riley was left facing the middle-aged woman. "It will be ok. They are excited, but they know better than to overwhelm you all at once. You'll meet them all, a little at a time." She turned and looked at each of them while she said this. "First, I think we need to get you cleaned up."

The woman guided her back to the sleeping area and handed her a set of clothing. "Here, take these and change."

Riley felt comforted by the women's no-nonsense tone. She was so used to being alone and trying to figure out how to survive that it was nice that someone else was taking charge without actually controlling her. Riley nodded and began to change. The women turned around and walked to the door.

"When you are done, come out, and we will take care of you."

Riley changed into the bright red shirt and the bright orange pants. She looked at herself and took a deep breath. The colors hurt her eyes, but she knew she would have to adjust. She was a Martian now, and it would just get brighter when she got to Mars. She tried to imagine a world full of color, unlike the darkness of Earth. When she finished, she tied the white cloth back up over her face.

When she returned to the community area, everyone was back to doing what they were doing when she first arrived. They seemed to have already accepted her place among them. She caught only small, curious glances before they turned back to what they were working on.

Riley stood and waited. She used the time to become more familiar with her surroundings, and she found a present pattern in the chaos when she was not the center of attention. Abruptly, the older women put down the clothing and stood up.

"Now that you are dressed, you need to know your way around the area." The woman started walking, and Riley hurried to keep up. They walked through the clusters of families, stopping to greet each one. They were using her new name, calling out to Sinta like she was already a member of their community. Riley looked at the older woman in surprise.

"You're not the first stray that this group has taken in. Be nice and say hi back, will you? These people are your community." Every person they passed required at least a greeting. Many stopped and shook her hand, informally welcoming her to their group. Riley found herself with a small grin as the greetings continued. She had never fit in anywhere, and people had accepted her sight unseen.

Riley also noticed that the young children gravitated toward the older women. Each one was treated with a hug or a hair tussle, and a few children seemed to have a unique greeting, where they touched their hands in elaborate motions. It was still startling to see people so openly touch, even those that had just come from Earth.

"How many of the people here are new Martians?" Riley asked the women.

"Oh, most of them. Most Earth-born Martians will not go back to Earth. Most would probably be killed if they did. Mars cannot take everyone, so we tend to take those most persecuted. About of third of those here are Martian natives." The woman turned back and focused her gaze on Riley. "Once a person sets foot on Mars, they are considered a native. There is still support for as long as they need, but the distinction on the ship doesn't last on the planet."

"Why are there any native Martians here? I mean, besides the ambassadors?" Riley asked. They had walked past the families and were now walking back toward their own families.

"When Earth-born Martians are given citizenship, they are adopted into a family. The family sends representatives to pick them up. We find it easier for Earth-born Martians to transition if exposed to their new culture on the voyage home. Even for those that are different, it can be difficult to see such differences so openly expressed. After all, they have had to hide who they are for so long."

"So many people were willing to spend over a year traveling to and from Earth just to pick up Earthens?" Riley asked in disbelief.

"They are family. Most will only make the journey once in their life. Some will choose to make it more. Many volunteer so they can see Earth. Once they leave quarantine, they spend a month seeing the planet and getting to know their new family. But, once they see Earth, most never want to go back again. Some go for work, to transport materials back and forth."

They were walking back towards the family now, past the households they had greeted earlier. Each unit was divided by strips of colorful cloth, but in a way that united all the families together instead of separating them.

"Matty told me about them," Riley said.

"Well, at least she managed to tell you something."

Riley looked at the women in confusion. She seemed upset at Matty.

"You have a lot to learn about our people. More than half the voyage is done."

"It isn't her fault. I started this voyage on the Earth side of the ship.

The woman just grunted. They had made it back to their family, and a rush of children greeted them.

Chapter 35

Matty

Present

Matty stood silently watching Riley work. Her short Earthen body was folded in on itself, wedged between the back of a tent and one of the built-in storage containers. She was wearing a disposable face mask and a pair of earplugs that Mama and Papa Hapots had requested for her. The reports of her panic attacks had torn at Matty, even more so since she couldn't come and visit. They couldn't give any indication to Earth that she was still alive.

The rescue had come too fast, and the time that Matty had been granted to see Riley was too short to convince her that she was actually alive. Matty wasn't upset at the deception, not if it helped to keep Riley safe, but the nightmares wouldn't leave her. She wasn't supposed to visit at all, but she had business nearby and had to make sure Riley was okay.

Matty watched her work for several minutes. Riley's face

was relaxed and focused, a peace she hadn't seen on Riley even while asleep. Her fingers flew across her pad, and her lips scrunched up in concentration.

"Riley," Matty yelled. She didn't move. Matty tried to climb past the crates and stored luggage to reach her. She couldn't help but wonder how Riley had ever found such a place. "Riley," Matty tried again. Finally, Riley shifted her weight, stretched her legs, and noticed Matty near her.

"Where have you been?" Riley asked. Matty should not have been surprised that she went straight to the point, but after three weeks apart, she had forgotten exactly how blunt she could be.

"I couldn't come. I'm sorry."

"Why? Did they change your work assignment?"

"Yes, but they did it so I would stay away from you." Matty noticed Riley pause and saw a slight disappointment in her eyes. "I wanted to come, but it would be suspicious if I visited here too often. It's not much longer until we reach Mars, and then it will no longer matter."

Riley didn't speak, and Matty thought briefly that maybe she should go, but she noticed that Riley's pad was lying on her lap. Matty had her full attention. "Mama Hapots says that you have been working on something a lot lately."

"Yes. I need to make sure it's done. Is she upset? I'm still making sure to help. I haven't forgotten that they took me in."

"She isn't angry, but concerned. She says you haven't been sleeping."

"I do sleep, at least some. Well, most nights. Sometimes I'm in the middle of something, and I forget."

"What are you working on?" Matty glanced down at Riley's pad. It was just a string of code that did not make any sense to her.

"I'm working on a way to help people. I'm trying to fulfill a promise to a friend."

"How do you plan on doing that?" Matty tried to keep the concern out of her face, but Riley must have sensed something because she didn't respond. "At least tell me you are being safe. No one can trace you?"

"Don't worry. No one can trace me. I've adapted what I've learned from your systems."

"Good."

"Is something wrong?" Riley asked.

Matty stopped looking at her and finally let out a sigh and began talking. "We aren't sure. We think they may not believe you are dead."

"Why would they think that? Everything went to plan," Riley said.

"We're not sure. We think that it may have been something Ron said that tipped them off, not right away, but as they kept listening to his story. They haven't been able to verify the logs because there is no DNA record."

"But it's ok now, right, since you came?"

"Nothing has changed. We don't think they can prove

you're alive. We have to keep you hidden until we reach Mars."

"Then why did you come?"

"I needed- I... just... had to see you were really alive." The words were barely a whisper.

"I'm alive," Riley said.

The words were said so matter of fact, seeming to discount all the worry and frustration that had built up in Matty over the last three weeks. "The whole time I was gone, you didn't question it, did you? Did you even miss me, or were you too busy with whatever you are working on?" The words came out sharper than Matty intended, but Riley looked at her in confusion.

"I missed you. You said that you would come and you didn't. That hurt. But I know that you have responsibilities, essential ones. And I have my work, and I'm used to being left alone for a while, so I decided to wait."

Matty relaxed at the words. She knew she couldn't expect Riley to feel the same way that she did. She had seen how much pain she had endured and wouldn't add to that. Riley was more sensitive than anyone understood. "I missed you too."

When Riley reached out for Matty's hand, she had to contain her excitement. It was the first time Riley had initiated any physical contact. Just feeling her hand inside of hers caused Matty's heart to race. They sat like that until Riley broke the silence.

"Are they going to find me?" Riley asked behind closed eyes.

"I don't see how they can," Matty said. "We will do everything that we can to protect you."

"I won't put them in danger." Riley looked up, her face as blank as ever, but her words were full of concern. "If they come here, I will surrender, so they don't hurt anyone accidentally or purposefully. If I leave, then they will leave them alone. There's too much at stake politically if they did otherwise."

"It won't come to that." Matty squeezed her hand as she said this. "I wanted to talk to you about something. Since you've been on this side of the ship, you have seen that people are different and that those differences are respected." Matty waited, but when Riley did not respond, she continued speaking.

"Before I went to Earth, I didn't think these things were different. They just were. I told you that we were allowed to find our own identity. That included deciding who we were attracted to."

"That sounds nice," Riley said.

"I saw you before we got on the ship. Not long before, when your shuttle landed for the quarantine period, I saw you and Ron get off the shuttle. I assumed you were married, but I still felt connected to you somehow. There is a term on Mars called Theia mania. It is an old Latin term, but on Mars, it has come to mean that two souls are connected."

"There is something similar on Earth," Riley said. "I think they call it soul mates."

"Did you feel anything like that when you saw me?" Matty asked.

Riley looked at her, her face expressionless. When she didn't respond, Matty began to ramble.

"It's ok if you didn't. You probably didn't even see me then, but maybe after at some point. I know you had a lot going on."

"You make me happy," Riley said. "I enjoy being your friend. I've never felt like that before. Is that what you mean?"

"Your friend?"

"Is there anything better than a friend?" Riley asked. "I have had so few of them in my life."

"I guess I was wondering if you were attracted to me."

"Do you mean if I want to have sex with you?"

"Yes, I guess that is what I am asking."

"No," Riley said this right away, and Matty pulled back from her. She started to get up when Riley reached out, grabbing her hand back. "Why would I want to do something like that to you?"

"Sex is a way of showing someone you love them." Matty stared at their interconnected hands. The feel of the other woman's skin against her own caused her to course with desire. Then she looked up at Riley's face. It had filled out during her time on the ship, but there were still signs of the years of abuse. "There are other ways people can show they love each other. It doesn't have to be sex. I would be happy to be friends with you."

"Sex is about power and pain. It is a way to get offspring and to show someone that you are stronger than them. It is horrible, and I will be happy if I never have to experience it again." The words were biting and filled with pain that Riley had never shown before.

"Sex can be many things," Matty spoke hesitantly, trying to find the words to share her experience while acknowledging the pain she saw. "When you don't have a choice, when it is used as a source of power, that isn't sex. That is rape. You never have to have sex, but when you find someone who cares about you, and it is a decision you both make together, it can be a way to show love and bring your partner pleasure."

"I'm not meant to be loved, not like that. When I was young, my father told me I was broken. I think he was wrong. I think I was just different. But now I'm broken. I don't know what I feel when I am around you. I know that when you are around, I am happy. I want to make you happy also."

"Being around you makes me happy. I'm glad that you walked into my life." They sat in silence, holding hands, until Matty's pad let out a ding. She picked it up and looked at the message from the High Priestex, letting out a sigh. "I should probably get going." Matty went to stand up again.

"I'll try." Riley's voice was full of desperation. "If that is what you want, I'll try."

"What do *you* want?" Matty raised her voice in frustration, and Riley flinched back. "That's not fair. I shouldn't ask this of you. I forget what happened to you. Of course, you need time."

"You're leaving?" Riley asked.

"I need to go. I don't want them to find you, not because of me." Matty wanted to stay and comfort Riley, but everything she said just seemed to make things worse.

"Will you come back?" Riley asked.

"I will, I promise. I don't know when, but I will be back."

Riley looked up and smiled. Matty returned her grin and then turned and walked away.

CHAPTER 36

RILEY

PAST

THE OUTFIT DID NOT FIT QUITE AS well as it used to. She had grown, and the pants were now an inch above her ankle, but ill-fitting clothes were not uncommon. The way her chest was starting to show under the shirt had her most concerned. Riley found herself holding up her messenger bag to cover her upper body. Posing as a messenger boy had been her cover the handful of times she managed to sneak into the second tier for a few hours at the hacker bar. Although, usually, those times were short trips when the bar was closer to the tier-one fence. Now, free from her fiancé, she was left wandering around with no idea where to go.

She stopped against the side of a building and pulled out her pad. It had been a while since she had a chance to track down her friends, and she didn't have the latest key, so she would have to start from scratch, tracking down the clues that she would need. Riley hadn't gotten very far when she felt a sudden pain in her shoulder.

"Hey, boy. What do you think you're doing around here?" A large man, muscular from years of labor, had grabbed her shoulder and was now squeezing it as if afraid she would slip away.

"I'm sorry," she stammered. "I got lost. I was trying to find directions before they noticed I was late."

The man looked at her with his dark brown eyes, a pinched expression on his face as if trying to match her low voice with her growing frame. She saw him take note of her bag and gave her a sneer, but he let go of her shoulder. "You're too old to be getting lost. Get away."

She took the opportunity and started running away as fast as she could, just as any messenger boy would. But he was right. She was getting too old for the part. Not that it mattered. Out past the gates, there were cities rumored to be free of corporations, and she was going to find one.

Riley didn't stop for another hour. By then, she had made it farther into tier-two than she had ever managed. Night had fallen, and the streets were dark more often than they were lit. The shadows started closing in on her, and every slight noise made her jump. She found the darkest corner she could and hid away. Riley was afraid to pull out her pad, knowing the light could be seen from all around, so she spent the night with her knees pulled up to her chest, too afraid to sleep.

When the sun rose the following day, she woke up. Riley wasn't sure what surprised her more, that she had managed to fall asleep, or finding herself not alone. Her dark corner turned out to be an alley between two small factories. Behind her were three children, the oldest no more than six. Although they were huddled so close together, it was tough to tell. All three were staring at her, uncertain what to do with this giant blocking their way.

"Do you have a wallet?" Riley spoke straight and to the point, her manner causing the children to flinch away from her. "Well, do you?"

The biggest of them gave a slight nod, causing his short blond curls to bob, and held up his hand. His fingers were covered in dirt, but there was a small metal band wrapped around his wrist.

"Well, come here," she said.

The boy looked at her and then tentatively walked towards her, giving occasional glances back at the other two children. Riley flinched back at first. The boy's pants were torn and old, and he wore dirt instead of a shirt. But it was the stench, like that of a week-old trash can, that Riley couldn't stomach. She held her breath and pulled out her pad, logged into one of her more secure profiles, and transferred some credits over to the boy. He looked down at his wrist, his eyes going wide.

"You're old enough to find work in some of the factories," Riley said. "They should be able to look after themselves while you are gone."

"They don't hire girls, sir."

Riley looked at the child again. It was so hard to tell gender just by looking at someone unless there were fluffy dresses involved.

"Is there anyplace you can go?"

"There is an orphanage in tier-three, but we didn't have enough to bribe the guards to let us pass." The child still spoke hesitantly, her eyes glancing down at her wallet in disbelief.

Riley looked back at her pad and pressed a few more buttons. The child's eyes stayed transfixed on her wrist. "Is that enough to get you through the gates?"

"Yes, sir. This is more than enough." Then the child took a deep breath, as if steeling herself for something unpleasant. "What would you like in return, sir?"

Riley was about to tell them it was just money and that it didn't matter, but she stopped, realizing that it probably did matter to some people. Given that the child couldn't stop looking at her wallet, Riley started to guess that she may have transferred over more than they had needed. She pictured the small group going around and telling everyone about her.

"I have a secret." As Riley spoke, the child moved back, afraid of what was coming next. "Can I trust you with my secret?" The child gave an uncertain nod. "I'm not a boy. I pretend to be one because I don't like being a girl all that much. I'm running away, so I need you three to keep my secret. Can I trust you to do that?"

"Is that all?" The child sighed in relief. "We can do that just fine, sir."

"Oh, and buy you all some face masks and gloves."

The children laughed at this as they got up and started to run away. Riley watched them, looking at their bare feet and bare hands and bare face and shuddered. Then she went in search of a place to work.

It was just her luck that the hacker bar was closed. The only message she could find was a warning that it was not safe to meet. The group needed a chat room, one secure enough that no one would be able to infiltrate it. Except she was going away, and it wasn't her concern anymore. Still, they really ought to have one.

Riley knew she couldn't go back, so the only way was to move forward on her own. She just had to get to tier-three, and then she was sure there was a way to get out of the fences. So, she walked.

The corporate city was large, as it was the president's primary location and housed many upper corporate members. The city had to be split into tiers because it was too large to have the entire population housed together. If there was an outbreak, there needed to be some way for it to be contained.

Except as she continued walking into tier-two, she couldn't help wondering if the boundaries were for more than stopping contagions. The houses were nothing like the condo that her family lived in. The housing units were tall buildings that looked like they could topple if you touched them. Various factories and workhouses surrounded them. The further into tier-two she went, the more broken everything looked, and the more people seemed to live on the edges of the buildings rather than inside them. The people watched her as she walked, as if sizing up if she was worth the hassle. By the time she made it to the tier-three gates, she nearly collapsed in relief.

She had learned that it was not as common for messengers to cross this side of the tier, but it still happened. So, she had forged her papers to indicate that she was headed to one of the transport sites. She approached the gates with the confidence and swagger of a youth used to being able to go where he wanted. Inside, her heart was pounding.

There was no line into the third tier, so she walked up, placed her hand on the scanner, and waited. Behind her, the guard cleared his throat, and Riley moved away slightly for fear of getting sick. He did it again. Riley looked up at him with concern.

"Didn't your employees teach you nothing?" The man's voice was deep and gruff.

Riley couldn't help but startle at his words and then stared, unsure how to proceed.

"You need to pay the tax to pass through. If your employer didn't give it to you when you took the assignment, that is on you. You will know better for next time."

"How much, sir?" Riley tried to deepen her words, but they came out quiet and hesitant.

"Five credits. And you should be prepared to have another five credits for the way back."

"Five credits," the words came out in disbelief. Riley recalled the children who couldn't cross because of five credits. The ribbons that were used to tie up her hair cost more. No wonder that kid had stared at her in disbelief. She had deposited over a thousand credits into her account.

Thankfully the guard took her outburst as outrage over the price instead of disbelief. "If you don't have it, you can return with your items undelivered. You'll lose your job for sure that way."

Riley didn't answer. Instead, she pulled out a small digital wallet she had hidden in her bag. She didn't think it would be wise to show the guard that she had her pad if he thought she would be upset over five credits. She transferred over the money and passed through the gates.

The signs to the transport station were clearly marked. The streets were clear of trash and people. These streets were bordered by buildings. Most were empty but kept in good repair. They seemed like a barrier separating this walkway from the area beyond it.

It was only a short walk before she saw signs of the transport agency. The area was fenced off with a guard station in front. Uncertain how to proceed, she decided to treat it like any other guard station. She walked up and placed her hand on the scanner. For the second time that day, it did not light up to let her pass.

"Kid must be new," one of the guards said. He was tall and lanky, leaning against a post.

"He's too old to be new. Maybe he isn't quite right," the other guard said. He was shorter and the kind of skinny that showed that he had missed a few too many meals.

"I'm not here to deliver anything. I want to buy passage." The guards finally looked at her then. It was a quiet assessment until they both broke out in laughter.

"The kid thinks he has enough money for transport."

"He really must not be right in the head if he thinks they would let the likes of him on a transport."

"I can pay," she said.

"Even if you could," the guard finally spoke directly to her, "it isn't just about money. Could you imagine if they let every tier-two bum on a transport? There wouldn't be enough workers left. No, you're stuck here like the rest of us."

"What if I pay you to cross?" Her voice came out in a desperate plea.

"Even if you had enough kid, we'd lose our job, and you

still wouldn't get on the transport. You best take your money and keep it safe. Maybe one day, you can buy yourself a wife and a space that isn't falling apart. That is the best one of us can hope for."

Riley stood there so close to freedom but uncertain how to proceed. The second guard stepped closer. He had pulled out his stunner and held it firmly at his side. "Listen to him. Don't make trouble."

Defeated, Riley walked away.

She wandered through tier-three, watching maskless and nearly naked people lounge around with a hungry look in their eyes. There was a man whose coughs racked his thin frame, and before she could help, he was picked up and carted away with the dead.

People watched her. She may have been dressed as a messenger boy, but the clothes were finer than anything anyone else was wearing. They eyed her face mask and gloves, and she knew it wouldn't be long before someone decided it was worth tempting their fate to have such items.

Riley wandered around, hoping to find a hotel or housing she could purchase. Most of the buildings in this part of town were unusable. Instead, people marked their space with discarded packaging or broken pieces of buildings. Even with her face mask, the place smelled of unwashed bodies and urine. As night approached, she thought about turning back and making her way to tier-two. The dark streets seemed a paradise compared to this world. But she knew that if she kept walking, she would eventually see the fence that would lead outside the city, and she didn't want to lose that.

When the sun was low in the sky, she found a building that was not only still standing, it was full of children. The block outside was full of more children running and playing. It was the happiest place she had seen since she had crossed the fence.

"What is this place?" she asked one of the children who had just emerged from the house.

"It's Amee's Orphanage." His arms were full of a wrapped bundle that looked like another child. He didn't stop, continuing on his way without looking back.

Riley approached the building slowly, uncertain what to expect. At first, she thought the front door was open, inviting people to enter. As she got closer, she realized the door was missing. The doorway opened into a room with a scattering of bedding all over the floor but was otherwise empty. She followed the noise to a stairwell and then past that to a busy room. Children were standing around, stirring giant metal containers. Others were busy dishing out an unappetizing mound of slop into bowls placed into trays carried out a door in the back of the room. Everyone seemed young except one woman who at least had to be fully grown.

Riley stood in the doorway, uncertain how to proceed. The woman was short, not much taller than some of the children. She had long, light brown hair that swayed as she orchestrated the running of the kitchen. Eventually, the women turned and noticed Riley standing, staring into the room. Her face went from a look of concentration to one of anger.

"Hey you, get out of here," she screamed. When Riley didn't move, the woman headed over; her hands held up as if to push Riley straight out.

"Please, I need a place to spend the night. I need somewhere safe."

"This isn't a hotel. I have enough kids to take care of. We don't need no upper tiers here trying to use this as a place to hide away from trouble."

"I thought you helped people," Riley's voice broke, and tears fell down her face. Her plan had utterly fallen apart, and she had no idea what to do. An image of her future husband flashed in her mind, and she started crying harder. "Please, can you please help me? Just for tonight, and I will leave in the morning."

At the sight of the tears, the woman stood still, standing a few feet away. "There is no more room, and these children need to be here more than you."

"What if I help?" Riley asked.

"I have more than enough help." The women gestured to all the small bodies working away in the kitchen. "There is too much help and not enough of anything else. I'm sorry, I am, but you need to go."

"I can pay," Riley said. "Tell me how much, and I can

pay. Just give me an amount of how much it would cost for me to stay for a few days. I'll stay out of your way."

"Right, then. For a hundred credits, you can stay the night. I'll even throw in a bowl of food." The woman laughed like she was making a joke.

"Deal," Riley said before the woman changed her mind. She pulled out her digital wallet and paid the woman.

The next day Riley paid again, and then the next.

While she was there, she tried to figure out a plan. During the day, she went walking, trying to find information on a way through the gate. At night she would return to a bowl full of mush and a corner to sleep in. After a week, she returned for the night to find the women waiting next to two of her father's guards. Riley tried to run, but they caught her before she had taken more than a few steps.

"Why?" she shouted to the women as they carried her off, slumped over their shoulders, but the women just let out a small sigh, turned, and walked about into the orphanage.

CHAPTER 37

RILEY

PRESENT

AFTER MATTY LEFT, the days seemed longer. Riley found herself glancing at every set of footprints. She wasn't sure if she was hoping to see Matty again or if she was afraid of seeing Earthen guards. Maybe it was a bit of both. Eventually the older woman, who had insisted Riley call her Mama, made her stay with the family for all but a few hours that she was allowed to claim as her own. The children were loud and demanding, so to quiet them, she started programming them simple games based on the code she had created in her childhood.

When Mama saw the younger children running around and trying to pop virtual bubbles projected by their pads, she informed Riley in no uncertain terms that the rest of the community could use her help.

The tasks people brought to her were simple but kept her occupied. More often than not, they just needed a technician, and Riley found that she had developed skills to do simple repairs over the years, as she'd had to maintain most of her own technology.

She spent time getting to know her fake son. She found she could make him laugh, then felt guilty that she had a stronger connection with this boy than she ever had with her biological son. But he was never hers, not really.

The community continued to be welcoming, and she began to get to know people. She became amazed by the women, many of whom were leaders in the community. The men listened to and respected them. If there was a disagreement, the leaders got together and discussed a decision. At one point, Riley asked how the leaders were chosen, and one of her new younger brothers laughed at her. They were not chosen. They just naturally were. Leaders had an authority about them, and it was expected to be respected. It seemed it didn't matter their age or gender as long as they had some quality that Riley was not capable of identifying.

Each day she felt her sense of self settling. The more that people expanded the gender roles beyond the narrow confines of Earthen rules, the more Riley found herself identifying less as a woman. She was without gender, having no connection with male or female and an association with both. The family seemed aware of this shift, never grouping her in with the men or the women but still using the familiar female pronouns.

One night the adults were sitting beside the electronic fire. The group was together, but each was working on their projects. Riley was engrossed in her project when she received a notification on her tablet. Mama had sent her over a book that focused on the use of pronouns throughout Martian society. It was a children's book, but Riley found herself engulfed in the pages.

One night Riley went and sat next to her fake son. He was sitting on the edge of the camp playing a game on his pad.

"Do you mind if I sit?" she asked.

"No," he said, continuing to play.

"I'm sorry that you were put in this position."

"What do you mean?"

"I can't imagine how you feel about me using your mother's name." Riley looked at his pad and saw he was playing one of the games she had made. It was a simple logic puzzle she had enjoyed when she was his age.

"It's kind of nice, even if it is pretend. I haven't had a mom in a long time."

"How old were you when she passed away?" Riley asked, then immediately regretted it. She realized too late that it was probably a topic that was too painful for a child. But like her, her adopted son had not had an easy life.

"I was eight. I lived on the streets for a while but got

picked up for stealing food. They tried to make my dad take me in, but instead, they put me in one of the Mars-run orphanages, and I waited to get picked up."

"Did you ever meet your dad?" she asked.

"I saw him once. I don't think he knew I was there. He came to the detainment center one time to try to prove I wasn't his. He was wrong. Most everyone in the gutter has skin like yours and my mom. I stuck out, but his skin was darker than even mine. I thought somehow that would connect us. He would pick me up and take me somewhere I wouldn't get strange looks just for existing. I was stupid back then. I heard what he said. Even after the DNA test proved he was my father, he walked out, refusing even to sign away his rights. I don't think I would have fit in where he was from either."

"You fit in here," Riley said, and she knew it was true. You could go to a new comm, and each would be full of people that were all different, but all connected. The boy smiled at this, and Riley felt nice for helping that to happen.

"How did you come here if we were in the middle of outer space?" he asked.

"I got on the ship at Earth. I just got on the Earth side."

"So you decided to move over here?" As they talked, he moved closer to Riley until they were sitting right next to each other.

"Yes," Riley said, uncertain how to respond to his sudden closeness.

"Why?" he asked.

"It wasn't safe for me there."

"Is that why you have to be someone else?"

"Yes, it is." They sat together, his head slightly leaning on her arm. He picked up his pad and started playing again until one of the younger children came up and dragged him off to play. Riley sat watching them, feeling a peace she had never felt before.

It was three more weeks before Matty visited again.

Riley was busy collecting all the dirty clothing to be taken to the wash. She wasn't allowed to take the clothing, as the nearest cleaners were outside of their comm, but it was something she found she could do to help out. While she picked up the clothing, she tided bed mats and put away toys. She jumped when she heard the familiar voice behind her.

"Did you miss me?"

Riley turned around a large grin on her face. Matty rushed up and hugged her, and for the first few seconds, it felt nice; then, she found herself tensing up and pushing away.

"Sorry," Matty said, her face now deflated.

"It's just still a lot," Riley said.

"I know. So how are things going here? How are the Harpots treating you?"

"They are nice. There are so many people. Is your family this large back home?"

"Let's sit," Matty said. She walked outside the tent and sat down in one of the chairs. Riley set down the laundry by the entrance and then joined her. They sat quietly for several minutes. Riley's eyes darted around the activity in the comm, her mind wondering what she had done wrong.

"It's just my mom and me, mostly." Riley turned to look at Matty, surprised she had spoken. "Not all Martians have big families, mostly just the ones that keep adopting Earthens. But for us, my dad died in an accident when I was young. She never remarried, and I was too much of a handful for her, anyway. We lived in one of the cave towns. Everyone is so close there that the town is like family. You knew everyone and everyone looked out for each other."

"Is she still there, your mom?"

"She is. I tried to get her to move closer to the administration sector, but she wouldn't come. She said that the town helped her when she needed it, and she needed to give back. She comes and visits a lot, though, and I visit her. At least when I am on the planet."

"It must be hard being away from her for so long." Riley reached out, extending her hand towards Matty. As if waiting for the invitation, Matty reached her hand out and intertwined their fingers. The sensation of their hand touching was overwhelming, like a fire burning across her skin, but a pleasant fire. One that she would happily let consume her. She had to pull her attention away from the feeling to try to listen to Matty when she began to talk.

"I didn't think it was going to be hard when I left. I was so excited. We would get to see everything we had heard about on Earth and bring all that knowledge back to help our world. It was idealistic."

"But that is exactly what you are doing."

"I was so short-sighted. I was on the planet for three years and had no idea what it was like. It seemed so easy to me. If your husband hits you, walk away. If you see a starving kid give them food. If someone likes someone of the same gender or no gender, don't care because that is life. I saw Earth from my perspective, and it limited my view."

Riley watched as Mama and Papa Hapots gathered the children and walked them away, probably to one of the makeshift playgrounds. The adults also seemed to have disappeared, leaving them alone in the camp.

"Everyone is like that, not just you," Riley said. "I lived there and am only now learning what it was like to live in tier three. Did you know they call it the gutter? It's some term from Old Earth where people would sleep on the edge of transportation lanes."

"If I had done better, maybe I could have helped you earlier," Matty said regretfully.

"When? You didn't even know I existed back on Earth. When it counted, when I needed you, you did help me."

"I wish that I could have done more. Have you finished working on your program?"

Riley startled at the mention of her program. She tried to

reach back in her mind to see if she had told Matty what she was working on. She couldn't have; Matty would not have acted so casually when she asked her. Riley finally decided that Matty must have just been making conversation, a way to ask Riley about her interests. It was a sweet gesture, even if it had flooded Riley with panic. "No, I've helped with some tech here and coded a few games for the kids. I've made some progress, but I'm not done yet."

They sat in silence again before Matty spoke again. "I wish there was some way to help Earth. I wish I had done more when I was there."

Riley thought back to her program, uncertain how to respond.

"Maybe we can create something on Mars, some way to help even from a planet away. There has to be something we can do," Matty said.

"It doesn't seem enough does it?" Riley said.

"What do you mean?"

"The Harpots came all the way to Earth and rescued less than a dozen kids. On this ship, there are probably about two thousand Earthen refugees. There are so many people on Earth that need help. Taking them all to Mars is not the solution. More people are turned away than accepted. Everyone here is lucky, but what about all the unlucky ones? There has to be a way to make things better on earth."

"It isn't our place. Earth has its own customs. We have to respect them."

"I don't."

"What are you going to do? You can't go back. They will kill you, which won't do anybody any good." Matty scouted out of her chair as if she suspected Riley would head back to Earth right that second.

"No, I'm not going back. But I have to do something."

"We'll talk about it, I promise." Matty's voice was almost pleading, as if still afraid for Riley. "I'll bring it up the High Priestex. I bet they have some ideas."

"Yeah, that sounds great." Riley tried to tone down her voice, to sound resigned to waiting for action. Matty couldn't know, not yet.

Riley didn't notice at first when Matty stood up. It was only when she let go of her hand that Riley startled back to the present.

"I have to go. I can't spend too long here, or someone may catch on."

"When can you come back?"

"Hopefully, in a couple of days. I have been put back on comm duty. The High Priestex decided it would look suspicious if I wasn't, now that my grief period is over.

Riley stood up. She fiddled with her hands, uncertain how to say goodbye.

"Can I give you a hug?" Matty asked.

"Yeah, ok."

Matty wrapped her arms around her, and maybe because

she was expecting it, or perhaps because Matty did not linger, the hug felt really great.

"I'll see you soon," Matty said as she started walking away.

Riley stood watching long after her figure had disappeared.

CHAPTER 38

MATTY

PRESENT

MATTY JUMPED out of bed and rushed to get ready when one of the other interns caught her and told her that the High Priestex was looking for her. Matty skipped breakfast and went straight to the command center. Inside five techs were all huddled around the screens.

"What's going on?" Matty asked.

The High Priestex looked at her and said, "They know she is alive."

"We already know they suspect," Matty said. "They haven't made a move towards her in months. What's changed?"

"Somehow, Riley's son found out she boarded the ship," one of the techs said. "He obtained a copy of one of Ron's interrogations. He doesn't believe Ron killed her and has asked for further investigations."

"Shit," Matty said. "Why didn't they just kill him already?"

"I'm sure Riley's husband tried," the High Priestex said, "but it is harder to have a man killed than a woman."

"You said you handled everything. You said they would never know. We shouldn't have put her at risk that way." Matty knew her outburst was not helping anything, but after everything they'd been through, Riley was still not safe. The need to move overwhelmed her, but there was no space in the room.

"The doctor disappeared," the High Priestex said.

"You can't just disappear on a ship." The disbelief was thick in Matty's voice.

"You can if you burn the body," one of the techs said. He had ginger hair and pale skin scattered with freckles. Matty tried to remember his name, but the tech heads all blurred together.

"They killed him?" Matty collapsed in one of the empty chairs. "They can't kill him. He had dual citizenship. Why won't they just let this go?"

"We don't know what has happened." The High Priestex spoke in a firm voice. "Maybe they have him somewhere that we haven't found yet. He may have been Earthen born, but he has been Martian for years. They know we could not let that go. I believe that they have taken him in for questioning. They probably plan to buy his silence."

The High Priestex stood in front of the group. Their presence was as solid as ever. The calm demeanor caused Matty's own anger to flair.

"I don't understand what this has to do with Riley. There are logs showing that her body was disposed of. Riley did it herself; no one here would be able to trace them."

"We covered our tracks," the High Priestex said. "All they have is the word of a man disgraced in their society, saying he didn't kill her. But they are not letting this go. I may have discounted exactly how important a position Riley held."

"Is she safe?" Matty's voice broke as she asked.

"For now, I think so. We haven't heard chatter that anyone knows anything for certain. It all just seemed like speculation. But I'm going to take you off Comms duty again."

"Won't that raise more speculation?" Matty jumped out of the chair.

"Not if I reprimand you and put you on office duty as punishment. You need to stay close to the command center."

"If you do that, then I can't see her."

"Exactly. For her safety, you must stay as far away as possible."

CHAPTER 39

RILEY

PRESENT

WHEN RILEY WOKE UP, the room was dark. She lay frozen in bed, waiting to understand what had woken her. It often happened now, her sleep interrupted by the noise of being close to others. Other times, it was the realization that there was no door to lock. There were just layers of cloth and other sleeping forms.

At first, there were no indications of what had woken her. The night was uncommonly quiet. Then she heard the light movement of footsteps, like a group of people trying to hide their presence, and Riley sat up in fright. She knew with absolute certainty these were Earthens. Martians did not feel the need to hide anything.

Riley threw a pair of pants on under her sleeping shirt and went to the tent's entrance. In her mind, she had already planned what she would do if this happened. So her actions came naturally.

What she did not expect was Mama Hapots to have woken up when she walked past. The women jolted up in alarm and went to follow Riley.

"Please stay," Riley pleaded. "They won't hurt you if I go with them."

"I won't let them hurt my child." Riley looked at the woman. Her hair was pulled back in a bright pink hair net, and she was wearing a nightshirt with some extinct hairy animal printed on it. She looked so small, but so vicious at the same time.

"Stay and protect the babies," Riley begged. "Protect my son."

That gave the woman pause, and Riley took advantage of it to slip out of the cloth door. Corporate guards surrounded their space. It was a joint effort. Riley could see a mix of corporate logos on the uniforms. It was unheard of, but maybe here in the presence of space, the mutual bond of hatred mattered most.

"It's her. I found her." One of the guards reached forward and grabbed her by the arm, even though they had all witnessed her come out. She didn't resist as other guards stepped forward, and they pulled her wrists behind her and bound them together. When they pushed her to the floor, she didn't cry out. Riley knew that they needed to show force, and the only way she would survive would be to be as meek as possible.

"Don't hurt her." Papa Hapots had woken up and was now standing at the entrance to the tent. Riley could see a collection of bare feet behind him.

"Please," Riley said. That was all she could say before one of the guards kicked her in the stomach. Papa Hapots went to rush out, but he stopped when he saw her eyes pleading with him. Mama Hapots whispered something in his ear, and he stopped moving forward.

After a few more kicks that were more for show than damage, they lifted her, and Riley had the first idea that she may survive the night. She watched them all, her new family, as the guards dragged her away. The tears in their eyes matched her own.

CHAPTER 40

MATTY

PRESENT

MATTY JOLTED AWAKE. She had fallen asleep in the command center, her head propped on her arm, her hand holding her pad. Her pad was now emitting a loud, shrilling sound that was also coming from the rest of the night shift pads.

Her eyes widened when she read the alert. Over thirty guards had breached Martian territory, entered a community, and taken one of their own. The alarm was a call to arms. Everyone able and willing was called to help protect and defend their space. It was a call to war.

Matty scanned the notice impatiently, needing to know just one piece of information, what way they were headed. Once she had that, she raced out of the command center and through the hallways.

It was slower going than usual. Every Martian was up and

flooding the hallways, but they knew Matty and got out of her way as quickly as they could. It was not fast enough. By the time she reached the doorway between their two planets, the soldiers were already gone. The door was sealed, and multiple Martians were standing guard.

It would not stop her, though. She pushed past the guards and started entering her code when a pair of strong arms pulled her away.

"We will get her back," a voice said, but Matty was too far gone to listen. She kicked and screamed and tried to claw her way out of the grip and towards the door. Several more arms reached out to hold her until suddenly she collapsed, her body unable to give any more, and cried.

She felt a hand rubbing her back, and the High Priestex whispered in her ear. "Don't worry, child, I won't let them take one of ours, and she is ours."

CHAPTER 41

RILEY

PRESENT

RILEY WAS in the same cell. At least it looked like the same cell. The bed was in the same position. The toilet, the sink, and the door were all in the same place. She had already tried the sink to make sure it worked and attempted the door to make sure it didn't work.

She sat on the bed and thought about dying. So much of her life had been spent trying not to die that she had never really thought about what came after. It made her chest tight, and her heart was racing. She had no answers, and she did not like the unknown.

Riley realized she had finally allowed herself to believe that she had gotten through and won. She'd become weak and attached to someone, getting her caught.

Yet, she didn't regret it. The last few weeks of her life were incredible. She had lived more in that time than she had before. Maybe that would mean something. Her only regret was that she didn't tell Matty what she was working on. Hopefully, after she was gone, Matty would find the backup copy she had saved on her server. Hopefully, she understood it. Hopefully, she used it.

Riley lay on the bed and closed her eyes. She waited for the nightmares to come. The images of the closets and rooms, the hunger and the thirst. They didn't come. Instead, she saw her adopted family. The children were laughing and playing. She was teaching her pretend son basic programming. The conversations at night with just the adults where they taught her about Mars, and she taught them about Earth.

She thought of the couple in the comm that had escaped Earth so they could finally be together. The joy on their faces when the two men held hands out in the open. She finally realized that even though it wasn't enough to save the few thousand here, it was something important. It was something that mattered to each person on this ship. It mattered to her. She hoped she had left some mark on them.

So she lay in bed, closed her eyes, and waited to die.

She did not have long to wait.

The light flashed in her eyes, and Riley woke up instantly. She didn't fight, not in the end. Riley knew that going quietly would mean that everyone else would stop having to bear the brunt of her actions.

She was surprised when she walked into the room and saw Ron. He was sitting on one of the four chairs in a clean, crisp dark blue suit and shiny brown shoes. When they made Riley kneel on the ground, he smirked and leaned back in his chair, happy to watch the show. It still amazed her how stupid he could be.

Riley held her head up and watched as the men began to fill the room. A lanky man in a tight blue suit shuffled in first. He looked down at her. His clean-shaven face had a boyish look. He sat down in one of the chairs, his eyes locked on her even as his face remained expressionless.

A middle-aged man in a fitted dark suit walked in next. He went straight to the seat, spread his legs, and crossed his arms. His gaze stayed fixed on the wall. He had olive skin and a short, manicured black beard.

Suddenly both men stood up, and Riley turned to watch a third man enter. He was dressed in a black judge's robe that accentuated his portly figure. His face was round with full, puffy round cheeks, but his eyes looked empty. As he walked in, he was flanked by three peace offers.

As the judge sat in the center seat, the two other men sat as well. Two of the peace officers stood behind the judge, but a third moved to stand directly behind Ron. Riley could still feel the gaze of the officer that had brought her in, drilling into her back.

"State your name," the man on the judge's right asked, the one wearing a blue suit that looked too small for him.

"Riley Medici." There was no point in not using her real name now.

"To whom do you belong?"

"Objection," the other suited man said. This one was in a classic black suit that seemed to fit him perfectly. It was not hard to see which one her husband had financed. "The woman has been officially declared dead twice. She does not belong to anyone, and my client would rather that his name not be included on the record."

"Agreed," the judge said. "But by doing so, he is officially declaring that this woman is no longer his."

"My client agrees." It was such a small thing, but Riley's heart was about to burst. She may be about to die, but for a few minutes, no man had a claim on her.

"What is she accused of?" the judge asked.

The blue-suited man looked down at his pad like he was examining something of importance, but Riley doubted that he didn't have her accusations memorized.

"The woman left the planet without the permission of her husband. She was accompanied by another man who had unsanctioned relations with her. She is accused of theft and resisting the will of the people."

"Begin," the judge said.

"Did you leave the planet in the company of Mr. Ron Edgewood, formally known as Ronald Bishop?" The younger man stood up as he spoke, towering over Riley, still kneeling on the ground.

"I did," Riley answered.

"How did you come to be in the company of Mr. Ron Edgewood?"

At the question, Riley realized that this hearing was no longer about her, at least not yet. She glanced over at Ron, who was blissfully unaware of what was about to happen. "I left my house and used a fake ID to move cities. I found Ron in a different community and offered to pay for his travel to Mars if he agreed to pretend to be my husband."

"How did you obtain tickets for the ship?" the judge asked.

"I bought them," Riley said. She moved her gaze to the ground, waiting for the sting of a needle in her neck.

"That is impossible," the outburst came from the man in the black suit. "To think that a woman could have enough money for tickets, let alone be able to purchase them. I can assure you that my client would not have left her in that position."

"Ms. Medici, who did the actual purchasing of the tickets?" Riley could feel the judge's gaze on her, trying to get her to say what they wanted to hear.

"I purchased them, of course," Ron said.

"Mr. Edgewood," the judge said. "I have given you strict instructions not to talk during this session. If you cannot hold your tongue, I will give you a sedative, and you can spend the rest of the trial asleep."

Ron slumped down in his seat, crossing his arms, but did not speak again. Riley wondered if he would ever realize that this was his trial, that if they put him to sleep, he would likely never wake up. She wondered if it would be better that way.

"I did." All three men turned to her as if they had forgotten she existed. "I had purchased them through a fake profile I created long before I found Ron. I was..." Riley paused, uncertain how to continue, then decided it no longer mattered. "There was someone else that I was supposed to go with. The police picked him up before we could leave. I needed someone else, someone who was desperate enough to go with me."

"I'm sorry, I just do not see how this is possible," the blue-suited lawyer spoke up. "I cannot believe a woman would be able to handle such a complex transaction. It must have been Mr. Edgewood."

Riley looked up then and focused her attention on the judge. She knew him or knew of him. She understood why he was serving on this ship, unwelcome on Earth but unwilling to step foot on Mars. "It isn't a secret that I can read. You can confirm that just by talking to the corporate wives. It was also known that I am eccentric. I doubt anyone was willing to see my true aptitude, but there are records in the corporation for a hacker nicknamed Swinglon, for his takedown of a company of the same name. That was the first time he came to the corporation's attention, but it was not the last. Some even claimed that this hacker was indeed a woman."

Riley stared at the judge, watching him keep his face as expressionless as possible. He held her gaze while the lawyers exclaimed her statement as nonsense. Ron sat in his seat, moving his head back and forth, trying to understand what had happened. But the judge never took his eyes off of Riley.

"This changes things," he finally said. "What role did Mr. Edgewood play in all of this?"

"He accompanied me. I offered him a ticket and the rest of my money when we arrived on Mars so that he could start a new life."

"He traveled as your husband?" the judge asked as more formality than interest, his mind preoccupied elsewhere.

"Yes, as you know, women are not allowed to travel alone."

"Quiet right, quite right," the judge said. "And for good reason."

"While you were onboard, did Mr. Edgewood take it upon himself to act as your husband in all things?" the blue-suited lawyer asked.

"He did." Riley could not help shuddering as she said this. The feel of his hands on her body came crawling back to her.

"I mean specifically, Ms. Medici, did he take it upon himself to be intimate with you?"

"He did." As Riley said this, she knew she had just sentenced Ron to death. Her husband may have released his claim on her, but she was still a Medici. No man would be allowed to partake of Medici property without the consent of the head of the house. Her son had not consented to the union.

Ron still seemed blissfully unaware. If anything, he seemed to puff up at the acknowledgment.

"Thank you. I think that helps clear things up," the judge said. "The judgment is death. Do either of you have any objections?"

At this, Riley looked up and saw the two lawyers nod in the negative. She then braced herself. This was it. She had finally reached the end. She turned and faced Ron, amazed that he had managed to stay quiet through it all. He had a grin on his face as he stared down at her.

"Officer," the judge said. "You may proceed."

Riley took a deep breath, trying to steel herself. Her mind wandered to all the ways that they may carry it out. Before she could decide what would happen, Ron fell before her. His eyes were open and unafraid, the grin still plastered on his face. She looked up and saw the officer behind Ron's chair take a needle and put it back into a plastic container, careful not to prick himself with the tip.

"Now that that is settled," the judge said. "What are we to do about her? Your client has relinquished all claims, so it would be difficult to charge her with theft of her personage if he has already claimed that she was dead before she entered the ship. Has the son pressed charges?"

"Not at this time," the black-suited man said.

"We have to be careful with this. The Martians gave her

sanctuary. It was verified by the Jeck corporation, not that they had any business verifying something that had nothing to do with their corporation. However, it has been done. And there appears to be some more things that need to be investigated."

Riley looked up at the two sets of lawyers. They seemed disappointed that she was still alive. As if to confirm her thought, the black-suited lawyer spoke.

"My client would like this handled before we reach Mars. As you know, he has a new wife to care for and would not want anything to get in the way."

"Yes, yes, not to worry. Talk to the boy, help him to understand the situation. For now, take her back to her cell. I will reach out to Earth and see if I can locate some information that will help. This has been a very enlightening day." The judge looked at her as if she was his ticket back to a planetside job. She knew he would take all the time he needed to ensure his case was built before he brought it forward. He wouldn't want to be wrong again. But the lawyers did not need to know any of that.

The lawyers nodded in assent and then stood up, talking to each other about strategy as they exited the room. Riley was left with the four peace officers and Ron's body lying still in front of her.

"Get up," the officer behind her said. Riley was happy to comply.

CHAPTER 42

MATTY

PRESENT

THE MARTIAN SIDE of the ship had transformed. Every hallway connected to Earthen territory had a patrol unit moving through it. Every doorway had a permanent guard. There were so many volunteers that they had to create a four-shift schedule. Some Martians apologetically declined, needing to stay with their family, but every new Martian put their name on the list. They had children as young as ten come to join the efforts and the High Priestex refused to turn them away.

Groups were armed with clubs. A few trained individuals were armed with stunners. In the off time, volunteer groups taught self-defense moves and what to do in case of an air breach.

The doors to the comms remained closed and guarded.

Even the Martian medical staff had been called in. There was a make-shift clinic within one of the mess halls.

Matty couldn't help wondering if the Earthens even realized what they had caused. She had spent the day listening to the ambassadors making calls through diplomatic channels. The High Priestex was on a call with the ship's captain and assembly of corporate presidents. Matty had been refused entrance to the meeting. They claimed she was too emotionally involved. But of course, she was. She had vowed to protect Riley and had allowed her to get arrested again. Not only that, they'd come into Martian territory, aiming stun guns at an entire community. Who knows what chaos would have happened if Riley hadn't gone willingly?

The other ambassadors kept staring at Matty as she paced through the small command center. With so many meetings, they wore localizers to limit the audio to their own hearing. It was maddening to be so in the dark. Matty knew the implications of this situation were huge. Earth had blatantly violated a police treaty that had been a precedent for a century. Tensions had been building between the two worlds for years. Too many people on Earth hid what Mars was capable of. They thought Mars was weak, and it was only a matter of time before tensions came to a head. Riley just happened to be the tinder that started it all. Only the Earthens that recognized and accepted the actual state of affairs of the relations between Mars and Earth were working to rectify this station.

The rest of the Earth was too caught up in their supposed superiority.

But Matty was just worried about Riley. All that mattered was bringing her back safe. Once that was done, then they could work on fixing what had been broken today or prepare to cut ties with the planet altogether.

Wait, she had been told. *Wait until the diplomatic channels had failed. Wait until they were closer to mars.* And she did wait because she knew Riley would never forgive her if any of her new family were harmed. After all, Matty was reckless.

She had visited her family. They had told her how she sacrificed herself to keep them all safe. Mama Harpot and Matty had clung to each other and cried until they realized they were scaring the children.

Now she paced. Her hands balled into fists at her side. She walked from meeting to meeting, hoping to glimpse how things were proceeding.

When the High Priestex entered the room, their robes a flurry around them and their pale face flush in fury, Matty knew it was finally time for action.

CHAPTER 43

RILEY

PRESENT

RILEY WONDERED if they had forgotten about her. After they locked her in the room, they provided her with a meal, one that she ate right away. There was a second meal, but this one was given to her after she had slept, and the hunger had eaten away at her. This time she remembered to ration the food. They hadn't been back since, and Riley was starting to wonder if it was time to eat some of the hidden food. But she wasn't dying yet, so she continued to hold off. Instead, she drank some water. The cool liquid filled her stomach.

As Riley drifted half awake and half asleep, her mind wandered to Matty. She wondered if Matty was trying to get her back. Part of her hoped she was fighting for her, ready to rush in and demand her release. The other part hoped that she had already forgotten her, so it would be easier on her after she was gone.

Riley heard a noise in the hallway, and her stomach growled in anticipation. She sat up, her muscles protesting, but adrenaline coursed through her. The door opening could mean anything from her next meal to her execution. She did not expect a figure dressed all in black.

"Come on. We need to get you out of here." The voice was masculine but unfamiliar. He was wearing a black pullover turtleneck and a a pair of black slacks. On his face he had a black face mask and a knitted black hat that was pulled low so only his eyes were visible. Even his hands were covered in black gloves. He was six feet tall with the stocky muscular build of an Earthen.

"Who are you?" she asked. But what she meant was who sent you.

"Hurry up. We need to be gone before the guards come back."

Riley hesitated. That was the wrong thing to say. Guards wouldn't just leave. Either the man had incapacitated them, or they had not bothered even to guard her. But for the man to not commit to either raised a red flag for her. She stayed where she was.

The man moved into the room. He pulled a stun gun from behind his back and aimed it at her. It was the same model that the peace officers carried. It had to be a setup; she would walk out that door and be shot trying to escape.

"Go, now." He aimed the gun at her. Staying didn't seem to be an option either.

Riley started walking towards the door. She walked slowly, trying to give herself time to think. It wasn't much of a ruse, her muscles hadn't been used often, and she was weak with hunger. The man, impatient with her pace, jabbed the stunner in her back. She stumbled, just barely catching her fall with the wall. The man grunted in impatience, but he didn't push her again. They continued to a part of the ship that Riley was unfamiliar with. The neutral Earth template gave way to the bright blue color of the Reaper corporation.

"Stop," the man said. "Here is good enough."

"Good enough for what?" she asked, trying to stall him as much as possible. "Who sent you?"

"Who do you think? You, idiot women, are all pathetic in the end, trying to question and haggle. What would you try to give me for your life?" He eyed her up and down, and Riley realized he wanted her to bargain her body for a few more minutes of breath. She wondered how many had given themselves to him, hoping he would spare them just to kill them when he was done. Riley did not doubt that he would end her life no matter what. But it would give her time to come up with something.

"What would you like?" she asked.

"Stupid women, what do you think I want?"

"Right here? Where anyone may walk by?" She opened her eyes wide, hoping she did a convincing fake shocked face. She was sure that no matter what she did, this guy would take her for an idiot. It worked to her advantage.

"Here is good enough. It won't take long."

He moved towards her, pushing her up against the wall. The gun was still in his hand, and she eyed it wearily. He grunted again and then moved the gun to a holster in the back of his waist.

She let him kiss her, his cold, dry lips pressed against hers. Then she kissed him back, moving her hands to caress him, trying to put on a show, like she believed that her performance would decide if she lived or died. Then, she reached around to untuck his shirt and felt the unbuckled latch of the stunner.

One hand moved to the front of his pants, and he grunted in pleasure. Her other hand pulled out the gun. When it was in her hand, she backed up from him as fast as she could. Before he realized she was no longer pleasing him, she was away and had the gun pointed at him. *And women were supposed to be the stupid ones?*

He rolled his eyes at her and moved towards her.

"Don't come closer. If you do, I will shoot. Leave now, and you can go unharmed."

"Like you would even know how to fire a gun. I was going to give you a nice clean death, but now I'm going to enjoy it." The grin on his face gave her chills, and he took that as a sign of weakness. He stepped towards her, and she shot. A pulse of energy ripped from the gun and caused his body to spasm. He looked at her in shock, and she shot him again.

He fell then, his body seizing until he passed out. Then

she went over to him and searched through his pockets until she found the poison meant to end her life. She stabbed it into his neck and dropped the needle on the ground.

Riley moved in measured steps unwilling to think about what she continued to do to survive. Instead, she looked around, making sure no one had come. Then she wiped off the gun with her shirt, as best she could, and placed it on the body. People would come soon, and she needed to be far away.

She thought about ducking into one of the rooms, but if they weren't already locked, they would surely be the first place someone would look. *Were those footsteps?* Desperate, Riley walked away from the scene as casually as she could.

Riley continued to look around her for a place to hide and noticed that one of the rectangular panels that periodically lined the halls was not flush with the wall. She pulled on it and was surprised when it opened like a hidden door. She climbed in and closed the panel back up, sealing it. The space was small, nothing more than a tunnel with built-in reflectors. Just tall enough for her to sit up in.

She sat near the vent and tried to hear what was happening on the other side but could not make out anything specific. Then she tried to look through the slants and realized it was not a vent at all. On this side, it was a smooth piece of metal.

Riley was afraid to move, worried they would hear her if she did. Her mind filled with visions of peace offers pacing the hall looking for her, and medics picking up the body of the man she had killed. Her body started to shake as the adrenaline drained from her. But she knew she wouldn't have made different choices. It was his life or hers, and she had chosen her own. There was nothing to do but move forward. Riley eyed the tunnel, uncertain of where it led. But she only had two options, stay here and get caught or crawl.

She decided to crawl.

CHAPTER 44

MATTY

PRESENT

MATTY THREW on some Earthen clothing she had bought for her mother. It probably wouldn't help her blend in much, she still had the tall, lean form of a Martian, but at least the consulate could distance themselves from her if she was caught. Then she put a stunner in her pocket and grabbed Riley's pad. She had started looking at it after she was captured and had noticed a lot of unique and very illegal codes. There had to be something to help her unlock the cell door.

They knew where Riley was being held. She had mapped out the security and the fastest way to get there. And she had a digital wallet filled with enough untraceable currency to make any Earthen guard abandon their post.

Matty looked at herself and couldn't think of anything else she had forgotten. She walked out the door and ran right into the High Priestex. Matty stood there, unsure of what she would do if she were told to go back into the room.

"You realize that even though technically Riley is under Martian protection, we cannot sanction this mission. Our planets are on the verge of war, which has to be my main concern."

"I understand," Matty said.

"If you are successful, then we can file a formal complaint. We will be able to put her in protective custody. We can make enough noise so that this will not happen again."

"If I am not successful?"

"Then the Martian consulate will disavow your actions. Earth will keep you as a traitor, and you will most likely be executed."

"I understand," Matty said.

The High Priestex took a second to look Matty over and then spoke. "I ask that you think about why you are doing this. If it is for the good of your planet, then I couldn't agree more. Riley is a valuable asset, more useful than Earth could understand. Her knowledge will allow us to break through Earth security that we have not been able to touch and make our own technologies more secure. Rescuing her will also show Earth that we will defend our own to the last. Unlike them, we consider each individual life important.

"If you are doing this as a friend, I also understand. I would ask you to make sure to stay focused. If you are doing this because you picture a happy ever ending where the two of you live side by side, then you should rethink what you are about to do. I have met thousands of Earthen refugees, and I have seen women who had to endure a fraction of what Riley has been through who were never able to function healthily. She is strong, but she is not unscathed. She may never recover from what they have done to her; most likely, she will not. It will always be a part of her."

"I know," Matty said. "It took me a while, but I realized. That doesn't stop me from loving her or make me any less her friend."

The High Priestex nodded their head and then clasped Matty's shoulder. "Good luck."

Matty left, heading to the territory doorway closest to Riley's cell to cross.

Once over, she still had a few floors to traverse. It helped that the earth was on its night cycle, and most people were either in their rooms or one of the entertainment centers. Earth wasted a lot of time on places to socialize, whereas Martians just combined housing and socialization. It seemed more effective to Matty. But she had to focus. Thankfully, the few humans she passed seemed nonchalant and didn't pay her much attention.

Matty was almost at the cell when she heard a faint echo. It didn't sound good. Matty ran the rest of the way, afraid she would be too late. Except when she reached the cell, the door was wide open, and no one was around.

Where would they have taken her?

Matty stopped and tried to focus on where the sound had come from. Then she started heading in that direction. She walked down the empty corridors, uncertain of where she was. The sound never came again, and Matty was unsure if she was walking in the correct direction or not.

Then a peace officer passed her walking briskly in the opposite direction. Matty pulled out Riley's pad, pulled up the official news bulletin for Earth, and didn't see anything. Then she pulled up Riley's encrypted version and saw that there had been a call about a body found. Her heart sank. She was too late. Either way, she had to see for herself. She pulled up the location and turned around.

She was not far off, and less than five minutes later, Matty walked into the crime scene. There were a handful of peace officers standing around. Two of them spotted her and motioned for her to stop.

"I'm the Martian representative, Matty. We understand that there may have been a situation involving one of our people."

"I don't know about that," the officer grumbled, then he ran an optical scan to confirm her identity, giving a questionable look to her Earthen attire. "The judge is over there somewhere. You can go clear this up with him."

"Thanks," but Matty was already moving forward, headed towards the body. It was storming with medical personnel, and she couldn't see much of anything. But it didn't look right. It didn't seem to be Riley. She pressed closer, wanting to be sure.

"Can I help you?" the judge asked. He was dressed in shirt and sweatpants that didn't quite cover his frame. Thin strands of hair fell down his face. He looked like he had come straight from bed.

Matty stopped, frustrated that she could not get a better view of the body. She had had to deal with this man in the past and found him to be incorrigible. They called him a judge, but he didn't care about justice. He just wanted to keep the world working to his viewpoint and collect as much money along the way as he could.

"I'm the Martian representative, Matty. I have come because I believe this situation involves a person under Martian care."

"Oh, no. You don't need to worry your pretty little head about this. This man was most definitely Earthen. I think we have enough problems between our planets without you to start sticking your nose into a situation that happened so far away from Martian soil." He looked at her in a way that told her he knew exactly why she was here, and he wasn't going to give her any more information.

Matty gave him her best smile and walked right next to him. "My pretty little head is just fine. Thanks for your concern. As you said, relations between our worlds have been strained pretty hard because you mishandled a certain situation. Now, you can tell me what I want to know, and I can go on my way. Or, you can continue to patronize me, and I can go back and report to my High Priestex, who will have no choice but to let everyone on Earth know exactly how this ship is being run."

The man scowled at her and then walked towards the body. "I assure you that this is nothing of your concern. This Earthen citizen was shot by an Earthen weapon on Earthen territory."

"Who shot him?" Matty inched in, trying to get a better look. Despite his use of male pronouns, she was still relieved that it was not Riley. She had never seen this man before, and he was undoubtedly of Earthen descent. She raised Riley's pad and snapped a quick photo of the body.

"We don't know." He inched up on her trying to be intimidating, but he was so short that Matty had an excellent view of the balding spot on the top of his head. Besides it was hard to take a man in pajamas seriously.

"You may not know, but you have an idea. Who do you think shot him?" Matty asked.

"It would be irresponsible of me to throw out theories until all the evidence has been collected."

Matty rolled her eyes and waited.

"It does not concern you."

"On my way over here, I happened to notice that there was an empty cell. Not only was it empty, someone had carelessly left the door open. I know this cell once held a woman who had been granted Martian sanctuary. She had been kidnapped by Earthen thugs and then kidnapped again by Earthen peace officers after the united corp board had already given her back. Then I find a dead man in the hall with no sign of the woman. I can't help but think that there is a connection. Where is she?"

"We have no reason to think the two incidents are connected."

Matty moved even closer and leaned down until she was talking right into his face. "Wars have been fought for less than this. Earth can sit and kid itself that Mars is this backward planet that can't defend itself, but you have been the presiding Earthen judge on this tin can for more than three trips. You know we let you control the travel between Earth and Mars to help boost your pride. More than anyone, you know what we are truly capable of."

The color fled from the already pale judge. Mars rarely talked about the truth. They were a friendly group and did not mind giving Earth a sense of security, but they were also a young planet still in its prime. But the point seemed to hit home to the judge.

"The man is a criminal. He was sentenced to work on Mars for his crimes," the judge finally gave in, his how demeanor relaxing as he started to talk.

"What was he convicted of?"

"Murder for hire."

"Earth executes murderers. Why was he exiled instead, and why wasn't the Martian government notified? I would have remembered if a murder was listed among the prisoners you sent to my planet."

"I am not speaking officially," the judge looked around and moved them away from the body. "He worked for families high up. They protected him. I only recognized him because of the work I had done before. You were not told he was here, but he wouldn't have been free to walk around the ship."

Matty looked at the judge, trying to determine if she believed him. "You think he was hired to take out Riley?"

"The husband wasn't happy with my decision to delay her execution. He may have gotten desperate."

"And why did you delay her execution?"

The judge looked at Matty. They were both from different worlds, but they each understood the position of the other. Finally, he decided to speak. "Do you know why I work on this ship?"

Matty had looked at his record before boarding. It was standard to know about who they would be working with. The judge had been punished to five tours between planets because he insisted that a woman was responsible for committing the takedown of a bank. "Oh," Matty said, making the connection. "You think she did it?"

"Not anymore. Now I know she did it. I just don't have the evidence."

Matty had to keep her hand from reaching into her pocket and touching Riley's pad. She was sure it contained everything the judge could ever want to close his case. "What do you plan to do about it?"

The man ran his hand across his thinning hair. "It doesn't matter, anyway. She is gone, and no one would believe me, even with evidence. Could you imagine if women thought they were better than men?"

Matty tried to decide if he was being ironic or if he had forgotten her gender. So, she ignored the comment and focused on what was important. "What do you think happened here?"

"We honestly don't know. One of the bridge crew stumbled across the body on his way to his quarters. The gun was lying right on top of him, but it wasn't what killed him. After he was shot, he was injected with a deadly poison, the same one we use to execute in transit. They were both wiped clean, but they had her DNA still on them."

"She shot him and then poisoned him?"

"I suppose, but it seems unlikely. How would she be able to overpower an assassin and then use his gun on him? We think maybe someone else came and took her. We thought maybe you people got involved." He leaned in closer even though they were already away from everyone. "Maybe someone on this ship with more clearance than you knows something?"

"There is no one on this ship with more clearance than me." She looked him in the eye, forcing him to acknowledge her.

"Oh well, then we are honestly not certain." He took a step back as he spoke.

Matty turned away from the judge and walked back to the body. There was no sign of a stunner or a needle. But the man's shirt was untucked from his pants. She lifted the end and saw that his pants were unsnapped. She looked up at the judge. "I think I know how she got his stunner."

She stood up and turned around. If she had overpowered him, then where was she?

As if understanding what she was looking for, the judge started speaking. "We have searched the entire area and found no trace of her. We think she made it down to Mars."

"I wish she had," Matty muttered. She thought of how Riley had found the small space between the tent and supplies in the community. She had a knack for hiding, no doubt due to her childhood. All Matty had to do now was find her and keep her safe for the last few weeks of the voyage.

CHAPTER 45

RILEY

PRESENT

THE TUNNELS WERE CLEAN. It surprised Riley, as dust would settle over time, even on a ship with good filtration. Yet she did not feel a high airflow through the tunnels. She was pretty sure that these were not used for airflow. Especially since their end led to a solid piece in the hallway. She was uncertain what the tunnels were used for. They had never shown up on any ship schematics, but she had only focused on the areas meant for human habitation. She realized there was probably a lot about this ship that she didn't know.

Riley kept going; she didn't know what other choice she had. Every time there was a corridor, she went straight. When she could not, she turned right and then left. Her body felt lighter, and soon she found she was not crawling as much as floating down the tunnel. She realized she must be heading to the center of the ship. Maybe she was on one of the axles that helped the ship to turn, creating gravity.

The only time that Riley had felt weightless before was on the shuttle ride up to the ship. Now, as gravity continued to decrease, she wasn't sure how to move. There were no handles, and even though the tunnels were small, she couldn't figure out how to hold on to both sides to move.

Riley thought about the irony of how she had managed to escape, only to end up dying alone in a tunnel. Her body would spend eons just sitting here frozen with no critters to decompose it. At least she would die free. She was so tired and hungry. The effects of dehydration were starting to set in. She just needed to stop and close her eyes. After a short nap she could figure out what to do.

It felt like she had barely closed her eyes when she was awoken. She opened her eyes to see a person's face before her own. They were poking her with their finger. The person had short black hair and olive skin. Their brown eyes looked at her with curiosity. They looked Earthen, or maybe Martian; she couldn't tell. Instead, she did the most logical thing and screamed.

The face moved back slightly and waited for her to stop. They didn't seem concerned. Riley realized that this far in the ship, no one would even be able to hear her. She stopped screaming and watched the person. She realized that if they wanted to hurt her, they could have done so already.

The person started talking, but Riley didn't understand

anything. They looked at her, waved their hands, and then managed to say something she comprehended. "Come, Come." Then the person started crawling down the tube in the direction she had been heading. They were fast, and Riley realized they were used to living in these tubes. They were probably the reason that they were all so clean.

The person stopped and turned their head to look at her. Then they turned around and started moving again. Riley realized that her only options were to follow or to stay where she was and die. She had no idea what she would find if she followed, but she had spent too much of her life fighting to give up now. So she followed as best she could.

The person stopped and watched her as she bounced from wall to wall, pushing herself forward like she was still crawling. His sudden laughter surprised her. She became defensive and frustrated, but after that impulse passed, she realized her clunky attempts to move were probably hilarious.

She gave a small smile and tried to catch up to them. They laughed even harder.

They stayed by her then, attempting to show her the correct way to build and remove momentum so they could fly through the tubes. When Riley over-corrected, they showed them again. It wasn't long before Riley was able to move in zero gravity. It may not have matched their grace or speed, but at least she could move.

Suddenly, the person stopped. They held out their hands and caught Riley. They had just come to a junction. It was larger than anything Riley had seen in the tunnels, wide enough for them to stand side by side and still have room for at least two other people. It moved up and down, and the walls were smooth as far as Reilly could see. There were no ladder rungs to help her, but then she realized that this part of the ship had never been on the ground. It had been built in space, and there was no up and down in space.

They held out their hand, and Riley stared at it, unsure how to proceed. They said the same words again, "Come, come," and took one of their arms and wrapped it around her waist.

Before she could even be shocked, let alone fight back, they had propelled her into the new corridor. They were moving up or down, like one of the trams back on Earth. Riley saw that there were corridors leading off as they moved. Each was marked with a symbol, but they were going too fast for Riley to read.

Riley moved her hands to the person's arm, afraid of being lost in this tunnel. She wanted to close her eyes and not see what was happening around her, but she was not one to back down from a challenge. She saw the person grab onto the edge of one of the openings to stop their momentum. They gave her a huge grin as they helped move Riley into another tunnel. Then they followed after.

"Come, come," they said, pointing to the tunnel ahead of Riley. She moved and continued in the tunnel, afraid they were behind her, laughing at her efforts. The tunnel opened up into a room full of people and equipment. And with awe, Riley realized she had made it to the engine room. Unable to stop, she flew through the end of the tunnel and straight into one of the electric tubes running through the room. She waved her arms to no effect, but right before she was about to hit a large tube, a hand reached around her ankle and caused her to stop. She looked around and saw the person who had led her. They started laughing again.

CHAPTER 46

MATTY

PRESENT

MATTY HADN'T SLEPT, not since Riley had gone missing. Instead, she had stayed in the communication room, drinking down stimulants and typing into computers. Riley had vanished. Tick had hacked into the Earthen communication channels and was actively monitoring them. They had nothing.

Although they did get to overhear a call from the judge to Riley's now ex-husband. He was an ugly man, uglier than even Matty could have pictured. His black hair was balding, and his face seemed to scrunch up. Matty wanted to reach through the screen and thrash him.

"What happened?" her ex-husband said. Even with improved communication, there was still a delay between messages—each coming minutes after the other.

"We think she may have killed the assassin you sent after her."

When his reply came, her ex-husband did not even bother to deny his part in the situation. "How would that be possible? She is a pathetic weakling. I kept her in line for nearly twenty years, and you can't manage it for six months. I need this situation resolved." After each message, the screen would freeze the respondent's frame until the new message was received. It was supposed to make for a more natural flow in conversation.

"I'm handling it. We are just trying to locate her. But I don't think you had her under control as much as you think."

"What are you trying to suggest?"

"We have evidence to suggest that she may have been involved in some illegal financial activities."

"Don't bring your conspiracy theories to me." The ex-husband's face grew red in frustration. "I promised to help bring you home if you took care of this. Instead, you lost her on a spaceship. Maybe you have become too passive on that ship of yours. Have you had too much contact with the Martian's 'love one another' bullshit?"

"I have served admirably on this ship for three tours, more than six years. It is time for someone else to come. You promised to bring me h—-." The transmission cut off before the judge finished, leaving his face frozen mid-scream.

"You will come home when the corporation tells you to, not

before. The way you are mishandling this situation is not going to get you a ticket back to Earth. I cannot have it known that she is still alive. Even if my marriage was canceled, its timing would still be hurtful. My current marriage could be called into question, and I could lose my wife's inheritance while my mangy in-laws would get to keep the name. It is unacceptable."

"Do you need proof of her demise?"

"What does that mean?"

Matty began pacing behind Tick, her hands thrumming on her legs with impatience. It reminded her of the way Riley moved when she was overwhelmed, and the thought made her stop. An intense longing for the woman enveloped her. She couldn't ever remember missing anyone so much. *This conversation better be worth it*, she thought.

"We think she crawled into one of the ship's tunnels," the judge said. "There is one near the scene, and, being very thorough, we found traces of her DNA inside."

"Then get someone in there and follow her. Check all the exits and see where she went."

"The tunnels do not lead many places." The judge's voice became pleading. "There is only a handful that connect to the Earthen levels. We have checked them all, and there is no sign that she ever reached them. It is possible that she made it to the few Martian openings. However, I have been assured that it would have been extremely difficult. She was starved before she even went in there. She was in no state to survive in the tunnels. Most likely, her body will never be recovered."

The ex-husband slammed his fists onto his desk. "I have been told she was dead many times over now, and each time, she resurfaces. I need this over."

"How can we do that? You must be aware that the tunnels no longer belong to us."

"That is your job to figure out. Just make sure it is done, or I will use everything in my power to ensure you never leave that ship."

The ex-husband hung up suddenly, leaving a blank screen.

"She went into the tunnels," Matty muttered. She tapped Tick on their arm. "Pull up everything we know about the tunnels."

It only took Tick a second before the information was streaming across the screen faster than Matty could read it. But she didn't need to read it; she just needed to remember. Something was nagging at the back of her mind.

"There, stop," Matty tapped on Tick's shoulder excitedly. "How could I have forgotten? There are people who live there, who maintain the ship. That is who we need to help us." Matty looked around the room, hoping that the High Priestex was out of their latest meeting. When she didn't see them, she settled for sending a high-priority ping on their pad. "While we are waiting, can you pull up everything we have on the people who live inside the ship?"

"They are called Spacers," Tick said. "I wrote my graduation paper on them. They are technical geniuses but are nearly hermits now. There has been limited contact for the last generation."

"Hopefully, we can change that. They are Riley's only hope. What else can you tell me about them?"

"They have been in space for generations and have adapted so they can no longer handle gravity. They place a high value on family since they are very tribal. However, when two ships are in orbit of a planet, there is almost always a shuttle request to transfer people between ships. We assume this is to ensure that the genetic line does not become too restrained."

As they talked, the High Priestex walked into the room and approached the duo. "What have you found out?"

"We overheard a communication. She is in the tunnels," Matty said. Her voice was high with excitement. "We hoped to reach out to the Spacers to help us."

"I greeted their leader at the start of the voyage. We have not communicated since. However, I will reach out. They are good people, and I think they will be willing to help."

"Do you think they can find her? They said she hadn't eaten in days." Matty's voice cracked as she spoke.

The High Priestex wrapped Matty into a hug, allowing Matty a few seconds of relaxation. "Keep the faith," they whispered in her ear. "She is a survivor."

"Right. I'm going to check our entrance to the tunnels. Just in case." Matty released herself from the High Priestex's grip and walked out of the room more hopeful than she had been in hours.

CHAPTER 47

RILEY

PRESENT

RILEY FLOATED, watching all the people move around her. They were going about their everyday life, some working and others passing through. Seeing them navigate zero gravity was beautiful.

The human helped her move to a hole on the other side of the room. They moved together from room to room, Riley holding onto the person, allowing them to navigate for them both. The rooms were a community with eating and socializing in the same room as engine repair. Nestled into an outcropping, a group of children stared at an adult. Most were floating still. A few had attached themselves to the wall with Velcro. One child was spinning in perpetual circles. The adult continued speaking through it all.

For the most part, her presence garnered very little attention. The workers would glance at her and then go back to their business. It was different with the children. Once one saw her, they pointed to the others, and soon a swarm of little ones covered her. She marveled at how they navigated zero gravity. Some of the children were young, maybe five or six. It was hard to tell since they were all so tall, taller even than Martians. Soon, the teacher and her escort had them away and back in their spot.

"Come, come," her guide said, and Riley followed them through another opening. A few doors down, they reached a room that seemed to be filled with books, actual books made with paper. There were built-in walls with shelves just the right size for the books. The shelves were covered in clear plexiglass, ensuring they stayed where they belonged. Most of the books were old. Riley had only seen a few printed books in her lifetime, and she came from a wealthy family. It wasn't done anymore. Trees were too precious a resource to waste on paper.

Her guide moved to the center of the room and waited for her to follow. She glided from bookshelf to bookshelf, unable to take her eyes away from the thousands of books. They moved toward the end of the room in an area that had been sectioned off.

She heard her guide speaking again, but she was too far away to see anyone. As she approached, another moved out of the hidden section to look at her. The figure looked so similar to her guide that she would not have been able to tell them apart. Then again, all those she passed had looked so alike.

All with their long slender bodies and white jumpsuits. Their hair was shaved off, and nearly all their skin had a deep olive complexion. There was nothing to distinguish one from the other except for the children, who were smaller.

The new person looked at her, then they both talked and kept pointing. Their voices grew agitated, and Riley feared she had gotten her guide in trouble. Then the new person addressed her.

He spoke in what Riley recognized as Martian from hearing the children's language lessons. Then he switched to Earth standard. "What language do you speak?"

"I come from the Molbin corporation," she said. "I speak Earth standard and some old English."

"How did you come to our part of the ship?" he continued speaking in Earthen standard. "Jint said he found you in the mid tunnels, far from the Earthen levels."

Riley looked at the man who had guided her and tried to see the signs of masculinity she was familiar with. His frame was so slim and untoned. Riley thought back to what Matty had been trying to teach her about gender and how to expand her expectations beyond what she knew on Earth.

"Will you thank him for me?" she asked. "He saved my life. I would have died in the tunnels."

The new person translated for her, and Jint flashed a big smile and reached and embraced her. Then he patted her head. He spoke more to the new man and started heading towards the door. Riley looked at him, uncertain if she should follow.

"He needs to go back and attend to his duties. You need to stay and answer my questions."

Riley turned her focus back to her new host. She looked at their shaved head and delicate features and could not tell what their gender was. Then she scolded herself. If she didn't know her own gender, why should she care about others? "I needed to hide," she finally said. "I saw one of the tunnel vents slightly open and climbed in. Then I got lost trying to find somewhere to get out.

"Where were you trying to go?"

"Someplace without people and with food." She wasn't sure how much to tell them. They may just haul her right back to the Earthen authorities.

She saw the person look her over. Their expression was unreadable to her. It looked like her presence either annoyed them or intrigued them. She hoped for the latter.

"Who are you?" Riley asked. After the words were out of her mouth, she realized it may not have been polite, but she was curious.

"I apologize. I should have introduced myself. The elders would be ashamed. I am Batle, and I use your masculine language. I am the Scholar." He spoke this as if it was a title that should mean something to her. "I maintain the knowledge of the Earthen world."

"Are you from Earth?" She knew she couldn't be correct, but the words had already left her mouth.

"Originally, we came from there. Our people were once part of the Reaper Corporation. We were hired to maintain the ship. But the extended stay in zero gravity made it impossible to return to a planet. Now, this ship is our home. We are our own people, independent of corporations. We keep the ship running in exchange for supplies and anonymity."

"You have lived here since the beginning of the ship?"

"I have lived here my whole life, just like my parents did. We have been maintaining this ship for over a hundred years. We are the oldest spacer clan. Each ship has its own clan that maintains it. Sometimes when a new ship is built, some of ours teach the new clans how to survive in zero-G properly. It saves them some of the death that our earlier generation experienced. But there has not been a new ship for over thirty years."

"You've lived for generations on this ship?" Riley's eyes roamed over the room, trying to imagine what it would be like to live her entire life in a confined space.

"It isn't so different than plans to send humans out in ships to reach other stars, except we only travel between two planets."

"Do people really want to do that? Riley looked around her at the rows and rows of paper books. "But why this? Why do you have a library in the heart of the ship?"

"Where better to keep old volumes safe than in space?

They do not wear as much, and we can preserve their knowledge for future generations. Now, why were you running away? No, wait. You can tell me over a meal. It looks like you have not eaten all day."

"Several days, actually," Riley said.

Riley followed Batle out of the library and through a few more tunnels. He was not as gracious as Jint, and Riley found herself failing to navigate the turns of a room. She ran into people constantly. They would right themselves and then correct her, helping her on her way. No one was ever angry with her. Usually, they patted her on the head and left with a laugh on their lips.

Word must have spread ahead. Every time she entered a room, someone was there waiting to help correct her. They all talked to her. The words were unknown, but their smiles and laughs let her know they seemed to enjoy the change from their routine. Each one patted her head as she left them to continue on the path.

The people seemed to work in perfect cohesion. Riley couldn't help but wonder at the culture they built being so close to each other, isolated in the middle of the ship.

At last, they arrived at what looked like a storage room. Modules covered the walls. It took a minute before Riley realized that this was a cafeteria and that each module contained food. Two people took items from the modules and placed them in a mesh bag. Then there was another person who had a container of prepared bags.

Batle glided up to this person, and after an intense conversation where the server seemed very interested in Riley, he came away with two of the bags. Batle reached up and handed her a bag, but she managed to turn the exchange into momentum that propelled her towards one of the walls. She bounced off of the containers, which seemed to be made with Velcro cloth.

She tried to reach out and stop herself, but she could not and bounced away, spinning around uncontrollably. One of the diners was able to catch her and guide her over to some loops in one of the walls. As she held onto a loop, the diner left and went over to Batle, yelling at him.

Riley looked at the other diners and noticed how they used the strap to allow them free range to eat. Batle arrived next to her, a look of shame on his face.

"I am sorry," he said.

"What was he upset about?" Riley asked.

"She was upset that I did not take care of you. She said I should have known that you have been adopted as one of our children and should have been treated accordingly."

"A child?"

"It is nothing to be ashamed of. It is a compliment that they have taken you into the clan. Jint must have been talking well about you. Children are our biggest joy, and they are spoiled in our culture. When they touch you on the head, they are showing their joy that you are their child."

"I'm not sure how I feel about that."

"I assure you, it is an honor. For now, you should eat."

At the mention of food, Riley's stomach cramped in pain. She looked at the bag that Batle had handed her. It was a mesh container full of packaged food. Riley found the pouch of water, extended the straw, and drank deeply.

"You must slow down if you have not eaten in days."

Riley finished the pouch of water, ensuring she had drunk every last drop. She enjoyed the feel of it in her stomach, even as it caused it to cramp. Batle reached into his bag and pulled out his water. He handed it over to her.

"Take it. There is plenty. Only drink this one slower. It is not so great to expel your stomach when there is no gravity."

Riley accepted the water and, picturing the potential mess she could make, aimed to eat slower. She pulled out one of the packets out of the bag. It was a package of dried bananas. She reached into the bag, pulled out one packet, and replaced it with another. It was all dried food, the cheapest that could be found on earth. Yet, no one in the cafeteria seemed to mind. They had probably never tasted anything else.

Finally, Riley opened the bananas and placed one in her mouth. The flavor filled her, the sweetness bringing her alive. At that moment, she could not imagine any food tasting better. She reached in for another piece, making sure to keep the bananas from floating out of the pouch as well as not overextending her stomach. She realized the packaging was simple, just white pouches with the item written in each corporation's language.

"They can read this?" Riley asked.

"Not the same way that you do. As our verbal language has adapted over time, our writing has not. Instead, we teach our children to read important corporate words as symbols rather than phonetically. I believe there was an ancient Earthen culture that did something similar."

"I wouldn't know. History is not something studied on our planet, at least within my corporation."

"That's a pity. You cannot truly know yourself unless you know your history."

Riley reached into her bag and grabbed another package. This time it was dehydrated peas.

"My people have decided not to worry about gravity walkers," Battle said. "We talk when we must, but otherwise, we are content to live on our own. I have read the books and know the stories. There is so much fighting and anger in gravity walkers."

"There can be, especially with corporation members. But don't any of your people ever want to be something other than an engineer?"

"There are other positions in the clan. Most are engineers, but there are teachers, food workers, and those who clean. I am a scholar. Some do wish to leave, and they go to other ships. Even if we wished we could not survive on a planet, so why concern ourselves with them?"

Riley carefully selected another pea from the bag and placed it in her mouth. She used the time to think about her next words.

"Earthen people are not taught their history. I think hiding that from us causes us to make so many mistakes. I understand why you may not want to interact with Earthens. They have lost their way. But Martians are trying. They have families like yours, and they tell stories so that their people remember. There are differences, but they try to be good." She looked around at the people in the cafeteria. They were laughing and so in synch. It was beyond anything she had ever imagined. "I could see why you would not want to jeopardize this, though."

"Who are your people?"

Riley realized her peas were gone and reached into her bag for another item. She was stalling again, but she was also hungry. The last item was labeled protein drink. She twisted off the top and started drinking in the sludge. The mixture was gritty and reminded her of dirt.

"I was born on Earth, but there were complications. So, I decided to relocate to Mars. While on the ship, I was granted Martian citizenship. Some people on Earth didn't like that. I was running away from them when I got lost." All that Riley had left was her extra water. She drank it down and then looked down at the empty bag.

"You will not starve here. Give your stomach some time, and I will get you more food." Batle said. "If Mars has accepted you, then that is where you need to go. We can help make sure that you make it back there safely."

"I've already been there twice." Riley sighed. "Twice, I have been taken away. Do you think maybe I could stay here? No one would think to look for me here."

"You are the first planet dweller on this side of the ship in over ten years. However, if you truly wish to stay among us, it could most likely be arranged. You would be cutting ties with planet life. You would never be able to go into gravity again. We couldn't risk the corporation finding out that we housed you."

"I don't want to put anyone at risk. When I was in the Martian levels, they came and pointed guns at the children. Those kids had been through so much to make it to the ship. They finally felt safe, and I put them in danger again. I can't do that. Not to them or you."

"Come, we will talk to the elders and figure out the best thing to do."

CHAPTER 48

MATTY

PRESENT

I WAS *able to get ahold of the spacers. They refused to do a tunnel search but asked to speak to you.* Matty read the message on her pad, her heart suddenly beating uncontrollably.

Matty closed the tunnel casing and rushed to meet the High Priestex in the command room. When she got there, she saw the language specialist seated with the High Priestex. The language specialist was talking to someone on the screen in a language unlike any Matty was familiar with. When they saw her, the language specialist vacated their seat, standing to the side. Without a second thought, Matty sat down. She saw an older adult with dark skin and a shaved head on the screen.

"Greetings," Matty said. Someone off-screen translated

her words. When they responded, the language specialist translated their return greeting.

"Thank you for talking with me," Matty said. "There is a missing woman. She is one of our people, but the Earthen government is trying to claim her as theirs. They want to cause her harm. We think she escaped in the maintenance tunnels. We want to ask you to help us search for her. I am sure we can work out some compensation in return if you desire."

"The sentiment is appreciated, Matty of Mars. However, we will not be searching the tunnels. It is not necessary."

"You already found her," Matty interrupted the interpretation. "The High Priestex said that you asked to speak to me. This means you have Riley, and she told you about me."

"I appreciate your understanding of why we did not tell you immediately. Our clan has adopted this person. We must keep her safe."

Matty's smile grew as the words were translated. "She tends to have that effect on people. I am relieved that she is safe, and I appreciate that you hold her life in as much esteem as I do. What can I do to help you to ensure her safety?"

"That is an excellent question. If we work together, we can find an answer."

CHAPTER 49

RILEY

PRESENT

"I need to go back." Riley thought about Matty's voice, the way it always seems to bring her peace. "I want to go back. I am happy here, but..." she faltered, uncertain how to continue.

"Your heart calls you to another. Matty is your mate, and it is proper that you should join her."

It had been three days since Riley had arrived, and in that time, the Spacers had welcomed her in as one of their own. But she knew this is not where she belonged.

"She's not my mate. I don't think I could be married again." Riley tried to think of the words that captured all of her feelings. "We are friends, more than friends. I'm just not sure that I am capable of anything more."

They were in the library. Riley held one of the paper

books carefully in her hands. Batle had moved out of his office space and was now facing her. "You have seen a lot of pain. You have very little reason to trust. But you can learn." Then he reached out and handed her a pad.

"What is this?" she asked.

"You constantly complain about how much you miss your pad, so I gave you one of ours. I think you will find that our upgrades are better than what you will find elsewhere. I have also included the digital files of all these books, plus hundreds more. You can learn about your history so you can help the future."

"I'm trying to help the future. Do you think I am doing the right thing?"

"We have been cut off for too long for me to tell you yes or no. If you need another opinion, I think you should ask your girl." He smiled as he spoke the words.

"When do we leave?" Riley asked. She closed the book, placed it back for the last time, and gave a longing look around the library.

"We are just waiting for Jint."

As if summoned, Jint floated into the library. He approached Riley and wrapped her in his arms. When he spoke, Batle translated. "The elders have declared you kin. You have the shortest childhood on record. They told me to wish you well and that, as kin, you should come back."

The trio made their way through the tunnels, Riley moving with a skill she had lacked days before. As the gravity increased, Jint had to help Batle, allowing him to hold on as they moved. By the time they reached Martian gravity, they were both helping Batle.

Riley felt the press of gravity in a way she had not noticed before. Martian gravity no longer felt light and carefree. Instead, it pressed on her. She glanced longingly back at the tunnels and visualized a life back in zero-G. Then she moved forward, Batle's hand pressing on her shoulder as they advanced.

The tunnel ended in a hidden room. The spacers had gradually removed their presence from the digital blueprint of the ship. With minor modifications, they had claimed space as their own, unknown from the Earthens or Martians. This room was a training ground. Young children were brought here starting in childhood to withstand the pressure of gravity in short sprints. Jint had been one of those children. It allowed him to move through the tunnels that separated the rest of his people.

Jint slipped out of the tunnel first, bringing a sort of chair for Batle to sit in. It had a mini propulsion system, similar to transports, that allowed it to move around Martian space. Even in the chair, Riley could see the strain that gravity was putting on Batle. Riley found herself overwhelmed that he was risking himself to be here with her.

"Thank you," Riley said. "I don't know what I would have done without either of you."

"You are family," Jint said, his words highly accented but

understandable. Riley responded the only way she knew, by reaching out and hugging him. A grin grew on his face, and he gave one of his laughs.

"I am going to miss you, all of you."

"You will not be forgotten," Batle said. "We will keep in communication. The children expect you to send them videos of the Martian surface. I think they like the idea that you have not seen it either. When we return, we will request a pass so that you can come and visit."

"Will the transports still run after I am finished?"

"Don't worry. The world will right itself, and we will be alright either way. The Earthens only think they control the ship."

They waited. Riley ended up sitting down tired after days of zero-G. She also was nervous. What if Matty didn't come? What if they had problems locating the room? The thoughts wouldn't stop spiraling through her head even while she tried to remind herself that there was no reason for concern. When the doors opened, she jumped and had to stop herself from hiding. But even then, she watched to see who would walk through the doors.

The High Priestex walked in with Matty and Mama Hapots. There were a few other faces that Riley felt should be familiar to her if she bothered to look away from Matty. Riley smiled tentatively at Matty, who instantly returned it with a relieved grin. Riley rushed over and, without thinking, gathered Matty into a hug. With Matty's arms wrapped around her, she finally felt safe.

"I'm so glad you weren't harmed," Mama Hapots said. "I was so worried when you left with them. I thought we would never see you again."

Riley reluctantly let go of Matty. "It was the only way. I didn't want any of the children to get hurt. How is everyone? How is my son?"

"They are well. He misses you. I hope when this is over, you will consider living with us on Mars. I know you can't come back now; it isn't safe yet. But on the planet, it should be. You are one of our family."

"Thank you, Mama Hapots. I would love that." Riley reached out and pulled her into a hug. "I would like you to meet more of my family. This is Jint, and this is Batle."

"We've met," Matty said.

The High Priestix walked over to Batle and put a light hand on his shoulder. "I want to thank you for taking in one of our own. If there is a way we can repay you, please let us know."

"Riley has a way of collecting family. We consider her ours now as well. However, she has helped us see that it may be beneficial to better communicate with planet dwellers. She speaks highly of you and those you lead. Our elders have asked me to extend an invitation for further talks."

"We would be honored."

Jint started speaking to Batle with a hit of concern in his voice. "He says it is time for me to go back. He would appreciate it if you would leave. We aren't ready to give up all of our secrets yet."

"Can I help?" Riley asked, concerned about how Jint would manage to bring Batle back alone.

"We will be fine," Batle said. "Go and follow the plan."

The Martian delegation started to file back out of the door, and Riley reluctantly left with them. The training room was in the Reaper corporate member area, Earthen space more by default than actuality. Outside the doors, Riley saw they had brought a handful of armed Martians as escorts.

The group moved slowly through the corridors. Runners were sent ahead to ensure the walkways were clear before moving forward. The walk was tense, but they made it back to Martian territory without any difficulty.

"I need to go back to the family," Mama Hapots said. When she hesitated, Riley gave her a hug.

"Thank you," Riley said. "Please tell the family that I miss them."

Most of the delegation left to follow Mama Hapots, leaving just a small group to walk together.

"Are you ready?" Matty asked.

"I'm ready."

The two walked to one of the built-in quarantine suites where they would be placed on lockdown for the next two weeks. There was no override to the system, meaning there was no way for Earthens to get inside. In two weeks, there may be an entire Earth army outside the door, but they would have to wait until the cycle disengaged.

It would be Riley and Matty alone for the next two weeks.

CHAPTER 50

MATTY

PRESENT

THEY WERE LOCKED in a family quarantine room with two small beds instead of one. It was slightly larger than their single quarantine rooms, but as Matty stood next to Riley, their arms nearly touching, the room felt even smaller.

As soon as the door finished sealing, Riley glanced at the walls and sat down on the floor, her head lodged between her knees. When Riley had hugged her, Matty thought things would be easier, or at least better. But as she watched Riley, already overwhelmed, she didn't know how to help.

Matty walked to the kitchen, trying to give her some space. She opened the cabinets, stocked before the ship had been boarded, and sorted through the food. She picked out two packets and put them in the rehydrator.

Riley hadn't moved from the floor. The only change was

her hands wrapped around the back of her head, her arms covering her ears.

The table was folded down into the floor. Matty reached down and lifted it, barely clearing Riley's feet. Matty realized that Riley no longer wore her earth-made shoes. She now had a thin covering gripped all along the bottom. She must have changed during her three days with the spacers.

With the table down and the stools extended, there was just enough room to walk between the table and the beds. It was going to be a long two weeks.

When the food was done, Matty took the meals and put them on the table. She ate hers as slowly as possible and then put the packaging in the recycling unit. She pushed up her stool and opened the drawers below the bed. Yesterday she had prepared the room, stocking it with everything that she thought they would need. She pulled out her pad and lay on the bed to finish some work.

When Riley stood up, Matty stayed focused on her work. She watched the women pull out a pad, one Matty had not seen before, and then lay down on her bed. They worked together in silence for the rest of the evening.

"Do you want to play a game?" Matty asked. They had woken up an hour ago. Breakfast had been eaten and cleared away, the table still raised.

Riley just stared. Matty loved how the women's eyes

spoke whole conversations, even if the words did not come out. Matty moved forward and touched the table on the side with her three middle fingers pulling up the directory. There was a game that she had learned on Earth that she thought Riley might enjoy.

"Have you ever heard of poker?" When Riley didn't respond, Matty continued. She pulled up the program and filled the table with holographic cards and chips. Matty tapped the deck, telling it to shuffle, then tapped it again to start dealing the cards. Riley put down her pad, and the two began to play. As they played, Riley's shoulders relaxed. She started talking and even smiled a few times. Riley won every hand and soon had taken every one of Matty's chips.

"How could you possibly be so good at that game?" Matty asked.

"When I was a child, I found an underground club. They taught me how to play."

"They let a child into a club?" Matty reached out and tapped on the button to lower the table.

"Anyone that could find the code could join. I just happened to be the youngest. It was my happy place. The older I got, the less I could get away with going." Riley sat on her bed, her back against the wall and her knees pulled up to her chest. But her pad stayed down.

"Did no one ever find out?"

"No one could imagine that I had hacked my way into an illegal club. Girls aren't smart enough for that. Although, there were times when they knew I went somewhere. They thought I was running away, even when I came back. No matter how harsh the punishment, going to the club was always worth it, even if it was temporary."

Matty sat down on the edge of her bed. "What did they do?"

"My father tried everything to get me under control. But I couldn't be who he wanted me to be. The worst punishments were when he tried to reward me. It was always with a new dress or a party, which I hate. He wasn't a great father but was nothing like my husband."

Matty watched Riley seem to shrink into herself. She moved before thinking and sat on the other woman's bed, her arm wrapped around her. Riley relaxed into her and put her head on her shoulder.

"He locked me in a room. They had done it plenty of times before, but this time was different." Riley's voice was so quiet that Matty had to focus on hearing it. "He left me there for a month. He was supposed to wait to try to kill me, at least until our son had reached adulthood. But he didn't seem to care if I died in there. The walls..." Riley shivered and stopped, unable to finish that thought. "I'm sorry, sometimes it still becomes too much."

Matty didn't know how to respond, so she kept holding onto the woman.

. . .

It didn't take long for them to get into a routine. They woke up, both of them not morning people, and didn't speak to each other until they had cleaned up, dressed, and had breakfast. Then they both moved to their beds and started working for the day. Matty tapped away at her pad, happy when she got to talk to someone instead of just answering messages, even if the conversations were elusive. At times she would glance at Riley, who was always intensely focused on her pad. She couldn't help wondering exactly what she was working on.

It was always Matty who ended work first. The High Priestex was hiding whatever was happening outside the room, only giving Matty simple administration tasks. She could have asked Riley to find out what was happening, but the woman was engrossed in her own work. And it was nice, just for a short time to pretend that nothing else mattered. It was just the two of them alone in their own world.

When Matty would declare the workday was over, they would pull up games on the table and play. Riley was especially good at games requiring logic. She beat Matty so badly at chess that they both decided it was not worth playing together anymore. However, Matty excelled at the more active games. She won at table tennis and pool, even though the holographic pool cues were challenging to handle. The system was not top-of-the-line.

After, they would put on some of the Mars entertainment shows. Matty tried to claim that she was further educating Riley about Martian culture, but they both knew she was trying to catch up on all the entertainment she had missed while on Earth. The programming had only started down-loading to the ship's system a few days ago, now that they were getting closer to mars. Matty would move over to Riley's bed, so they were both facing the same way, and the story came to life over the table with people a meter high and scenery going up to the ceiling. At times Riley would relax, and the two would sit side by side. Matty would forget about the show and instead focus on how warm Riley was and the fluttering in her stomach.

After the first week, Matty was already starting to feel the loss. They could not stay in this room, cut off from the rest of the worlds. Soon they would be reaching Mars, and all of this would have to end. Neither talked about after, both of them too afraid of what would happen when the door finally did open.

On their last night together, Matty pulled out one of each of the rehydrated meals until the table was covered in main courses and desserts. The odor of the meals combined to fill the room with a tangy sweet scent. Then Matty turned on some music, a Martian band based on Earth's classical period. The notes flowed through the room.

"If it is too much, I can turn it off," Matty said.

"The music is smooth. I like it." Riley put down her pad and noticed all the meals for the first time.

"We reached the orbit of Mars today," Matty said. "In the communities, there will be a party happening. Everyone will be pulling out whatever they managed to save from the voyage. The kitchen will cook a feast, using everything that won't last for the next voyage. I didn't want us to miss out."

Matty watched Riley look at all the food on the table. Her eyes were wide like she had never seen that much to eat. She was full of contradictions, having grown up rich but simultaneously overwhelmed by basic needs. "Let's start the party." Matty started dancing, moving slowly to the music, swaying in the small space between the table and the beds. On instinct, she grabbed Riley's hands, holding on to them as she moved. The other woman stood stiff, but there was a slight grin on her face, so Matty moved closer, rubbing against Riley.

When Riley's hands let go, Matty stopped, afraid she had pushed too far, but then she felt hands on her face pulling her head down until their lips touched. A fire exploded inside her, all the desire she had tried to keep at bay. She sat down on the bed, pulling the other woman on top of her. Matty's hands slid under Riley's shirt, inching it slowly until her entire stomach was exposed.

Matty pulled back, afraid to get so lost in desire she would let this situation go too far. "Do you want this?" she asked. "I won't do more than what you want."

Riley leaned forward and started kissing her again; their tongues intertwined, the warmth of her body making Matty aware of every sensation. Then Matty's brain caught up with her hormones and pulled back again. "I need you to tell me. I won't do anything unless I'm sure you want it."

Riley leaned back slightly, her hips grinding against Matty's, causing her to let out an involuntary groan. But she moved her hands away from the woman and onto the bed, using them to prop her up, so she was now looking up to Riley. Her auburn hair was growing back, but she had kept it short above her shoulders. Matty bunched her hands into the bed sheet to resist running them through the strands.

"I," Riley sputtered before she lost the ability to speak.

"It's ok," Matty said as she pulled the woman closer to her. "I will still be here."

The food lay forgotten as the women fell asleep in each other's arms.

When the doors opened the following day, the room was clean, and their bags were packed. When Riley had pulled away in the morning, Matty had let her go.

CHAPTER 51

RILEY

PRESENT

RILEY BRACED herself as the quarantine doors opened. She spun around, looking for something to protect herself with, and saw Matty standing calmly. Riley reached out and grabbed her hand, using her to help steady herself. Then she grew concerned at her forwardness and pulled away, but Matty held on tight.

When the doors finally finished opening, only three people were standing outside. There was the High Priestex and two others. Matty stood unconcerned by their presence. Riley looked past them down the corridor and, when she saw it was empty, felt her body relax.

"Your shuttle is scheduled for tomorrow, first thing. We thought it best not to send you today," the High Priestex said.

"Have there been problems?" Matty asked as she stepped

out of the room. Her hand slipped from Riley's, and she felt the loss immediately.

"Nothing we couldn't handle." This came from one of the two Riley did not know. He was tall and bulky, with skin as pale as the High Priestex. "We think everything has been sorted out properly. However, we are taking extra precautions. We stopped taking asylums."

"All of them?" Matty asked. "But this is when people come to us to remain safe."

"We had to make choices," the High Priestex said. "We have records and will follow through on the planet as soon as possible. But, even with the heightened security, the threat was too high. It wasn't just for your safety. Bombs do not do well in outer space."

Riley stood there and listened to them talk. It wasn't that they had forgotten her; it was just that they allowed her to be a part of the conversation without having to join in the conversation. Riley found it relaxing that they didn't make her try so hard all the time and didn't make her feel less for being who she truly was.

"What is the plan until then?" Matty asked. "Where should we go?"

"You will have to go through the departure process," the third person spoke. She was slightly taller than Riley, with dark skin and hair cut close to her scalp. "It should be relatively simple. We have you under false names, just in case, and we found another doctor willing to help us out. We will make sure this one arrives on Mars safely."

As they started walking down the corridor, and Riley stayed where she was. When they did not notice her absence, she slipped out the door and began moving in the opposite direction. She had memorized the route, reviewing it each day inside the room.

There was a vent three floors down. It wasn't difficult to get there, and no one paid her any attention. Everyone was so busy packing to go down to the planet. When she reached the entrance, she stood around looking at her pad, waiting for the people to move away.

When the hallway was empty, she removed a small tool from her pants pocket and slipped it under the door frame. The latch was right where the scholar had told her. The door opened, and Riley climbed in, closing it before anyone appeared. It was hard to turn around in the small space, but she had learned enough from the spacers to manage it.

She took a deep breath and closed her eyes to center herself. She was back in the tunnels, but it was her choice. For once, she wasn't just passively standing around letting people do what they wanted to her. For once, she was fighting back. She had to do this, even if it was the last thing she managed to do. She thought back, briefly, to last night. The feeling of Matty next to her, of finally being able to let herself go without worrying when she would upset someone. It filled her with a sense of peace, and she continued.

The tunnels were no longer a strange mystery. The guide had taught her to read the symbols hidden in the wall, but she knew the way. A short time later, she opened up a new hatch, another one that only appeared on the spacer's records. She stepped out and looked at the computer center for the entire ship. It was one of the most advanced computers ever created. Riley paused, appreciating the rows of towers, with the casing mostly removed to allow for the upgrades the spacers had completed over the years.

It did not take long for her to connect her pad and transfer over her program. However, it took longer for her program to work itself into the central communication system of the ship. Then it had to transmit back to Earth. Seven minutes later, she received notification of its success. Still, she waited. She had programmed it to wait until it had made it into the central system of each corporation. Some were more sophisticated and would take longer. Riley did not want to risk them getting tipped off and being able to disable her program before it had fully integrated. Twenty minutes later, she received a notification that her program was ready.

Riley was still unsure if what she was doing was right, but she knew it was the only decision she could make. She couldn't just walk away without trying.

CHAPTER 52

MATTY

PRESENT

IT DIDN'T TAKE Matty long to realize that Riley was no longer with them. They had barely made the turn in the corridor when Matty stopped walking to allow Riley to catch up. Except she didn't, and a sinking feeling settled in her stomach. Matty turned around and raced back to the quarantine room. Riley's bag was on the floor, but Riley was nowhere to be seen.

Matty pulled up her pad and sent out an emergency notification to every Martian citizen. They were fairly deep in Mars territory, and someone would have had to see Riley before they could get back to the Earth levels. It had only been a few minutes, and there had to be enough time.

The High Priestex took their pad and threw their screen onto the nearest viewscreen. It took Matty a minute to realize that this was an entirely new set of security protocols.

"When was this created?" Matty asked.

"You didn't need to know. Now you do." The High Priestex waved away Matty's concern. "We were not going to lose one of our own again."

There was surveillance footage on the door. It showed Riley setting down her bag and walking away. They switched to new camera feeds as Riley moved. Not every area was covered, and Matty lost her for a few minutes at a time, but it was easy to find her again. Each time she was alone, with no sign of an outside influence. Matty felt the hurt that Riley was walking away after everything. Although, a part of her was also not surprised. There had always been something that Riley had been keeping to herself.

The feed was being sent to all the ambassadors and every Martian citizen that had been deputized since the Earthen invasion. Yet, they had noticed her missing too late. Riley had moved with a purpose, knowing exactly where she was going. By the time they found the footage of her entering the tunnel, Riley was nowhere to be seen.

"I don't understand," Matty said. "If she wanted to stay with the spacers, why did she come back?" Some of her was concerned that Riley was running away after their night together. That Matty had misread Riley's feelings and now felt she had to escape from Mars as well.

"There is a way to find out," the High Priestex said. She turned and started walking down the hallway. Matty watched as the security feeds disappeared from the wall screen, then turned and followed.

Matty ran through their last few weeks together. Maybe she had pushed too hard. Perhaps she had forced Riley to run. Nothing added up in her head. One thing that Matty was certain of was that Riley would not risk anything to end up back in earth's hands. There had to be something else going on that Matty was not getting. The only thing she could think of was that whatever was going on had something to do with what Riley was doing on her damn pad.

At the command center, Matty nudged one of the other ambassadors out of the communication terminals. She then reached out to the spacers. It only had taken seconds before the familiar face was on the screen in front of her. They were expecting her call.

"To what do we owe the pleasure?" he asked.

"Where is she?" Matty didn't bother to explain. She was sure that he knew something.

"We have not seen her since she left our company. Was there a problem?" The man's eyes darted off-screen, and Matty could picture Riley sitting there listening.

"I just need to know she is safe," Matty said. She reached up and wiped away the unwelcome tears.

"Riley learned a lot during her brief time with us. She can now navigate the tunnels almost as well as a spacer. I'm sure she had an excellent reason if she went back into them."

Matty focused on what he wasn't saying more than what

he had. Going back had always been Riley's plan, and Matty wasn't supposed to be told about it.

"Is she with you? Let me know, and I will leave her in peace if that is what she wants."

His eyes darted off the screen again, but a new face moved into view. It was the other spacer that had accompanied Riley. They spoke together briefly, in their own language, and Matty waited why they decided what to tell her.

"Riley will always be welcome among us. However, it is clear that her heart wishes to be with you." He spoke hesitantly as if trying to be careful about what he was saying. "Sometimes, there are duties that we think we must do before we can move on to new adventures. Once Riley is finished, I am confident she will make her way back to you."

The two men started speaking together again. Both were looking at something else off-screen, and Matty felt confused about what was happening. "I think," the man started speaking again, "if you turn on your news feed, you will better understand why Riley is not with you now."

The video shut off, and Matty became aware of a shift in the room. The people were bunching around the various screens, and Matty looked up at the large wall screen and saw flashes of pictures popping up. It was all too fast for her to follow, so she pulled up the news feeds on her pad. There were more news stories than she could process coming out of Earth. Something massive must have happened. Matty selected one of the videos at random. A man was sitting at a desk with the Mortan corporation logo behind him. He began to speak.

"This just in..." The man was sitting stiffly behind a desk, his hand clenched in front of him. "Files containing serious allegations against high-level corporate members have been forced downloaded across both the corporate and private feeds. Allegations are not limited to one corporation but implicate hundreds of men from all corporations. We go now to a statement made by the Mortan president."

The scene on the video changed to show an older gentleman with light skin, a square chin, and short white hair sitting in an expensive grey suit on a chair in front of a fireplace. "I want to assure all corporate members that the allegations are false." His voice was steady, and despite the calm environment, he commanded respect. "The corporation will find who is responsible and punish them. The corporation is family, and disobedience will not be tolerated." He looked into the camera until Matty felt like he was looking directly at her. "The corporation has declared these files as contraband. They should be deleted from all devices at once. If you are found in possession of these files, then you will face repercussions."

The video clip ended, and Matty pulled up one that was more recent. The video was from the Reaper corporate channel and had a newscaster that looked wide-eyed as he spoke. "All corporations have declared the files as contraband.

Anyone caught in possession of them will be severely punished. However, users report that removing them from their devices is impossible. If a copy is rooted out, then another copy takes its place. Corporate members have been abandoning pads, telescreens, and other devices in mass. There are piles of them on street corners as people huddle in their houses. The file seems to be taking over everything."

Matty switched to the TKR corporation, catching their live feed, delayed due to its travel to Martian space. The newscaster was a woman with straight black hair, cut chin length, and light brown skin.

"However, one allegation is most prominent. It seems that one Nesili Medici of the Molbin corporation was married to the daughter of the esteemed Mr. Medici, second of the Molbin corporation. Mr. Medici's son inherited the entire estate on his name day last year. Financial records show that Mr. Medici was substantially in debt at that time. Since then, Mr. Medici has remarried the daughter of the Director of Trinsdale. However, there have been some questions about his wife's disappearance, who was last seen at their son's coming-of-age party.

"Since the release of these files, allegations by past household employees have been coming in claiming that Mr. Medici had willfully contributed to the death of his wife by blocking access to food and water. The corporation has officially disputed these claims from low-level employees. However, cremation records are suspiciously absent, and the medical examiner has now come forward to claim that he was threatened and bribed to falsify death documents.

"Now the question is, is Mr. Medici's first wife still alive? The implications of this would send waves through the entire corporation."

Matty let the news feed continue. The words flowed past her, but she was too stunned to listen anymore. The entire Earth's corporate system seemed to be unraveling. Matty knew Riley's family was high in the corporation, but she had not grasped how much her being alive would cause such a scandal. Somehow Riley had to be involved in the leak of this information. Something in the newscast caught Matty's attention, and she continued to listen.

"They are now calling this the TRUTH virus. As more information is being uncovered, mass demonstrations have started in third and second tiers across all the corporations. At the cornerstone of the movement seems to be Mr. Medici. Video has now been found in the files documenting the treatment of both his first and second wife. While the footage will take quite some time to review thoroughly, it has been deemed too disturbing for us to show.

"Videos are being leaked across the feed showing Mr. Medici's first wife hours after her supposed death. It will take some time for these videos to be validated, but there is speculation that Mr. Medici's current marriage is not valid.

"For now, the authorities have called Mr. Medici into questioning. The Trinsdale Director has also filed for reclamation of property, stating that the marriage to his daughter was made under false pretense, as it appears that Mr. Medici is currently married. The Director is asking for damages and the rights of their family to keep the Medici name, allowing Mr. Medici's second child, due in six months, to keep the Medici name."

The door to the conference room opened, and Matty saw Riley framed in the doorway. She hesitated and then walked towards Matty. The news feed continued in the background.

"You did this?" Matty asked.

"Yes."

"This was the code you have been working on?"

"Yes."

"Did you know it would cause this much mayhem?"

"They hide," Riley said, her eyes focused on the floor. "They keep everything in shadows, so no one has to notice. I knew if I made them stop hiding, they would have to face what they did. I designed it so they cannot get rid of the information. It will always be there, their sins, for everyone to see. It is flexible. Anytime they go to attack it, the virus will adapt."

The High Priestex had joined them. "You blended Martian and Earthen coding?" They asked.

"Yes."

"Why?" Matty asked.

"I couldn't leave Earth like that. Not with all the secrets, all the women being hurt, and the children starving. I couldn't just walk away. The system needed to change."

"So you took it upon yourself to change it?" Matty's voice was quiet as she spoke.

"No, I just took it upon myself to start the change." Riley looked at Matty then, a pleading in her voice. "I won't be there to see it through. I am running away to go hide on Mars."

"You didn't have a choice." Matty reached out and grabbed the other woman's hand. "He wouldn't have let you live."

"I had a choice. It was the right choice. But so was this."

"They are just going to bury it. Nothing will change." Matty did not turn to see which ambassador had spoken. Her gaze was too fixed on Riley's.

"Everything will change." Riley turned her head as she spoke, and Matty realized that everyone in the room was now focused on them. "The corporations are not stable. Each is vying to take over each other to gain power over all of the world, not just their section. Even within companies, everyone is out for themselves. There is no loyalty, just ambition. It has been fostered until all that matters is money and power. People will do anything to obtain it. They will struggle to get to the top with the information in their hands, and the entire structure will collapse."

"How many people will get hurt in the process?" Matty asked.

"How many people are being hurt now?" Riley's eyes begged Matty to understand. "They knew he was trying to kill me, and they did nothing. They do not punish for what people do, only for people getting caught. Now they have all been caught. All their secrets are laid out for everyone to see. Do you know how many murders there have been that have been bought off and covered up? Do you know how much money is taken from the third tier to line the pockets of those that already have everything? People are dying now. All I have done is given them a chance to fight. I had to do it. I left them all there to fend for themselves to save myself. It was the last gift that I could give them."

Matty stood up and tentatively reached out. Riley sank into her arms, but only briefly before moving away.

"Do you think many will die?" Riley asked.

"Many were already dying," Matty said. "Now you have given them a chance."

CHAPTER 53

RILEY

PRESENT

RILEY TRIED to stay out of everyone's way. She tried sitting down at the end of the table, but she had to stand when the workstation was needed. Now she moved around, trying to find a space that wasn't occupied.

She could have left. Everyone was too busy to stop her. But, she felt an obligation to see this through. She watched the news footage as it was shown on the screen and overheard frantic messages that the ambassadors were sending out. She bore witness to the chaos she had caused.

It is for the best. Riley had to remind herself of this. *The Earth had to be taken apart before it could be reborn. Only how many would get hurt in the process?*

The ambassadors had stopped receiving responses to their communication hours ago. The corporate news channels had gone dark, one by one dropping off, until only the TKD news feed was left. Communication from Mars had been blocked, and Riley watched the Martian technicians attempt to re-establish the connection. They worked together, and it reminded Riley of the hackers, the one community she had on Earth. *At least they knew what was coming.*

When an ambassador arrived, half out of breath and clothes and hair in disarray, they learned that the shuttles had stopped being cleared for departure. The launch bay doors had been sealed.

Riley watched as a team was sent out to connect with the ship's crew. They arrived back quickly with reports that the doors between worlds were locked down.

Slowly, the chaos in the room turned into defeat. The ambassadors slunk in chairs or leaned against walls. The only thing left was for them to join Riley and stand as observers to the upheaval coming through the sole news feed.

When the communication request came through, Riley knew her time to observe was over. She waited for it to be answered, but the ambassadors stood looking at each other in stunned silence. Finally, the High Priestex accepted the call.

"Hello," they said.

CHAPTER 54

MATTY

PRESENT

MATTY WAS TIRED. She had spent the last nine hours trying desperately to connect to someone. The entire solar system was changing, and she was locked in this room, separate from everything. As she worked, she would glance at Riley. She wanted to make sure the other woman was still there, that she was still safe. Matty's need to protect was strong, even though she was hurt that Riley had done all this without talking to her.

Eventually, Matty admitted defeat. There was nothing else any of them could do. She abandoned the console she had been using and went to stand against the wall, as far away from Riley as she could manage in the small space. She watched the current situation on Earth unfold before her. There was rioting. The Reaper president was believed to be dead. Other high-level officials were in hiding. In many cities, the gates between tiers had been torn down completely.

When the corner of the news feed lit up to indicate an incoming communication, Matty didn't process it. She had come to terms with being disconnected. Eventually, the audio of the news report was interrupted to announce an unknown caller. Matty started to return to herself and saw others doing the same. Then the High Priestex reached out and accepted the communication.

The view screens filled with an unknown person. Their shaved head, lean build, and olive skin made them instantly recognizable as a spacer. "Greetings, Martian envoy. I am Commander Splink." Her voice filled the conference room.

These were not the people they had communicated with earlier. In all that time, they talked about elders, but not once had they mentioned that their people held a ranking system. Matty glanced at Riley, whose demeanor hadn't changed. It was like she knew this call was coming.

"Greetings, Commander Splink," the High Priestex answered. "Your communication is most welcome. We have found ourselves cut off beyond this room."

"That was necessary. I am sorry if you were inconvenienced, but there were other pressing matters I had to attend to before I could contact your people. We have taken ownership of the ship. I assure you that it was not done by force."

There was a collective gasp in the room, and Matty could sense the fear coming off her colleagues. She did her best to stand as a reassuring presence. Matty did not have much experience with the spacers, but what she had didn't make her worried. This also explained the locked doors and unlaunched shuttles.

"How do you plan to move forward?" the High Priestex asked.

"We apologize for any concern that we have caused." The commander radiated a political coolness that Matty recognized from her work. "We felt the steps were necessary to ensure that the Earthen crew made it to the negotiation table."

"They are well?" The High Priestex's voice was hesitant as they asked.

"Quite well. We came to an understanding. Riley had given us a few files that were not released, and they were quite willing to negotiate."

Matty glanced at Riley again. She wasn't sure what she was looking for, but Riley seemed utterly unaffected by the conversation.

"The spacers are now the owners and operators of the transport fleet," the commander said.

"The entire fleet?" Matty asked, the question flying out of her mouth.

"That must have been some information," the High Priestex said.

"It was. However, I think the general instability of the Reaper corporation helped to sway them. Most of the crew will remain in their current positions, working as contractors. We have instigated a morality clause into their contract, so hopefully, it will be easier to work with them moving forward."

Matty could see the High Priestex pause to assess the situation before replying. "It seems that the Martian planet will need to negotiate with you as well."

The commander laughed. Matty found the sound unsettling, not the laugh as much as hearing it after watching so much chaos and destruction.

"We both know that your people are not dependent on the fleet."

Matty noticed Riley move for the first time. As much as she had rooted out all of Earth's secrets, Mars still appeared to be a mystery to her.

"The spacers understand your people's secrecy," the commander continued. "We agree that using fleet ships will reduce unnecessary friction and decrease aggressive behavior, at least for now. It has been agreed to continue to offer the use of our ships. Except we will no longer require any payment for relocation."

"What do you require?" the High Priestex asked.

"As you are aware, Earth is dependent on Martian mining. They are dependent on the fleet. When the current upheaval settles, we will finalize our contract with those left in authority. The contract's base will be the requirement to participate in a commission designed to make new standards, including basic human rights and environmental regulations."

"I'm not sure I understand how that impacts our planet."

"As Riley has recently reminded us, we are all one people. We want Mars to be part of this commission. Before you agree, I must tell you that my people will be pushing for the continuation of the Omega project."

Matty's eyes widened at hearing that name. The ambassadors started muttering around themselves. The room went from quiet to shocked chaos.

"Wait, what's the Omega project?" Riley moved away from the wall and towards the screen.

"Multigenerational ships," Matty answered. The information wasn't secret; Mars did not believe in secrets. However, they were not often talked about.

The screen changed. Mars filled the screen, and Matty knew this was a direct feed from the ship's cameras. In orbit of Mars were the space station and the three ships created for travel within the solar system. Then the view zoomed out, the Martian moons now visible. There, circling each one, was a large multigenerational ship.

"They're already built?" Riley asked.

"Kepler and Proxima Centauri, each named for the planets they are scheduled to travel to," the High Priestex said. "But, if you know about their existence, you know that we abandoned the project because it was deemed too high risk. The likelihood of reaching the planet would be small.

The psychological burden and solar radiation were too great a risk."

A square appeared on the top right side of the screen, showing the commander's face. "I think you forget that our society has lived in space for generations. It can be done with our help. Earth currently houses 15 billion people. The last plague killed 30 million people, and another million die from climate-related issues yearly. The planet is trying to kill humans before humans kill it. But all this will be a conversation for the commission to have."

"Those are your only conditions?" The High Priestex said. "That we no longer be charged for saving people off Earth and that we join a council on Earth's survival?"

"Yes, those are the only conditions. However, we have two requests. Riley explained to our youth about food that is wet and sometimes even warm. They would like to try this. We would ask that you allow us to eat at your dining halls. I assure you that there will not be too many that will take advantage of this situation. Even the youth cannot manage the Martian gravity daily."

"Wet food?" Matty asked as she turned her head towards Riley. The woman was now standing next to her.

"All they have are dehydration packets," Riley said. "They don't even give them the kind that self-warm."

"You are always welcome to sit at our tables. As we have recently been reminded," the High Priestex turned and glanced towards Riley, "we are all interconnected. However, we want to work with your people on other feeding options. Our ancestors learned a lot when we moved to Mars, and we have done research for the multigenerational ships."

"Yes, well, I'm sure that is a conversation that could be had." The commander's lip turned up, and her nose wrinkled as she spoke

"Was there another request?" the High Priestex asked.

"Yes, our last request is that Riley and her mate join the council."

Jealousy spiked through Matty. Many people had multiple partners, but the thought of sharing her with another was something she was not comfortable with. Then just as suddenly, it dawned on her that the commander was talking about her.

"We understand that Riley's presence may be difficult for the Earthens," the commander continued, "but she is the only human that has lived in all three worlds. That, and her talents, make her a benefit to the council. We understand her mate is a trained Martian ambassador, and her skills will also benefit the council."

Matty grabbed Riley's hand, looking for any objections, and when she didn't see any held on tight. "I'm your mate, huh?"

"In their society, that is how they see us."

"And you don't have a problem with that?"

Riley shot her a small smile, and any anger Matty had melted away.

"I will need agreement from the coven," the High Priestex said. "But I do not think there will be any problems."

"Excellent. The shuttles will be continuing shortly. We have taken the liberty of revising the departure schedules."

With that, the screen went blank, and everyone in the control center sat unmoving, trying to process everything that had just occurred.

Riley felt a nudge in her abdomen and turned to face Matty. "So, Ambassador Riley, I bet you didn't see that one coming."

CHAPTER 55

RILEY

PRESENT

MARS FILLED UP THE VIEWPORT. The rusty brown surface was so different from the darkened blue and brown of Earth. At first glance, Riley found herself disappointed, even upset. The planet was just a dead rock. How could it support the people she had grown so attached to over the months? But the more Riley watched, the more she understood her new home.

At the polls, there were the northern and southern oceans, a significant part of the current process to terraform the planet so its surface could be walked unaided. Across the surface, there were the lights of some of the cities, the newer ones that were able to be built above ground. There were also structures scattered across the planet, various scientific contraptions large enough to be seen from space and created to help humans adapt to this planet. Riley knew that hidden beneath the surface was more life, including Matty's home.

Matty walked up to her and took her hand. They stood side by side, watching the latest shuttle detach from the ship and start its landing. Out there, hidden by the planet, was a space station that housed hundreds on a rotating basis. And orbiting around the planet were ships built to allow expansion further in the solar system. Beyond that, there were settlements already set up on the asteroid belt. And the two generational ships circling the moons ready to take them out of the solar system forever.

"Are you ready?" Matty asked.

Riley looked at the scattering of Martian personnel who were left. The spacers were somewhere deep in the ship, busy making plans for the future. It was then that Riley realized that everything she had worked for since she was fourteen years old was done, and she had made it out alive. And here by her side was a woman who had fought for her and never given up. Together they would create a new plan.

"I'm ready," Riley said.

Get a FREE Short Story!

Join My Newsletter

Sign up at mj-james.com

More Science Fiction By MJ James

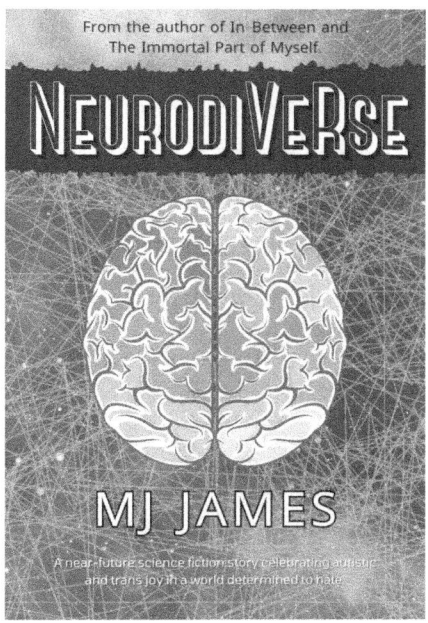

Jupiter J'nell just wanted a place to belong since their own family kicked them out while they were still in high school. They thought they had found their place in Long Beach, CA, working as an educational consultant on games designed for autistic kids. Being autistic themselves and an avid gamer, it was their dream job. Instead, they were too autistic, and the West Coast was not as accepting as they had hoped.

Would they ever find a place they could belong?

Fired and more uncertain of themselves than ever, they were

contacted by a mysterious individual, Stanley, who offered them a job at Austin School District (ASD), an elusive school system that was founded by the openly autistic tech genius who had built the biggest tech company ever - Austin Technology.

To get the job, all Jupiter had to do was pass one test.

What they received was a virtual reality headset that was an urban legend of the internet. It was said that this device made virtual reality nearly indistinguishable from the physical world. Only a few influencers had ever gotten their hands on one, and even fewer had gotten it to work. Holding the device in their hands, Jupiter knew they had to make the biggest decision of their life, and either way, things would never be the same.

NeurodiVeRse is a story of self-acceptance celebrating autistic and trans joy. But even as Jupiter learned to love themselves, the world fought to take it away. Except Jupiter now had more than themselves to fight for, and they found there wasn't anything they wouldn't do to protect the students of ASD.

Read Now!

Acknowledgments

A huge thank you to my youngest kid, who listened to me plotting the book and endlessly reading chapters out loud. They also patiently worked with me in creating the cover. It still amazes me that they can draw Mars that well.

Writing can be such an isolating experience. Thankfully, I have met many wonderful writers and readers on social media. I appreciate all your feedback and encouragement while I was writing this book. Thank you to everyone who read In-Between and sent me positive notes. Imposter syndrome is real, and you helped me create a book I am proud to have my name on.

I also want to thank everyone who supports trans authors and reads trans books.